Neeta Lyffe, Zombie Exterminator in

Zombie Death Extreme!

Karina Fabian

LASER COW PRESS

Laser Cow Press

Merritt Island, FL

2024 Dedication

To Kim Richards and Allen Shoff
Because you believed in me and in this book.
Thank you!

Original Dedication

To Audrey Shaffer and all my friends at The
Writers Chat Room.

Because you educate, you inspire, and you give
"door-knobs" a whole new meaning!

Contents

Chapter 1

Zombies were eating Eidelberg.

Dammit! Neeta thought. I was still training him.

The zombies gnawed on his beautiful leg, after tearing off its protective covering like, well, like the cling wrap he'd used to make it. Meanwhile, he screamed and blubbered and somehow still managed to flip his surfer-blond hair stylishly over his shoulder.

Not that anyone really noticed. The zombies had more interest in his meat than his pelt. There were only eight, but that was still too many for a bunch of unwashed trainees, particularly with the idiot film crew hounding them and getting in the way.

Around Neeta, seven panicky apprentices flailed with their tools, forgetting everything she'd taught them over the past six weeks, while through their headpieces Dave shouted directions that had more to do with good drama than good tactics. One cameraman continued to film while another had abandoned his camera and had fallen to his knees vomiting.

Zombies grunting, plebes screaming, someone calling for her mother...

Wait, that was Neeta. And she wasn't calling; she was apologizing. She just knew Mom was spinning in her grave.

"Fall back!" she shouted into her mike. "Roscoe, Katie—take point and keep the path clear. Everyone else, orderly retreat. Move, move, move!"

Neeta dashed to the front line, wielding her chainsaw as much to badger her students into action as to keep the zombies at bay. She kicked the kneeling cameraman with her heel.

"Come with us if you want to live!" she snarled.

"I do want to live! I do want to live!" he blubbered and dashed into the center of her retreating students.

"Help me!" Eidelberg wailed. A zombie was now pawing at his hair. Young thing, not long turned. Probably some surfer boy's dream girl once.

Neeta Lyffe, Zombie Exterminator, lunged forward with the chainsaw and severed the zombie's hands—and Eidelberg's head with it. The titanium teeth of the saw made a clean cut, but that didn't mean it wasn't messy. Guts and blood splattered her rubber hazmat suit and coated the visor of her faceplate.

Didn't slow her, of course. She let go of the saw with her right hand, swinging it to the left and removing something's arm, and wiped her visor, while still backing up. All part of the job.

Meanwhile, her trainees, finally remembering their training, had formed up in a neat diamond pattern, stepping back in rhythm. Katie and Roscoe swung their blades like paired ninjas. LaCenta and Spud kept their flamethrowers shooting out at regular intervals. Gordon on the right lunged forward low and severed one shambling undead at the knees.

"Score! OOH-Rah!" he shouted, as he pulled back into formation.

On the left, Nasir's cheap Craftsman Treesplinterer 5000 shook so hard he'd only sever something by accident. Gordon shouted for him to keep the blade up. "Remember Heisman!"

Nasir replied in what Neeta thought were Arabic curses. She made a note to learn them. There weren't enough swear words in the English language for her job.

Inside the diamond formation, the on-location film crew huddled and moved with her team. Only one cameraman remained outside.

Neeta ignored him. If Ted got brained, wasn't her problem. Guy was a lunatic, anyway, whooping and getting into the fray. Still, he had good instincts: she'd seen him skip out of the way of a flailing arm just in the nick of time, and once, he used his camera to knock a zombie off Katie before it tore her helmet off. He wore an industrial-grade protective suit and helmet, too. Reckless, but not stupid.

As the last of her trainees cleared the building, Neeta made a wide sweep with the chainsaw, causing the horde to pull back long enough for her to jump out and slam the door. Gordon and Spud braced it shut while she reached into her pockets and pulled out a napalm bomb.

Director Dave screamed, "Stop! No, Neeta, those things are expensive!"

Ted the cameraman crouched low to get a good angle as Neeta pulled the pin. Behind the faceplate, she could see him grinning encouragement. Gordon had pulled out some of his own grenades.

She shouted, "Napalm sticks to zombies!" for effect and because, well, Ted was kind of cute.

Spud eased up on his door, and she and Gordon tossed their grenades in, thrown high, like she'd taught them. Then they ran.

There weren't any dramatic flames, and no exploding door. Nonetheless, Dave yelled for them to run ten feet then dive to the ground dramatically.

"Screw that! Keep running!" Neeta told them. Only after they put several yards between them and the building did she spin around, chainsaw at the ready.

The door burst open.

Rather than a horde of flaming zombies, only one walking ball of flame, groaning "Brains!" emerged to fall mere feet from the threshold.

Neeta waited. One minute, then three. At five, she clicked off the saw and lowered it to her side.

"Good job, Gordon," she said.

"Cut!" the director snarled.

Katie Haskell stared straight into the camera, trying to sniffle without sounding gross. Why did they have to film this now? Couldn't she blog it later, when she could talk without her nose dripping?

"I…I can't believe it. He's gone, just gone. One minute, he was all, 'Let's do this thing, baby!' then they were gnawing on him and he was screaming and Neeta just…" She bit her lip to stop herself from shrieking.

From where he sat behind the camera, Dave motioned, *Go on.*

"I can't. I just can't! I mean, what am I doing here, anyway? Is it really worth a million dollars? Bergie had a shot—more than me—and now he's dead! And—and he'd be even worse than dead if Neeta hadn't..."

She buried her face in her hands and sobbed, uncaring of the sloppy sounds she made.

Gordon spit out the chewing tobacco as Dave ordered, glaring at the director as he did so. Didn't he understand he needed something to cool his nerves? Asshole was watching the whole thing from a nice safe location. He wasn't there! He didn't know!

Use the anger, man. Use it and don't let it use you.

"Bergie was an idiot," he told the camera. "Broke formation, mugging it up for points. I did six years in the Marines, man. Taught me the importance of listening to your CO. I seen stuff make your short hairs stand and scream. But what they was doing to Eidelberg..."

He shook his head. "Neeta, though. She's got monkey's brass balls, she does."

And you ought to be fragged, he thought at the grinning man sitting beside the cameraman.

"Oh, my gawd," Roscoe ran his fingers through his still-wet hair. He'd just left the shower, where he'd washed four times to get even the thought of that zombie vileness off, and was doing his video blog, like he promised Dave, in his towel. Dave had liked the casual, risqué effect, and it certainly fit Roscoe's persona. Still, he was careful about how he kept his legs. Didn't want to give the girls too much. Or the guys for that matter.

"That was just perfectly horrifying, you know? I totally can't blame Neeta, though. Bergie's uniform was so wrong. I mean, I tried to warn him. If you want to show the legs, it's transparent Kevlar all the way! More expensive, sure, and it doesn't breathe, but really! I'd rather be able to breathe after the extermination, you know?

"But, oh, gawd, didn't he have beautiful legs? If I were a zombie, I'd have eaten him up, too."

Dave Lor, King of Reality TV, Czar of the Candid Outtake, stood outside the conference room and shook himself like a runner preparing for a race.

"Producer's in there. Gotta look sharp, stay positive," he muttered to himself.

One deep cleansing breath, then two, then he shot out his arm toward his personal assistant. Sharon slapped an Electrolyte Jolt drink into his hand with the efficiency of a surgical nurse, then pulled her DoDroid SuperSmartPadPhone from her purse and called up the myriad of notes and raw footage from the dailies, transferring files to his own DoDroid. No one would have guessed that she'd just spent the last two hours screaming into a couch cushion. Days like this, she regretted her second-grade pledge to DARE to stay off drugs.

She just finished calling up the footage Dave had already set aside for the blooper reel when he stuck out his arm again, empty bottle in his hand. She traded it for the phone. He gave her a roguish, caffeinated grin.

"In the words of the late Donald Eidelberg, 'Let's do this thing, baby!'"

She pushed open the door for him, trying hard to imagine herself into a cocaine high.

"All right, people!" Director Dave said as he strode toward the table which the producer shared with two depressed writers, one resigned lawyer, and various cameramen and production crew. And of course, Neeta herself, whose hands kept gripping and ungripping, as if missing her chainsaw or longing to close around someone's throat.

Dave didn't notice. No, Neeta amended herself, he noticed but chose to pretend he hadn't. Very little escaped his director's eye, she'd learned during the past six weeks of filming *Zombie Death Extreme*. Instead, he projected an image from his DoDroid onto the large screen so that Eidelberg stared helplessly at the people around the table, his mouth frozen in a scream, his head resting in the lap of a teenage zombie who was running her fingers through his hair.

One of the writers, Gary, gagged. Neeta quickly passed him a bag. It wasn't the first time.

Dave waited, a paradigm of patience and sympathy. Neeta would have liked to slice up some of that paradigm and feed it to him fist-first. *Mom, I'm sorry!*

"So, let's talk about what went wrong," Dave said when Gary had wiped his mouth with a muffled apology.

"Wrong?" Neeta growled. "Where shall we start? How about when you said, 'Let's give them a budget and have them *design* their own gear'? How about we start there, Dave!"

As usual, Dave looked deeply concerned while his "people" jumped to the rescue.

Lawyer Larry decided to jump in first. "We clearly stated that every uniform meet OSHA standards."

"OSHA?!" Neeta slammed her hand on the table and pushed herself up. "Do you know when the first zombie infestations were discovered, Larry?"

He sighed. "My name is Eugene."

"When, Lawyer Larry?"

"Twenty-three years ago," he snapped.

"And the first OSHA regulations concerning the make of protective gear, types of tools and general working environment?"

"Twenty-two, as dictated by the Zombie Extermination Authorization Act of—"

"And when was the last time they were updated to reflect what we've learned about zombies?"

He faltered, "I fail to see—"

"Never, Lawyer Larry! Twenty years of research and raw experience by people like my mother, God rest her soul, and the only thing the OSHA standards have even addressed are 'environmental' issues suggested by know-nothing big-lobbying companies like Bioclowns—"

"Bioclonz," Wang Bastille corrected. His partner, Gary, looked at him with wide eyes as if to say, *Are you freaking mad? She's on a roll!*

Gary was weak, but at least he wasn't a fool. Neeta turned on Wang with a snarl. "Thank you, Wang the Waste! And where were the specifications I told you to write into the script?"

Wang chose the better part of valor and turned to the producer for the answer.

Alberts leaned back in his chair and spread his hands. With as many heavy gold rings as he had on his fingers, she was constantly amazed that he could move them so easily. "Neeta. Be reasonable. No one could have afforded to make the kind of suit you specified."

"Larry" continued for him. "Ever since the UN Environmental Accord and the subsequent US Petroleum Product Limitations Acts, industrial grade, man-made rubber is hard to come by and expensive to obtain."

"Which," Director Dave concluded, "was the genius behind this week's challenge!"

"Challenge? Try fiasco. Eidelberg died!"

Dave shrugged. "Well, sure. You cut off his head."

Wang passed Gary another bag.

Neeta spoke quietly. "Dave, do you really want what would have happened to Bergie if I hadn't?"

The room got very quiet.

When Dave spoke, he, too, used a hushed voice. "Neeta, this is a dangerous business. You told us that yourself, right? The turnover rate is, sixty-five percent a year, right?"

She glared at him.

"You've lost two partners already. That's part of why you came to us—to find a new partner, right?"

"I didn't come to you," she growled.

He held up placating hands. "I misspoke. But that is the beauty of this partnership, right? Think about it: you've trained twelve people, and only one has died!"

"Half-trained. They're too raw."

"*Yet only one has died!* Even better!"

"Tell that to Heisman."

"Come on. They're growing him a new foot."

"And Goldie?"

"Responding well to medication—isn't that right, Sharon, baby?" He turned to his personal assistant.

Sharon, whose blank smile and unfocused gaze implied that she was on some serious drugs herself, nodded.

Dave made a *See there?* gesture with one hand. "Alexis walked after the first training video. Just imagine if she'd actually signed up with an exterminator before she'd learned it wasn't for her. And Hu… Well, the whole incident with the toilets was unfortunate, but no harm done, right?"

"And it'll look great on your blooper reel, right?" Neeta said, grinning with all her teeth.

"Right! Now you're—oh, Neeta! Neeta, Neeta, Neeta." Dave shook his head and tsked. "Is that what you think this is to us? Just good TV?"

He clasped his hands together as if in prayer and pressed them to his lips. When he again spoke, he pointed his fingers toward her. "Neeta, I've seen entire neighborhoods ravaged by out-of-control undead. Stood by helplessly as people burned their homes to the ground rather than risk contagion. It's heartbreaking, you know it is. I don't need to tell you.

"But Joe Public doesn't get that. Zombies are just another filthy pest that only happen to other people. And keeping us safe? Just another dirty job no one wants to know about.

"Neeta, baby, you're their wake-up call. The zombies are real, and they are now! They could strike anywhere, from the mattress factory in the industrial district to the Pilates studio uptown. And zombie exterminators—people like you—like your mother, God rest her soul—*your* people, Neeta, are all that stands between us and certain annihilation."

Suddenly, he spun around so that his prayer hands pointed at Bergie's terrified face. "And if this! Yes, this! If this is what it takes to wake up the sleeping masses to the problem of our very survival, then I say God bless Bergie! God bless him!"

Sharon let out a loud wail and spilled out of her chair, grabbing Dave by the knees and sobbing. Producer Alberts regarded him with a proud, watery smile. Gary and Wang wept openly, as did some of the support crew sitting in the back, and even Lawyer Larry sniffled. Ted turned away, but whether to laugh or cry wasn't clear.

Neeta pinched the bridge of her nose and let out a growly sigh.

"I won't have another stupid death," she said. "There are better ways to wake Joe Public."

"Of course," Dave said, scraping Sharon off his artificial-leather jeans and sitting at the table, leaning forward to show his earnestness. "Low budget uniforms. Bad idea. Never happen again, right, Wang?"

"Never!" Wang sobbed.

Neeta removed her hands from her face and steepled them in front of her. "It wasn't just the uniforms. You pitted us against eight zombies."

"But there were eight of you."

"And I told you up front that one zombie is worth three trainees."

"But Neeta, babe, you alone are a match for five zombies!"

"Not when I'm babysitting plebes, gaffers and cocky cameramen. One of your own almost bought it."

"I saw that! 'Come with me if you want to live!' I got chills! Didn't you get chills?" Dave looked around the room, gathering nods.

"Old school," Wang said.

"Classic!" added Alberts.

Neeta slammed her hand on the table, making everyone jump. "No more! From now on, I choose the number you pit those plebes against. I will not be overruled on matters of safety. Your cameramen will train with the crew. Those that can take it can film. If they can't, you'll remote the rest of us and make do with what you get."

"Whatever you say, Neeta. We can work with that. Give the whole show a gritty realism. I'm seeing it! I am!"

"There's nothing more dangerous than a defeated plebe," Neeta pressed. "It's one thing to be aware that you might become the zombie blue pate special; it's another when you've seen someone else's pate become the special. The next challenge has got to build them up. I will decide what it is and how they prepare. In the meantime, if any of them want to walk, you'll let them—and pay them a nice bonus besides."

At this, the simpering stopped. "Er, how much?"

"Twenty thousand. Each."

"That's a thousand dollars a minute air time."

"Plus, whatever therapy they need to get past the nightmares."

"Be reasonable—"

"Reasonable?" Neeta had moved past yelling. People around her backed up against their seats. "How about you put on a homemade suit and come with me on a run? Then you can tell me what's 'reasonable.'"

Dave opened and closed his mouth a few times. Finally, Alberts, with a look back at the image of Eidelberg, held up a hand.

"Deal. But ten thousand comes from your pay."

"Five."

His mouth twisted into a frown. "Five."

"Well!" Dave said, clapping his hands together and beaming at his team like a schoolteacher proud of his class. "We've accomplished a lot! But now we need to turn our minds to closure. We have lost a dear and popular member of our cast today. I know our trainees are going to need to mourn, to express their feelings, to understand just what meaning this could possibly have. They need you, Neeta, to lead them through this troubled time. You must speak with them. Tonight.

"And I know the perfect location to film it!"

Much as Neeta hated to admit it, Dave had been right about the place. Eidelberg would have loved the twilight memorial on the beach.

The location crew found a nice little spot above the tide line, not far from a scrubby overhang. Dave sent people ahead to rake and clear the area of trash, animal debris and dead seaweed, and to move the federally mandated signs warning of the many dangers of swimming in the ocean (including cramps, chills, stings of naturally occurring wildlife that are really quite shy but have every right to defend themselves, shark attacks, porpoise buttings, and the completely understandable but nonetheless unsanitary bathroom habits of the ecologically rightful inhabitants). The four-by-four signs took two people each to move, but Dave insisted that their reflective surfaces would interfere with the lighting.

Just outside the ring of logs, they'd set up a shrine to Donald "Bergie" Eidelberg: his favorite surfboard rose from the ground like a California tombstone. The production crew had enlarged a photo of him from the first episode and framed it with leis, which they hung on the board. They'd spread one of his beach towels in front it, and everyone had set some item on it that reminded them of him: a canister of Sex Wax (ironic, considering that he claimed celibacy was absolutely necessary for champion surfing), the sunglasses Neeta had refused to let him wear into the warehouse (not that it had helped), the surfing trophy he'd kept by his nightstand (Second Place), the painting he'd been working since the beginning of the show (they thought it might be a wave), the keys to his classic 1978 AMC Pacer (he'd bragged that once he won the million, he was going to give it the overhaul it deserved). Lawyer Larry had already put it up for auction on eBay, with the proceeds to go to the Retired Surfers Association, in accordance with Bergie's will.

Neeta and her plebes had trooped to the site, accompanied by the filming crew, just as the sun hesitated over the horizon, like a swimmer preparing to enter a cold pool. As the sun dipped, then sank, they ate hot dogs, drank sodas, and shared stories about their fallen teammate. Roscoe waxed poetic about his legs; Katie admitted to a secret crush. Gordon laughed how Bergie was going to teach him surfing when this was all over in exchange for learning how to dum-dum bullets. LaCenta rolled her eyes and declared Bergie a damfool, but her eyes misted when she said it. Spud, silent and thoughtful, said he'd go visit Bergie's mom with Neeta before heading back to Idaho, and Nasir offered to join them.

Within the circle of logs, the campfire roared merrily, bathing Neeta and her plebes in its warm light. Soon, they'd each light a candle from that fire and hold it close as they discussed the day's tragedy. Dave was having paroxysms of joy over the effect. Neeta wondered if he'd gotten permits, planned to pay the fines, or had bribed someone to arrange this cozy beach scene. Since the California Carbon Footprint Reduction Act, such "eco-destructive luxuries" like campfires had been banned.

From her log apart from the others, LaCenta was complaining. "All I'm saying is that my family lost everything in that fire and then the judge fined us for starting it, but oh, the Hollywood man wants his 'authenticity' and they turn a blind eye."

Roscoe sighed heavily. Perched on the log with his feet flat on the sand, knees together, wrists resting on knees, wearing a tailored white T-shirt and matching boat shorts, he looked like an out-of-place model. He insisted white was the Chinese color of death and symbolized purity and nobility of the spirit, but Neeta suspected he just wanted to stand out in the dim light.

"Give it a rest, Placenta," he sneered.

"It's *La*Centa, and if you can't come up with a more imaginative insult, Roscoe, you should just shut your hole."

"Which one, honey?"

"Stop it!" Katie shrieked. "We're supposed to be saying goodbye to Bergie!" She buried her head into Spud's shoulder and sobbed.

He patiently reached into her backpack and handed her a tissue from the boxes she'd brought with her. They'd started the fire using the dirty ones as kindling.

Good ol' Spud. Calm, dependable, and about as exciting as potatoes. He could be good at this job, Neeta thought. Yet every week, Dave complained about his low ratings on the online polls. "Sure, people love potatoes!" he'd ranted at one writing session. "But who really thinks about them?"

Gary spoke up. "They like them with something. Cheeseburger *and* fries."

"Steak *and* potatoes," Wang added.

Dave grinned that maniacal grin. "Potato *and* gun! Yes! Yes! I'm seeing it! So, what do we hook him up with? Who is our 'steak'?"

The next day, Neeta had walked by LaCenta's trailer just in time to see Wang go flying headfirst out the door.

"I may have been raised in the hood, but I ain't no Hollywood whore!" she shouted.

Neeta had rounded up Gordon, and the two of them had found Dave for a sandwich and a talk. Rather, Neeta talked while Gordon held Dave sandwiched between himself and the wall. Afterward, Spud found himself teamed with Gordon as a weapons master apprentice, none the wiser of the behind-the-scenes dealing. Dave had had to settle for potato gun.

Now, thanks to Bergie's death, it seemed Dave might get his steak and potatoes, too.

She was really growing to loathe Dave.

She glanced across the fire at Gordon, who looked up from sharpening his hunting knife to roll his eyes. Behind him, just inside the dim light of the fire, Nasir was finishing his prayers. He'd spread his little prayer rug on the sand near the memorial, facing Mecca and Medina, and was moving through the motions of standing, kneeling and pressing his head against the ground, murmuring the prayers in his native tongue. One of the cameramen moved in for a butt shot, but Gordon had leaned back and waved his knife at him threateningly, and he'd backed off. Some things ought to stay sacred.

Unaware of the commotion around him, Nasir finished and settled on the log beside Gordon, the prayer rug rolled up beside him. Neeta picked up the candles and passed them around. Each took one and leaned toward the fire to light it. Spud lit Katie's from his.

Neeta gazed into her candle, gathering her thoughts. She was tired. She'd spent the afternoon combing the warehouse with another exterminator, a colleague from Anaheim, Jason Hollerman, to make sure there weren't any more surprises lurking in the shadows. Fortunately, Jason was a big Dave Lor fan; he'd done the job for a chance to meet his idol and the promise of getting a part in a future episode. As they'd scoured the warehouse with flamethrowers and cleaning products, she'd mulled over what had happened, what she would say about it and most of all, how she was going to salvage the disaster.

"Don't think of it as a disaster, Neeta," Hollerman said. He swung about suddenly, flames spewing, then laughed as he realized he'd charcoaled a rat. "A hard lesson, sure, but nothing like the ones your mom and I had to learn back in the day. Six of your trainees survived, and together, you kept four more civilians safe. Your mom and I didn't see successes like that until probably our second or third year."

"It was different then, and it should have been different now. This should have been a controlled situation." She held up a hand. He moved in to cover her while she checked out some zombie spoor: dried skin, a rotting finger, what looked like part of a nose. Must have been some sneeze. Still, it looked old, from before the episode. She scraped it into a hazardous waste bag, then wiped the area clean.

"Nothing's 'controlled' where the walking undead are concerned. If you believe that, then you've forgotten what your mother taught you, Little Girl."

Looking at the faces around the campfire, she resolved never to forget again, and to make sure these people never forgot, either. Still, she had to make sure they knew they could win this fight, too.

"Today should not have happened," she started.

Immediately, Roscoe jumped in. "Oh, gawd, Neeta. No one's blaming you!"

"Shut up!" LaCenta snarled. "This is not the time for your kissing up."

"Oh, so you're blaming Neeta, are you? Maybe you'd better look in the mirror if you want to assign blame. Did you even bother to shoot that flamethrower where she told you to?"

"And how was I going to do that when all I could hear was Caterwauling Kate?"

"Stop it!" Katie squealed. "There's plenty of blame to go around."

Gordon snorted.

Neeta cleared her throat, and they fell silent.

"Katie's right. This whole thing was a rats' nest of mistakes. Our intel was bad, and we went up against twice as many zombies as we'd expected. Eidelberg left the group. Whether he thought he'd impress someone or he got hit with the Exterminator's Berserk, we'll never know. Our civilians panicked first, got in the way. When Bergie fell, no one doused him. Where were you, right wing?"

Nasir studied his candle, but Gordon just snorted. "Come on, Neeta. Splash him with toilet bowl cleaner? Who really believes—"

"The exterminators whose lives have been saved by a couple of gallons of commercial grade Porcelain Sparkle, that's who. You have to believe in your tools, or they will fail you because you fail to use them well. Undiluted household cleaner repels zombies. It's not faith; it's fact."

"It doesn't make sense," Nasir muttered. "There's no reason that should work."

"That we know of, Nasir. There's no reason that we know of that thousands of dead are clawing their way out of their graves and seeking out the living to gnaw on, either. But they do. That, too, is fact."

She looked past them at the shrine they'd made to Bergie, which some production crewman had lit with candles while they were talking. Everyone turned to follow her gaze. Katie sniffled.

Neeta started again, "Today, you learned another fact of this job. People die. Good people, people who…" She stopped mid-sentence, her mind suddenly playing its own episodic flash backs of people she'd seen die: Bergie, and Michael, Threadgill with the red hair and thick Scottish accent, timid Lois, Auburn and Peaceglove…

Thinking like that could make a person mad from grief. She forced her mind to the present. "People who chose this job, not for fame or glory or promise of a million dollars. It's because they saw people die, and come back, and kill. Or because they saw soulless bodies denied their eternal rest. Or, like my mother, like me, they saw a threat to our world that we are uniquely qualified to fight against.

"I'm twenty-six years old. My initiation into the biz was when a zombie broke out of a faulty containment unit and knocked my mother down from behind. I drove it back with a bottle of window cleaner in one hand while I doused my mother in shower scrub with the other. We lived because I responded the way my mother trained me.

"Nonetheless, odds are I'll die before I'm 40 from a job-related incident. When I do, I want to be buried holding my severed head in my hands. I will not come back.

"The good news is, we know more about zombie behaviors now than we did when my mother exterminated them. Every advancement in knowledge, properly applied, translates into another week, another year our people survive. However, zombie extermination is not a science. We could have done everything right today, and Bergie could still have died."

All eyes were on her now. She'd ordered Dave to keep the cameras out of everyone's field of vision, yet she could feel the lenses focusing in on her face. She ignored it. Dave had been right about one thing: these plebes needed her if they were going to get through this with their lives and sanity intact. And the world needed them.

"Each of you has chosen this career, and not just for the money or whatever glamour you think you'll find. Each of you can do this. I wouldn't have selected you, otherwise. However, this is not a game.

"I promise you: you have just faced the toughest challenge of this show. I guarantee this: you have not faced the toughest challenge of your career. And just because this was the toughest challenge, doesn't mean someone won't get hurt. Won't get killed."

She paused. She figured they'd think she was giving them time for her words to sink in, but really, she was trying to remember how she'd phrased her next statement. By contract, she couldn't mention Dave or the network or anything else that blew the illusion of reality. If she did, they'd have to re-shoot, and she knew darn well Dave would take that opportunity to exert his influence. She set her candle down and leaned toward the firelight. From her pocket, she withdrew six envelopes.

"I've arranged for any of you to leave now. No obligations. No penalties. With twenty thousand dollars to thank you for your efforts. You can return home to a standard apprenticeship. You can start on a whole new career. All I ask is that you remember what you've learned these past six weeks. If that's what you want to do, come here, pick up your contract, and throw it into the fire."

A moment of everyone shuffling and looking at each other. Katie pushed away from Spud, picked up her backpack and walked to Neeta. She stuck out her hand. The light reflected off her tear-streaked cheeks.

After they watched the flames devour the envelope, Neeta stood and gave her a hug.

"I'm sorry, Neeta," she whispered.

"There's nothing to be sorry for."

They broke apart, and Katie turned to look at each of her former teammates.

"I'm sorry," she told them. "I want to help people, I really do. Zombie extermination is so important. But I can't. I can't watch another person die. I just can't!"

She heaved a heavy sigh, lifted her chin and strode out of the circle toward Bergie's shrine. She kissed her fingertips and pressed them to his picture, then headed toward the waiting cars.

"Well," LaCenta said, "There's one liability gone."

"I heard that, Placenta, you witch!"

"Beautiful!" Dave said into their headpieces.

Home once again, Roscoe leaned back in his computer chair and turned on the webcam. After checking his hair in the image projected on his screen and mashing his lips to give them more color, he set it to record. "Okay, so LaCenta said it first, and she was a totally out of line for saying it when she did, but honestly…"

He leaned in close, sharing a secret. "…we were all thinking it."

He checked the file, saved it and uploaded it to his *Zombie Death Extreme* blog.

"And then there were five!" He wove his fingers together and moved into a yoga stretch.

Oh, gawd, was there any high better than surviving another episode?

Chapter 2

Notes from *The Zombie Syndrome*

A Documentary

By Gary Opkast

Episode One: *The Zombie Syndrome*

Romero-zombies lurching toward fleeing crowd (NOTE: Use actual footage from *Night of the Living Dead*? Ask Larry Eugene about rights issues.)

> NARRATOR
>
> Zombies. The shambling undead of the horror films of old. They're not a new concept. From the 1920s, writers such as W.B. Seabrook and H.P. Lovecraft have written harrowing tales of the mindless un-dead, reanimated with a thirst for violence and a

hunger for human flesh. (Too much? Maybe better tone it down for prime time?)

The first, best known zombie movie, *Night of the Living Dead*, was criticized for being too terrifying to watch. Over time, however, the zombie genre moved from horrifying—

Photo from movie or book cover (Not Living Dead—Re-Animator, perhaps?)

NARRATOR

to friendly—

Scene from Disney film *Hocus Pocus*

NARRATOR

to comical—

Scene from *Shaun of the Dead*

NARRATOR

Cool—

Scene from Michael Jackson's *Thriller*

NARRATOR

and even classical—

Scene from movie Pride and Prejudice and Zombies

NARRATOR

Never, however, did we believe that someday, reality would reflect literature—and it would be the nightmare stuff that had once had audiences trembling in their seats.

Movie scene of people in a theater, jumping, screaming crying.

FADE THROUGH to footage of the Superplex 20 Infestation of 2021.

Switch to footage from expert interviews. (Note: Be sure to get Neeta in there. She's hot!)

When Gary heard the knock on the door, he called the person in with a "Yeah, yeah!" and kept typing. He had some footage of Neeta he thought might fit perfectly, though he'd have to ask her…

When he looked up to see the actual Neeta walking in with Ted by her side, however, he yelped and slammed the lid of his laptop down.

"Are we…interrupting something?" she asked.

"No!" his voice rose and cracked for the first time since high school. He cleared and tried again. "No, nooo. Not at all. Something I can help you with?"

Neeta set a greasy paper bag and a 40-ounce cup on the long table and leaned back against it. Los Angeles was experiencing a record high summer, and all of the studio's AC credits were being used to keep Studio G cool for the filming of *Global Warming/Global Winter*. In deference to the heat, Neeta wore a tan tank top and cut off denim shorts. Just looking at the sheen on her skin made the temperature in the room rise another five degrees in Gary's mind. Not like he had a chance with her, considering all the barfing he'd done over the past month. Would she ever see past that?

On the bright side, he had lost that writer's belly that came from too little exercise and too much BICHOK. (Butt In Chair, Hands on Keyboard)

"Can you keep a secret?" she asked.

He glanced down at his closed laptop. "Uh, yeah. Sure. Why?"

She traded a glance with Ted then reached into her bag, pulling out the thickest pastrami sandwich he'd ever seen. She bit into it, chewing slowly as she regarded him with narrowed eyes. He was being weighed, he knew it, yet all he could think of was how good she made the simple act of chewing look.

Yep, he'd been without a girlfriend for too long. He vowed to trawl the internet that night and get himself signed up as a guest speaker at the next reality TV convention he could attend.

She followed up the bite with a long sip of her drink. "All right. I've got a problem with the plebes. They know how the tools work, but they don't believe in them."

"You mean like the chemical stuff?" He felt his spirits lift when she smiled and nodded. Maybe he didn't have to look like such a dufus in her eyes. "Well, what if we reintroduced the stuff in a different label? Told them it was improved?"

When she pinched her nose in that annoyed way of hers, he knew he'd missed the mark.

"Gary, that won't help them—and it doesn't help anyone else. People need to understand that if a zombie invades their home, their best line of defense isn't the butcher knife on the counter, but the cleanser under the sink. I mean, that's part of what we want to do, educate people, right?"

He thought about his documentary, hidden in his folded laptop. He wondered if she would say that again for him on camera. "I want that, I really do."

She dropped her hand, relaxing again now that she knew he was on board. "Good. Because I was thinking. There's a research and training center out east near Palm

Desert. Very under-the-radar because they're afraid of community outcry, but I have connections and I think I can get a small crew in if we keep any identifying factors edited out. They have a small captive zombie population there. Our people—and the viewers—can see things like window cleaner and political handbills in action. Problem is, I'm not sure it's exciting enough for Director Dave."

"And you want my help convincing him?" *Political handbills? Those really work? Thought that was urban legend.*

"Ted here has some ideas for some visuals, and if we can add your input on the script…"

I could do a segment on that for my documentary… Zombie defense: Legend and Fact… and the people I'll meet—real front-line experts…

"Gary?"

"Sorry?" He pulled himself back to their conversation.

Neeta leaned forward and peered at him closely. "Are you sure you're up to this?"

He forced his eyes not to stray from her face. "Yep. Fine. Why?"

"This hasn't been an easy show for you."

She noticed! Sheesh, how could she not? He thought of bluffing, but decided she'd respect the honest approach. "Well, true. But there won't be any…eviscerations or that kind of grossness, will there?"

"Some of their stock has been there a long time. You'll see varying levels of decay. I can't make any promises about their experiments. I don't think you're eating well. Do you sleep?"

"Like a baby." A colicky one, but she didn't need to know that. He swallowed down the bile the mere word "decay" had produced. "I'm your man."

"Yeah? Prove it." She tossed her lunch bag on his desk.

He looked at it, confused.

"There's half a pastrami sandwich in there, from the best pastrami place you'll find on this coast. Let's talk shop while you finish it off."

"You want me to eat it? Your sandwich?" *Which your lips have touched...*

"Can you handle it?"

He opened the bag, pulled out the half-wrapped thing. A strip of meat escaped and spilled onto his lap. He could see the half-moon indentation where her teeth had nibbled... *She asked about my health. She shared with me her food.*

He bit down hard, his eyes rolling with pleasure.

"See? Good stuff, right?" Satisfied, Neeta leaned back against the table. "So, I figure we have to start the usual way, with me explaining where we're going and why..."

In the studio mixing room, Dave leaned over the technician's shoulder as he put together the personality segment on LaCenta for the next episode. The screens around them displayed news footage of the fire that had destroyed her home, stock footage of zombies as they leered and shambled, and bits of LaCenta from previous episodes, usually sneering, but sometimes in action, running the obstacle course with a spray gun or slicing an artificial tree with the chainsaw.

In a corner, Sharon had her head bowed and eyes focused on her DoDroid, which played a children's documentary about a free-range rabbit farm. Alberts had taken her aside and told her people had noticed her "change in behavior" this season. He'd offered to check her in at the Lindsey Lohan clinic, but she'd promised to find a better coping mechanism. So, bunny videos. Bunnies were cute and soft and only went for the throat in Monty Python movies. And they were so fuzzy!

Occasionally, her coos caused the technician to glance back with annoyance.

Dave grunted. "Okay, let's see that last clip again."

LaCenta gave the camera her best, "Do I really have to deal with you?" pout and tossed her cornrow braids. "Hey, I stand by what I said. Katie was a liability. All that sniffling and screeching. Probably gonna blow that twenty grand on tissues! I mean, Neeta told us often enough: You want to do this job, you've gotta be tough."

"Good!" Dave said. "Now, let's move to the flashback…"

The camera panned a low-income housing neighborhood in the depths of east LA. Small houses, irregularly kept; the camera focused in on one whose stucco was chipped in spots and which boasted sheets for curtains, but whose yard was mowed and weed-free. Lights shown through the sheets, revealing music notes and faded silhouettes of a long-gone pop star. In the background, traffic sounds competed with the clear voice of a woman yelling for her kids to get themselves ready for bed. On the screen flashed the words "Dramatic Recreation."

In the control booth, Dave said, "Cue narrator…"

"Twilight, and the Dane family prepares for bed. Monique, single mother of three, has had a long string of bad relationships, but never has that interfered with her devotion to her children or her pride in keeping a well-run home."

A lovely thirty-something black woman washed the face of a grubby boy of ten and called out math help to her six-year-old son, while her older daughter set lunches into their bags. LaCenta's voice spoke over.

"I don't even remember my daddy. None of us do. And the 'uncles' she brought home…Those that didn't hurt us still weren't worth much anyway. It was always us and Momma. She wasn't smart about men, no lie there, but that don't mean she was dumb, neither."

Unnoticed by the family, a slow-moving shadow lurched across the window.

The narrator intoned, "That night, one of Momma's 'bad choices' came back—in a most unexpected way."

The kitchen door crashed in, and a tall, black zombie with a dreadlock-laden scalp half hanging off its head staggered in. The children screamed and rushed behind their mother. They pelted it with everything they could find: knives, lunchboxes, math book. Monique dashed for the refrigerator. She shouted instructions to her children as she grabbed something. Her youngest son, Moe, grabbed the bottle of roach kill from the shelf and started spraying the air around them. Jamal, her older son, dug through the drawers and tossed her a pack of cigarettes. She threw it and the large ball of meat she'd pulled from the refrigerator into the small closet off the kitchen. When the zombie stumbled in after them, she locked the door while her son shoved a chair under the knob.

LaCenta twisted dials on the stove. Meanwhile, the narrator explained.

"LaVon Butler, thirty-two at the time of his death six months prior. He'd left their home in a fit of temper and had been killed in a bar fight later that evening. Now, some instinct had brought him back to the last home he'd had.

"This time, however, Monique was not going to take him in. Thinking fast, she lured Butler into the pantry with the hamburger she was defrosting for the next day's dinner and a packet of cigarettes. LaCenta, meanwhile, turned on their gas stove. Grabbing a rag and a bottle of rum as she hustled her children out the broken door, Monique fashioned a makeshift Molotov cocktail and set her own house on fire to destroy the contagion within."

The scene faded out as the family stood on the sidewalk, watching their house go up in flames, then faded in to a clip of LaCenta, twenty-one, talking to Neeta on her audition.

"They say, 'You can't take it with you,' but Uncle LaVon always insisted he would. Damfool did it, too. So, yeah, I got motivation to exterminate these vermin. Rather do it right, before someone has to burn their house down, too, that's all I'm saying."

Dave watched as the technician did a digital close up on LaCenta's face. He slapped his shoulder.

"Brilliant. Well done. Sharon, baby!" He snapped his fingers.

Sharon ran to his side, eyes on the ground, muttering, "Pretty bunnies. Fuzzy, fuzzy." Once she'd crossed the room to him, her eyes snapped up to his face, clear and focused. She hovered her stylus over her DoDroid. "Sir!"

"We're sure Uncle LaVon was destroyed in that fire? No chance of his coming back?"

"None, sir."

Dave sighed. "Shame. Would have made a hell of an episode."

The main story of the morning news was the opening speeches of the latest UN Conference. A well-groomed man of nondescript heritage in an expensive suit and artificially whitened smile slammed his fist onto the podium and spoke with measured passion.

"We can no longer afford to ignore the detrimental effect of Man's unchallenged industrial development. Our struggling world, unbalanced into a repetitive cycle of Global Warming/Global Cooling…That itself is not enough, rather the poisons that developed nations have poured into our skies, our water and our ground have sparked an unprecedented devolution! A species-wide threat with immediate ramifications to our continued survival!

"Too long have we dug among the sediments of international politics and burrowed deeper into the intricacies of text and the minutiae of fine detail. Clearly, we must, as my predecessor once said, 'soar above the ever-widening disconnect between an opaque and seemingly remote multi-lateral negotiation and the challenge at hand. '"

The picture shrunk and moved to the right side of the screen, revealing an anchorman with an artificial tan and equally artificial smile.

"With these strong words, the Umm Durman Environmental Rescue Conference began, with the radical goal of stabilizing the temperature of the Earth and reducing carbon emissions and industrial waste by half by the end of 2050. Among the list are phosphates, various chlorines, and—"

Neeta switched off the TV with a snarl. Once again, people who thought they were helping eliminate the zombie threat were going to make it harder for her to eliminate the zombie threat! Here she was, forced to play in a reality TV show in order to pay off her debts and stay in business, hopefully training up a couple of apprentice exterminators while she was at it. But what good were a half-dozen exterminators against the might of well-meaning nations? It was enough to drive the average man to drink.

Good thing I'm neither a man nor average, Neeta answered the thought. Still, she had to do something before she threw her remote at the television. She glanced at the clock. She had an hour or so before the field trip. She tossed on some grubby shorts and went to her workout room.

The workout room had a weight set and an elliptical in one corner, but Neeta ignored them. She needed more vigorous exercise than that if she wanted to burn off her emotional funk.

A control panel hung from a wire just past the equipment. She flipped the switch, and the lights came on across the large gymnasium with a satisfying series of heavy-duty clunks. Some typed commands, and the lighting began to flash and darken in a random pattern. Heavy metal music and undead groaning camouflaged the sound of gears and pistons that moved the zombie targets in their programmed pattern.

Neeta fitted the special covering over her chainsaw blade. Rather than chew through the zombie dummies, it would mark them with a self-dissolving ink. She could check her accuracy after the workout, and the next day, have clean targets to start again. She couldn't help but grin. The special effects guys had done an excellent job preparing this for the third-week challenge, and she'd made sure she got to keep it after the filming. They'd even returned afterwards to add a few "special touches" just for her.

Of course, none of the plebes had done the routine she'd just set for herself. It didn't really reflect the reality of zombie movements, either. Although the crew had designed the targets to look much like actual undead, they moved too quickly, changed direction too suddenly, lunged and retreated in ways zombies couldn't imitate. They zigged and zagged, dropped from the ceiling to zoom back up, flung themselves from the ground to trip the unwary. For once, this wasn't about training.

Neeta steeled herself, found an opening and dove in with a roar. She swung high, tagging the first zombie with the edge of her blade just as it got within her reach.

This was about reflexes...

She jumped over the arm that sprung up in front of her, doing the splits as she brought down her chainsaw to slice the hand off at the wrist.

...about burning aggression...

She spun a full circle, moving the saw in a sine wave. She took one target out at the knees, sliced another sideways across the chest, beheaded a third.

...about moving beyond thought and planning and negotiations with writers and directors and people who cared more for ratings than lives...

She lunged, spun, kicked and swung, her battle cries a perfect accompaniment to the pounding music.

A buzzer sounded, and the lights brightened and steadied. The targets stopped their frenetic motions and presented themselves for her to examine. She dropped the saw where she stood and braced her hands against her knees to catch her breath. Her arms felt like lead. A good feeling. She moved among the grimacing targets, noting the strikes that would have severed limbs, the ones that would have beheaded...When she came to the long-haired one with the pot belly, she gave a feral grin.

She's landed the blade in perfect position to slice Dave's manic smile right off his face.

Chapter 3

Notes from *The Zombie Syndrome*

A Documentary

By Gary Opkast

Episode: Zombie-ism: Causes and Cures

Interview clip: Dr. Myron P. Leadbetter, biochemist, author. Conservative, male, mid-30s, wearing a lab coat over a shirt and tie, Leadbetter sat with his legs crossed, ankle on knee. He kept shaking his foot so that the tassel on his shoe shook. Off screen Gary asked him twice to stop, as it made his whole body wiggle. Leadbetter finally grabbed his shoe with one hand, but then he started playing with the tassel. (Note: crop that out.)

LEADBETTER

To me, the cause is as plain as the nose on your face—provided you're living and still in possession of your nose, of course, hahaha. But seriously, let's look at history. 2009: the world is hit with the worst swine flu epidemic in a century. But thanks to modern medicine, we survive with only a few thousand deaths.

Leadbetter released his shoe and made air quotes around "thanks."

LEADBETTER

Between eight and ten years later, the first zombies emerge here in the United States, the most medically modern country in the world. I think the connection is clear.

Off camera, Gary prompted, "Could you just state it for our viewers?"

LEADBETTER

Vaccines! The COVID vaccines were simply produced too quickly and distributed too readily. Pharmaceutical companies saw the opportunity for massive profits, and congressmen had their careers at stake. They hurried it along to assuage public fears. I have documents and anonymous statements from people deep in the chain of command who say that even then, they knew there was something wrong.

I studied biochemistry in college, but when it comes to flu season, it's homeopathy and handwashing for my family!

Gary marked the end of the clip for use but continued to let the video play.

On his computer, Leadbetter had paused. "Can we go off the record a minute?"

"Yeah, sure. What's up?"

"Camera's off?" Gary had lied with his nod, and Leadbetter leaned forward and spoke quietly, anyway. "Listen, my publicist wants to know when this is scheduled to air. My book, *COVID and the Zombie Contagion*, comes out this fall, but we can tweak the launch date to match your airing."

"Uh, well, I haven't actually sold it yet."

He sat back, blinking. "Oh? Well, get on it, man! This is vital information. Here, let me give you my agent's card. If you're interested later in expanding this segment into a full hour special, I'd be glad to collaborate with you on it."

Gary stopped the video and shuffled the papers littering his side table until he found Leadbetter's agent's card. Was it worth giving Leadbetter an hour for his theory?

Neeta thought about Gordon while she showered. He'd make it, she knew that. He was efficient, thorough, and took orders well. He didn't have any problem destroying what had once been, and still looked like, a human being.

"There's something very satisfying about killing things," he'd told her in his audition interview. "Don't get me wrong—I'm not into murderous rampages or anything. But when something needs to get taken out, best to do it right, do it permanently, and move on."

She didn't know why he didn't get into extermination right off the bat, but instead, he'd wandered from job to job—martial arts instruction, police work—getting fired at each when his philosophy made itself known. Fortunately, before anyone was permanently taken out, the North Korean war broke out, and he'd joined the Marines, where he distinguished himself again and again for five years. Couldn't handle the peacekeeping, afterward, though.

Neeta leaned her head back into the spray, enjoying the feel of the water sluicing the shampoo out of her hair. Her mind turned to the e-mail she'd gotten from the Marine psychologist who'd out-processed Gordon.

*SSgt. Gordon "the Rock" Makepeace (discharged) possesses the natural tendencies of a serial killer. I can only credit strong parenting with the fact that he didn't spend his childhood pulling wings off butterflies and tying dynamite to cats' tails. The discipline of the Marines kept him from berserker antics in the war—though there was the incident at (**Classified information. Text redacted.**), but he ended up saving the lives of his fellow Marines. Semper Fi!*

*Zombie work sounds ideal for Rock. However, he will need a strong hand, firm orders and by no means should he be let loose around (**Classified information. Text redacted and added to Article 15 file. Please do not inquire Lt. Biloxi about it; he's in enough trouble already. OOH-Rah!**)*

Neeta turned off the shower, squeegeed off the glass, and sprayed the entire stall with disinfectant. She followed the same routine in her decontamination chamber—adding the radiation, of course. She'd never feel clean otherwise.

She was toweling off her short hair and thinking about growing it out and about what it was she needed to keep Gordon away from and if it might be kimchi, which could be a problem this afternoon, and, wow, she was hungry… So, when the doorbell rang, she answered it without thinking that she should probably have changed out of her bathrobe first.

Ted grinned at her, his eyebrows raised, while a half-step behind him, Gary gaped and blinked.

"Am I late for something?" she asked.

"Not at all," Ted said, all but purring the words. When Neeta squinted at him, he cleared his throat. "It's just that Dave changed his mind last night, said he won't shoot the—quote—educational boredomness—unless there's a real challenge involved. But Gary and I came up with an idea, so don't get your robe in a twist."

"Robe?" Neeta glanced down and blushed. She tried to hide it with an exasperated sigh. "Come in. Let me change."

She turned and headed into the bedroom, shutting the door. She resisted the urge to whack her head against the closet wall. She also forced her mind to stay away from the image of Ted smiling at her. The last thing she needed was to give Dave an off-stage romance to exploit. Even if Ted did have a cute grin.

Dressed in a pair of Bermuda shorts and a T-shirt with her company logo (Lyffe Undeath Exterminations), she emerged to see Ted flipping through one of the professional magazines that littered her coffee table along with her opened-but-unanswered mail, while Gary looked around the room with a dazed expression she couldn't figure out.

"Have you eaten today?" she asked him.

He blinked at her as if she were an apparition. "Some toast. We've been kind of busy."

She jerked her head toward the kitchen. "Come on. I'll make you a Pre-Run Special. Guaranteed to be easy on the stomach and quick to digest."

She gathered the ingredients and started chopping them into the blender while her guests watched, Gary with that weird look, and Ted with a small frown. Did he think she was going to poison him? He didn't have to drink it then. She turned her back on them.

Gary's phone rang, and he excused himself to the other room. As she reached into the dishwasher for three clean glasses, Ted moved to stand beside her.

"Uh, Neeta? This was in your magazine, marking the article on budget sprayers. I'm not trying to pry, but…"

She glanced at the letter in his hand; a second past-due notice on her mortgage with a 30-day foreclosure threat.

She hated the concern in his eyes. "Don't worry about it. It's taken care of."

"It was really that bad?"

"Why do you think I'm doing this show?"

He sighed and mashed his lips together. The silence stretched.

She broke it with the blender just as he was breaking it with a question. She snapped it off.

"What?"

"I said!" He stopped, began again at a lower volume. "I said, 'This is going to be awkward now, considering,' but I was wondering if you'd teach me to use the equipment. I'd pay for lessons."

"I don't need your pity!"

"See? Awkward! Who said anything about pity? I've been watching you guys have all the fun for the past six weeks—"

"That's what you think this is about? Having fun?"

He gave her his most rakish grin. "Looks fun to me."

Her next angry comment died in her throat. She opened her mouth, closed it, looked from his eyes to the magazine he held, folded to an ad for flamethrowers, then back to his face. Why'd his grin have to turn her insides to jelly? Not what she needed right now.

"Know what? Fine! Twenty dollars an hour, plus fuel and damages."

"Woooo!" Ted hooted as Gary walked back in.

"What? What?" he demanded as Neeta poured the smoothies into three cups.

Ted handed Gary a glass, then clicked it with his. "Neeta just agreed to give me private extermination lessons!"

"Oh." Gary's face fell.

Nasir sat in front of his laptop and made sure the camera could see the large poster of the mountains of Afghanistan and native bowl and artifact that sat on the stand beneath it. The poster was a blow-up of a photo he'd taken on a vacation, but Dave had had the props department make the objects from pictures from the Metropolitan Museum of Art. He'd written into Nasir's contract that he had to show them prominently in the background of all his blogcasts and interviews, along with wearing the turban and scarf when not in exterminator uniform. Still, if it made him competitive for the million, he didn't care. He'd managed to get a small bonus up front for butchering his grammar, however. He had some pride.

"Oh, yes," he told the screen. "I am very much excited to be visiting the Zombie Extermination Research and Development Center. I will being especially interested in effective low-budget extermination supplies and techniques. You see, a million American dollars is a lot of money in my country, but it is still not an incredible lot. I am not just to being my own business, but to start a national training center."

He paused, pressing one fist against his mouth and staring out his window at the palm-tree dotted parking lot of the cheap motel he'd found near the studio. When he spoke again, he didn't look back to the screen. "My country has been torn by war and insurgency for as long as we can remember. The British, the Russians, the Americans. The Taliban between. When finally, we were on our own, rebuilt, growing strong, the zombies emerged from the mountain hideouts to threaten our peace.

"We don't want to ask the world for help. We want to be left alone, to do for ourselves on our own. But if I don't win, I don't know if…"

He switched off the camera. Maybe he'd post it. He'd need to think.

He was still thinking when the bus came to pick him up.

The Zombie Extermination Research and Development Center looked like any off-campus lab building: large, square, with pastel brick and tinted windows, positioned off the highway and surrounded by a large xeriscaped campus with the mountains in the background. Not until one approached the entrance did the building's purpose make itself known and then only by a small, nondescript logo of the initials ZERD.

The *Zombie Death Extreme* viewers saw, however, an imposing military complex of cement blocks and steel, surrounded by six-foot fences topped with concertina wire and lined with surveillance cameras.

This suited the employees of ZERD just fine.

Inside, Neeta, her plebes, two cameramen, and a somewhat green but determined staff writer followed their tour guide through another set of double doors. The rubber waders they wore over their clean room suits squeaked on the tile floor. Roscoe somehow managed to walk without squelching. They passed rows of people working at computers and microscopes, their backs to the tour group. With their white jumpers and caps, they looked ominous and official. They didn't need to wear clean suits in this area, but no one wanted to go to get thrown out of the PTA or Rotary Club because they'd been identified on *Zombie Death Extreme*. East Palm Desert, after all, prided itself on its standards, and zombie work did not meet those standards.

Dr. Corriander Spice, who insisted everyone call him Dr. Hansen for the show, waited until they had all gathered around the large plate-glass windows, currently darkened. They couldn't avoid filming him, but the producer had agreed to use a computer-generated avatar in his place. As such, he was conducting the tour wearing a green-screen leotard with motion sensors dotting its surface. He tried very hard to ignore the giggles of his workmates and to keep his stomach sucked in. At least the director had agreed to replace him with a likeness of Duane Jones. He'd always harbored a secret longing to be just like the hero of *Night of the Living Dead*.

"So, to recap: We've seen the vivisection room—feeling better now, Gary?—and we've learned that removing appendages and even evisceration will not do more than slow your zombie down."

"Gawd, yes! The way that legless one kept crawling on, groaning, 'Flesh wound! Flesh wound!' was just totes creepy," Roscoe interjected.

Gary placed a hand over his mouth and his cheeks puffed. LaCenta rolled her eyes at him.

Spice wanted to ask him if he needed another bag, but the director had already chided him several times about talking to anyone but Neeta, the plebes, and the camera. He couldn't help it; the kid looked so pitiful. He decided to distract him instead.

"'Creep' is just the word!" Spice laughed, and Neeta chortled, but the rest looked blank. "Sorry. Exterminator humor. You'll learn it. So, the lesson there is, sever the upper spinal column, or…"

He held up his hands like a conductor.

The group chanted, "When the head comes away from the neck, *then* it's over."

He clapped his hands together. "Exactly! And, in fact, federal law now requires that all dead have their spines surgically severed before burial. Now, I know Neeta loves her chainsaw, but really, flamethrowers are the most effective destructive tool in your kit. Embalming fluid is highly flammable, especially where older corpses in advanced states of decay are concerned."

Neeta growled, "Which is all well and good until you singe some lawyer's precious back porch."

"Just so," Spice said. "There are too many places where napalm and fuel-injected inferno just don't fit."

"No truer words," Roscoe crooned. LaCenta slugged him.

"Not to mention the fact that a flamethrower in every home really isn't the best of ideas. So, we at ZERD are exploring safer means not only of extermination but of protection. We have been doing some very exciting work with antihistamine foam."

Gordon snorted. "Allergy meds for zombies? You've got to be kidding me."

Spice grinned at him. "Watch." He pressed a button on the wall.

The windows cleared to show a large room empty except for various mechanical arms suspended from the high ceiling, bearing a variety of spray nozzles and hoses. On one end, a small tray holding a pound of ground beef slid out of the wall. On the other, a door opened, and a female zombie clad in the ragged remains of a filthy calico dress staggered into the room. She hesitated, her head jerking about as she took in her surroundings, then she staggered for the meat.

About halfway across the room, a sprayer whirred into action, coating a line of foam between her and the meat. She jerked to a stop, wavering, her groans growing into panther-like screams.

"You trained it," Gordon scoffed.

"You can't train a zombie," Spice countered. "The part of the mind that processes cause and effect is atrophied. There's not even enough left for a Pavlovian effect."

As the zombie paced the line, screeching with frustration, Spice continued. "We aren't ready to deploy this tool yet, unfortunately. The concentration of antihistamine is way beyond FDA tolerance levels. Unless the exterminator is wearing a full hazmat suit, including gas mask, she or he will experience dry nose and mouth, irritability, and, of course, drowsiness, which is a bad thing when dealing with the undead. And of course, no one exposed should drive or operate heavy machinery for four hours afterward."

The zombie had started to calm and poke at the foam with her toe.

"Unfortunately, as you can see, the effect does wear off as the foam disintegrates. It's not ready as a long-term preventative until we find an agent that releases the chemical slowly. However…" He pressed another button.

The mechanical arm whirled toward the zombie and hosed it down with pinkish foam. The zombie's hunger screams rose into panic and it flailed at the stream. It staggered back, clawing off its own face, until it collapsed on the ground, jerked once, and stilled.

"And it's going to stay down?" Gordon asked skeptically.

Spice looked away from the prone corpse to answer but saw Gary's pale face. "You okay, there, Gary?"

Gary's eyes rolled into the back of his head, and he collapsed.

"Cut!" Dave snarled as everyone gathered around the unconscious writer.

"Look, I know none of you watchers are going to see him, but that writer Gary was pissin' me off! Gagging and swooning like he had the stomach flu—what's he doing writing for this show? And *what* was he doing on our tour of ZERD? Damfool probably looking for his fifteen minutes of fame. Well, if you get fame for barfing and falling on the floor, he got it, that's all I'm saying."

Dr. Corriander Spice settled into the leather office chair and adjusted the mike on his lab coat. "You're sure you don't want to use the green suit again? Really, I don't mind, especially here in private."

Off-camera, Gary answered. "No, sir. This is a different project. We'll digitize your face and disguise your voice."

"All right then. You know, I'm not ashamed of the job I do. It's just that we attend my wife's church—the Second Generationalists of the New Tomorrow. They don't believe in zombies."

"Uh, what do they think they are, then?"

"Demons, plain and simple, animating the bodies of the damned."

"Actually, that's not a bad description."

"Oh, it's useful enough—until you try to tell them that a five-gallon jug of TidyToidy works better at stopping them than a five-hour prayer revival. I like what the Baptist Convention said: Just because they're evil incarnate doesn't mean we can't fight them with secular means."

"The Pope said the same thing." Gary made a note to find a news clip.

"Well, common sense isn't tied to a particular religion. So, what shall I talk about?"

"Tell me more about your research—something you didn't cover in the tour."

"Well," Spice said as he rubbed his hands together, "one of our most challenging pursuits has been the search for Zombie Zero."

"Zombie Zero?"

"All right, plebes!" Neeta gazed seriously at her trainees and tried to ignore the camera looming behind them. She stood with her back to the observation room, its plate-glass windows again darkened. Beside her, a large divider with the ZERD logo hid a table. Her trainees all wore rain suits and wide-brimmed rain caps. So did Ted, though she had no idea why. He wasn't going anywhere near the tank. Still, she tried not to think about how he made cheap plastic look good.

"You've toured the facility. You've seen the tools and the experimental devices, but more importantly, you've seen common household items in action.

"They say seeing is believing, but *I* see in some of you that that isn't the case." Dave told her to pause while the cameras closed in on each face for their reaction: Gordon, skeptical; LaCenta, annoyed as usual; Roscoe, horrified; Spud and Nasir, thoughtful.

"Go!" Dave spoke in her earpiece.

"That's why we've designed today's challenge. On the table beside me, you will find a variety of everyday objects. Some repel zombies; others don't; still others may or may not. You will select five different items.

"Next, you will be put in the testing room. You must stand in the circle inscribed on the floor. Do not leave the circle! See that red line? It's eight feet from the circle. You will be two feet from the door. Six zombies will be released—"

Her plebes immediately shouted protests.

"What?" shrieked LaCenta.

"Neeta, are you mad?" Roscoe followed up.

Neeta held her hands up, and the noise died. "There are fail-safes in place which I will explain in a moment. Six zombies will be released. You will use the five objects to stop or stall all the zombies before any of them cross the line and keep them stalled for 30 seconds."

"And if we don't?" LaCenta demanded, her voice straining in disbelief.

"This room is designed for live trials. As soon as a zombie crosses the red line, an acrylic wall rises between you and the zombies. You will also be doused in shower scrub. If that's not enough, the entire room will be coated in antihistamine foam, and you can spend the weekend with a vaporizer. But if you experience irritability, don't take it out on me."

"Not like we'll notice," Roscoe whispered *sotto voce* to Spud, jerking his head LaCenta's way. Spud bit back a snort.

"What was that?" LaCenta growled.

"Neeta!" Roscoe raised his hand like a teacher's pet. "What if we run out of objects before time is up?"

"Then you'd better get creative. Nasir, I see a frown. Problem?"

"Neeta, we know zombie instincts are acculturated, and my culture—"

"Cut!" Dave screamed. "Accent! Take two!"

Nasir heaved a sigh and started again. "Neeta, I am being most certain that these items will work on the American zombie, but the Afghan zombie, he will not be so interested."

Neeta smiled. Gary had thought of that and planned for it, right to this scene. "We realize that, Nasir. That's why Cory—shoot! Sorry! Take two?

"We realize that, Nasir, that's why *Dr. Hansen* and his team have set up a special table for you." She moved aside another screen to reveal several somewhat different objects.

"Each of these have been tested by ZERD's sister laboratories in Baghdad and Riyadh. Obviously, we couldn't import Afghan zombies, but the ZERD team has treated each item with chemicals that will simulate the effect."

Nasir hadn't seen the table before this. He stared at it, speechless, reaching out to turn an object here, prod one there.

Neeta said, "Zombies are mindless. You can't negotiate. You have to handle them on their own terms. We get that, and we want you to go home able to do this job, and to do it well."

"I'm...I'm touched." He replied, voice horse, accent forgotten.

For once, Dave let it slide.

They drew names, and LaCenta went in first. She shook as the door opened, but once the small horde had shambled out, she burst into action. She threw her pound of hamburger into the center of the group. They all clustered around it, but too soon, two established dominance and the other four came at her while the two split their winnings. She ripped the packet of cigarettes and threw one half to each side. One zombie lunged for them, taking another out in the process. The rest skirted the fallen case, making the fake coughing sounds of the militant non-smoker. These she took out with well-aimed shots of chemical cleanser from a super-powered water gun.

The buzzer rang, and the wall came up just as she was running out of cleaner. She hustled to the door.

Her cheering comrades met her just outside. She gave Gordon a high five.

"Oh, honey, that was hardcore!" Roscoe enthused.

Neeta nodded. "You only used three of your items."

"Tried and true! It worked for Momma, it'll work for me!" she replied.

Nasir went next. Even as the door was sliding open, he ripped the cover off the package of bacon and tossed them in a messy row just on the zombie side of the red line. He wrapped the political cartoon around a package of cigarettes and threw them hard so that they landed in the middle of the horde. As with LaCenta, the zombies stopped and bickered, but two females quickly broke off and staggered again. He lobbed his bottle of eyeliner and the novel, *Under My Burka*. It stopped one, but the other sneered and ignored it. She, however, paused at the line of bacon, her head shaking spasmodically.

The buzzer rang, hailing his victory.

"W-what's the story with the b-bacon?" Spud asked.

LaCenta rolled her eyes. "They're Muslims, fool!"

Gordon went next, but alone, he moved without a clear plan, tossing his items in haphazardly, running out of distracters before he ran out of time. As a linebacker-sized zombie, still clawing Drano out of his eyes, stepped over the line, the wall went up. A trapdoor opened in the ceiling above Gordon and a bucket of TidyToidy emptied over his head.

True to form, Roscoe and LaCenta met Gordon at the door with jeers.

"Oh, boyfriend! Chlorine and lavender are so not your scents!" Roscoe howled. He and LaCenta leaned on each other laughing.

Gordon glared at them, hands balled into fists.

Quietly, Spud stepped forward. "W-w-wasn't so bad," he said. "You moved in t-to-too kw-quick is all."

Gordon rounded on the skinny Idahoan. "I don't need to listen to a stuttering hick tell me how to do a job!" he snarled and stormed off.

Neeta pushed herself off the wall to follow, but Nasir stopped her. "Go on with the challenge. I will speak to him. Maybe he'd rather listen to an Afghani accent, hm?"

Neeta watched as Nasir caught up with Gordon, keeping a respectable distance, nonetheless. The second cameraman, a new guy, followed. She didn't want to see it aired, but she did plan on asking Dave to let her see the tape.

"Okay, Spud, into the room with you."

If Gordon moved too fast, Spud moved with almost too-slow deliberation. Not that he was stupid, of course. He stopped four zombies—two male and two female—

by turning the TV from the Spike to the Oxygen channel, then throwing the remote at them. The other two, he held off with measured shots of 409 until the buzzer rang.

"Now that's how it's d-d-done!" he hooted.

Roscoe slapped his shoulder with the back of his hand. "Plenty of ways to do it. Just keep your baby-blues on me."

Roscoe, however, didn't have as much luck with his set of zombies, and with ten seconds on the timer, he'd exhausted his items and still had one zombie shambling toward him. A pre-teen in the late stages of decay, she advanced with slow, forced movements. Frantically, he unsnapped his raincoat and started feeling around his pockets.

"Hey! Can he do that?" LaCenta snarled.

"He's allowed," Neeta answered. She stepped closer to the windows, watching him intently. "Whether he can do anything that way...we'll see."

Roscoe took out his cell phone, shook his head, and put it back. He pulled out a thin tube and with a flourish, yanked off the lid off and flung it toward the last zombie.

It fell at her feet. She staggered, stopped, and with what could only be described as a joyful cry, flopped onto the floor and started rubbing the stick on her lips, flaying off bits of skin in the process. The buzzer sounded.

Roscoe sauntered out of the room.

"Lip balm?" Neeta asked.

He winked at her, making sure his face was angled toward the camera. "Well, the poor dear looked a little chapped."

For the first time on the show, Neeta burst out laughing.

Gordon stared into the webcam with narrowed eyes, his jaw set and so tense he had to force the words out of his mouth.

"That whole challenge was BS, man! Sitcoms and magazines and Chapstick! I'm not going into a horde of zombies with intent to stall! Go in, take them out, make sure they don't come back. Maximum firepower, maximum carnage.

"I'm not stupid. This was a confidence-building exercise. But I've got to tell you, a pansy-assed exercise like this wasn't going to build my confidence. Back in the Marines, you failed at something, you got put right back into the line of fire. That's how you build confidence. OOH-Rah!

"Speaking of pansy…Chapstick? And Neeta gave him *points* for that?

"BS. It's all BS, but that won't stop me. I will embrace the suck! I will persevere! I will win that million! OOH-Rah!"

Chapter 4

Notes for: *The Zombie Syndrome*

A Documentary

By Gary Opkast

Episode: Zombie Zero

Film clip of a zombie clawing its way out of a grave (NOTE: Check YouTube; InsaneCandid is supposed to have a good one, and his family may sell the rights to pay for his funeral expenses.)

NARRATOR

The world has been living under the zombie threat for over two decades, yet where did this threat originate? Did it begin with a single human, or a simultaneous uprising? Did the zombie syndrome migrate to other countries, or did it spring simultaneously, as it were, from the grave? The answers to these questions could give scientists a much-needed break in isolating and resolving the cause of zombie-ism. So, the search continues for that elusive first case—the one that scientists call "Zombie Zero."

(Need background visuals—something non-zombie-ish but interesting enough to detract from digitized face effect)

DR. BEN HANSEN (CORRIANDER SPICE)

The problem we're coming up against is in the reporting. Sure, now, you call 9-1-1 and tell them there's a zombie on your lawn, and the Z-mat team comes right away. But who would have believed this twenty-three years ago?

Cut to re-enactment of 9-1-1 call. Note on bottom: 9-1-1 call, Pleasantville, KY, Oct 31, 2019, 11:35 p.m.

9-1-1

9-1-1, how may I help you?

BARBIE MUNCHAUSEN

Please! Help me! There's a, a zombie and it's…

9-1-1

Where are you?

BARBIE MUNCHAUSEN

I'm in a barn off Countryside Lane! My boyfriend and I were on a drive, and we ran out of gas and now—

9-1-1

"Ran out of gas"?

BARBIE MUNCHAUSEN

Shut up, okay? There's a zombie, and it broke the window and pulled Billy out of the back seat and—

9-1-1

Miss, have you been drinking?

BARBIE MUNCHAUSEN

Shut up and help me! I'm in the barn, and it's coming after me, and I think Billy is too!

9-1-1

Miss, could it be they're just playing a joke?

BARBIE screams.

Cut to clips of the barn, the bodies with sheets over them, one hand, obviously zombified, peeking out.

NARRATOR

It was no joke. Barbie Munchausen, 17, and her boyfriend, Billy Stakes, were discovered by police officers lurching hand-in-hand down Countryside Lane. When they attacked Policeman Lance McRue, his partner, Dougie Marsh, a longtime fan of zombie films, decapitated them with an ax. Even so, officials were slow to believe the zombie story until McRue himself re-animated an hour later. This was the first confirmed case of zombie-ism in the United States, but was it the first?

HANSEN

Not a chance. We have found veiled references to the undead back to the mid-2010s. Before that, we had some vampire sightings, but we're pretty sure that was part of the Twilight craze. Vampires! Come on—who's going to believe that old tale?

"Neeta, baby! So, glad you could make it! We've got important work today—a real crisis."

Dave held out his hands in welcome.

Neeta sidestepped him, flopped down onto a plastic chair and plopped her feet onto the table. She nursed her second cup of coffee and resisted the urge to tell Dave where he could stick his "real crisis." What could he know about a crisis? Maybe she should let him live her life a while; then he'd know about crisis. As Dave nattered on, her mind replayed the phone call that woke her at six that morning.

"Ms. Lyffe, this is Brian Wanker from Wanker, Wanker, and Twiddle."

"What do you want? I made my payment to your client on time."

"Yes…just barely. We felt it prudent to remind you the next one is coming in two weeks, and that your license to re-kill depends on your prompt compliance to the schedule. After all, your little flirtation with fame won't protect you from the real world."

Dave addressed the room at large. "This is *real*, people! We've got trouble. Potentially big trouble! Sharon, chart!"

Sharon tapped a key on her DoDroid, and a bar chart showed up on the wall screen, showing viewers vs. time. Neeta gave it a disinterested glance as Dave flung his hand dramatically toward the screen, his laser pointer shining at the lowest spot on the chart.

"'Flirtation with fame'?" she'd sneered at the lawyer. "Listen, Wanker, what you call my 'flirtation with fame' is a lot of pain-in-the-butt, dangerous work that is barely—just barely—keeping a roof over my head and your 'schedule' kept. Meanwhile, I just heard that Twiddle—or should I say 'your client'—is using my money to put in an in-ground pool. You want to explain that?"

Dave didn't shout, but spoke with harried, urgent tones. "A thirty-three percent drop, people! How do you explain that?" He went on without waiting for replies.

Wanker had said, "Ms. Lyffe, zombies fell into it. You could hardly expect them to use it after it'd been contaminated with those…remains…"

"I get splattered with remains on a regular basis. They wash off more easily than lawyer ghwal."

"Perhaps you should calm down…"

"I don't care if Woodland Forrest chose that time to announce that he's thinking about running for President! 'Thinking about it?' That should not even compete! Sorry, sorry. I am doing my best to be calm, people. But we are talking about millions of viewers who simply clicked away from our show. You promised this wouldn't happen, Gary. Perhaps if we'd listened to my instincts…"

"Perhaps you should remind your client that if it hadn't been for me, he and his guests would no longer be in the real world. Who

in their right minds sets out pickled beets in this day and age, especially when they live so close to a cemetery?"

"Which does not negate the fact that you set fire to their home."

"The back awning! And I did not set fire to it! I flamed a zombie, which staggered onto their porch, and if some idiot hadn't thrown vodka on it, it would never have set their awing on fire!"

"Mrs. Wanker was only trying to help extinguish the fire."

"I have been putting out fires all day," Dave complained. "Producers, network people. Our sponsors are complaining about losing out on millions of viewers. LaserScrape Oral Hygiene was especially concerned."

Gary spoke up, "But the ratings went back up! We only had the dip between seven-fifteen and seven-thirty. People returned for the challenge, even though it was in the middle of Forrest's speech."

"Wait a minute!" Neeta pulled her feet to the floor with a thunk. "Are you telling me that right when we were discussing home defense, the part of the show people most needed to see, they were off watching some aging actor spout off about how he should run this country? That's the most important segment of the show!"

"No, Neeta, baby," Dave countered. To Neeta's ears, his tone mimicked the patronizing tone of Wanker. "The most important segment of the show is where your trainees go up against the zombies."

"And those ratings are fine!" Gary repeated.

"Ratings?" Neeta stood to scream across the table at him. "What is wrong with all of you? People are getting killed out there. They are dying—then coming back! Millions of people missed the chance to learn how to defend themselves, but you're worried because some company selling electronic tongue scrapers is upset?"

Dave reached out to touch her shoulder. "Neeta, baby, we understand—"

She flung his arm off her hard enough to knock him into his chair. "Don't talk to me about what you understand!"

She stormed out of the room.

Only after she was halfway down the hall did she realize she'd left her coffee behind. She stomped to the soda machine and fed a ten-dollar bill in. It spat it back out.

"Please insert exact change," the machine's mellow female voice intoned. "I can accept all forms of American currency. If you need help determining what to use, please say, 'I need help making change.'"

"Kharbachiya!" Neeta shrieked one of the swear words Nasir had taught her.

The machine replied. "Thank you. You may insert your money at any time. The price is seven dollars and thirty-five cents. You may insert one five-dollar bill, two one-dollar bills, a quarter and a dime. Or you may insert seven one-dollar bills, a quarter and a dime. Or you may insert—"

"Allow me." Ted came up behind her. He squeezed in between her and the machine. He looked right and left to make sure no one was watching, then began to push selection codes in a quick pattern and kicked the side of the machine.

"Mmmmm. Thank you!" the voice purred. "Please, choose anything!"

He pressed a button and a cola popped out the bottom.

"Oh, yes! Thank you!" The machine hummed and went silent.

"How did you do that?" Neeta asked, her anger momentarily forgotten.

"You can't tell anyone. Got a friend who programs these. He put in a cheat code. Only works once every thirty days, though."

He leaned over to grab the bottle. Neeta couldn't help but grin at the view.

"And kicking the machine is part of the code?" she asked.

"Nah. I just hate this machine." He handed her the soda with a flourish.

"I wanted a diet." She unscrewed the cap and swallowed down half the contents anyway.

He wagged his finger at her. "Aspartame causes brain cancer and induces post-mortem zombie-ism."

He led her to the chairs. His hand felt warm on her elbow. His smile teased. Why couldn't she have met him under different circumstances?

"You don't really believe that, do you? Doesn't matter. When Mom died, we buried her with her severed head cradled in her arms. My aunt had a fit, but the people really close to her understood. I want to go the same way." She took a long drink.

For a moment, he didn't say anything, just watched her with that intense, thoughtful look she'd seen him wear when blocking out a scene to video. She rolled the bottle between her hands, thinking of Mom, thinking of him, not sure what to say.

Finally, he spoke, his voice calming. "They came back for the challenge, Neeta. They saw the stuff in action. That's going to convince them more than Hansen's lecture."

"Yeah, maybe."

"There'll be reruns. Trust me, *Zombie Death Extreme* is going to be a streamed for a long time."

"Okay."

"Hey, did you know Gary is making a documentary about the zombie uprising? He's calling it *The Zombie Syndrome*. He's taping all kinds of experts. He's already gotten Hansen, and I think he's planning on follow-ups with him."

Neeta felt a spark of happiness warm away some of the tension of the morning. "Really?"

Ted grinned. "He was in heaven when you suggested ZERD. Listen, no one's supposed to know about it. He considers it his opus, and he's very protective. Scared Dave will try to take it over and make it a blockbuster movie with exploding bodies and bikini-clad women or something. I only found out because he needed to borrow the camera during break."

"Hmph!" Neeta sighed. "Wonder why he hasn't interviewed me." She realized only after she said it how self-pitying that sounded.

Ted, however, laughed. "Are you kidding? He's still trying to work up his nerve! He's got a serious case of hero-worship."

Her eyes widened. She nearly dropped her soda. "Hero worship? Me?"

Again, Ted laughed. "You know, Neeta, you play this right, you could be an action figure. Zombie Exterminator Barbie!"

"With her own chainsaw?"

"Sure! And a bottle of spray cleaner for emergency home defense! See? Now, feeling better? Because we have to talk about the next challenge."

Neeta felt her stomach drop and her smile sour. "Is that why you came after me?"

He spread his hands. "Someone had to talk you off the ledge. Besides, it's a great chance to get in good with my sensei."

She leaned back and crossed her arms, still holding her nearly empty bottle. What are you about? she wondered. She nixed the thought; it didn't matter. With her job, her debt, and her vocation, she could hardly afford a romance.

Maybe she could animate Zombie Exterminator Barbie and retire to a real life.

She stood. "All right, then. Let's go. I've got bills to pay and dolls to pose for."

"That's the spirit!"

Once inside, Dave all but pounced on her. "Neeta! Cooled down, then? No, no—no apologies. We all need our Diva Moment."

Diva? Anger began to smolder the happiness Ted had brought out in her. He may have "talked her off the ledge," but they hadn't solved what drove her there.

"Don't worry! I've got the perfect idea for the next challenge! We'll rescue this ratings fiasco yet! Work with me here: We get a boxing ring: ropes, audience, girls in bikinis, the whole enchilada, right? Can you see it?"

Neeta clenched her jaw to keep from gaping. *Ledges sound like a good idea. Wonder how hard it would be to get Dave out on one?*

"I see in your eyes that you're sharing my vision! Now, brace yourselves, everyone. Ready? Zombie... Tag team... Wrestling!" He looked around at his slack-jawed, horrified audience. "Do you have chills? I get chills!"

Ledges? Ledges are too good for him. I'm taking him to the Bedder Rest Mattress Factory and dropping him through the roof!

"Okay...I see that some of you have doubts. What if we made it a hot-tub sized tank of Jell-O? Even up the odds? What do you say?"

Neeta growled. "How about 'criminal negligence'? Where's the list of challenges I submitted?"

"Come on, Neeta, baby!" Dave cajoled. "I don't like these vibes! Turn that frown upside down! It takes more muscles to frown than smile, you know!"

She leaned in close, her hands clenched. "How many to handle a chainsaw?" she hissed.

He blinked. "Um...more?"

She looked him up and down. "Could be worth it. Ted, want to get the camera and my gear? Sounds like one for the blooper reel."

"All right." Dave backed away, hands up in surrender. "No need to be so negative. We're all brainstorming here."

"Remember what I said about your last brainstormed episode—the encounter in the warehouse? You disregarded my objections—and what happened?"

"Okay, so your instincts were right on that one. I totally trust you now, all right?"

"Good. The list."

"Neeta…"

Neeta reached into her pocket and pulled out her keys. She held them toward the room at large. "Right side of the van, mounted on the wall. Bring the gas can, too. Gary, you might want to leave—this could get messy," she said.

Even so, Dave didn't relent until after he saw the half-dozen people, including Gary, get up and reach for the keys.

"Er…Sharon, baby, got that list?"

Sharon had already called it onto the screen and high-lighted three of Neeta's ideas.

She explained, "During the recess and discussion, I logged into the *Zombie Death Extreme* Chitter account and ran a poll. I've highlighted the three most popular story ideas."

Dave frowned. "How many replies?"

Sharon hesitated. "Only 157,980 chits, but we're talk-ing about fifteen minutes of poll time, sir. Also, I removed the ideas that would take longer than a week to prepare."

"All right," Dave sighed heavily and considered the list with a frown.

Behind him, Sharon rolled her eyes at Neeta and winked.

Gordon settled back in his desk chair with a beer and turned on the webcam. Dave had ordered them all to make a blog today about the Forrest candidacy. He had something to say, and no doubt!

"Forrest? For President? Give me a break! Look, I liked him well enough in *Unwashed Unholies* Six, but he ain't exactly the tough character he plays. You think he's going to do anything about the real zombie problem? Probably have the country high and eating tofu first year in office." He snorted and took a swig of his beer.

"Who's he going to get for a running mate? Maybe he'll find Nancy Pelosi all zombiefied and hook up with her. Now wouldn't that be a hoot."

Roscoe sighed deep from his heart, his eyes misted. "Oh, gawd, I'm such a fan of Forrest. Such a fan—and not just of him as an actor. My parents actually met in his leaf bar. They were there when he was arrested in a rally for government subsidized marijuana. Of course, I grew up watching that classic series, *Rainbow Crossing*.

"He's just so commanding in front of the camera, yet so natural and so frank. And sexy! He oozes charisma! When this show is over, I am joining his campaign. If there's anyone I'd trust at the helm of this nation, it's Woody."

Roscoe replayed the blog. Hm, it was missing something. American flag in the background. His "The White House Needs Woody" campaign button showed prominently on his shirt. He could probably have lingered more lovingly over the wedding photo of his parents... What was he saying? That was perfect! No, something else...

He snapped his fingers. Of course! He dashed to the television and called up the first "Best Quotes from *Unwashed Unholies* Compilation" he found. He set it to play low in the background, and as Forrest as Aspertaim spouted his famous one-liners, he re-recorded his blog.

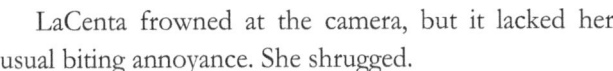

LaCenta frowned at the camera, but it lacked her usual biting annoyance. She shrugged.

"Listen, I'm not all that up on politics, okay? But we've had women running this country for the past twelve years and America is finally on the way up. Should we really mess with a good thing? That's all I'm saying."

She raised her hands in an "I'm done" gesture and switched off the camera.

Spud shifted uncomfortably in his seat before the computer. He hadn't blogged much for the show, and the ones he had made mostly talked about how he felt he'd performed. Dave kept scolding him to "get emotional! Get controversial! Give me julienne fries, baby!" He didn't know what that meant, so he kept his posts to a minimum. Besides, these things made him nervous; and the more nervous he was, the more he stammered. He hated stammering.

This blog entry, however, he couldn't escape. Dave had been clear on that point.

He took a breath, remembering Mom's advice: speak slowly, think about your words. Don't let yourself get nervous. Pretend you're talking to me.

"So. I heard these gu-guys talking in the snack bar. One asked how W-woody Forrest could run for P-president if he was from Athens. The other one said, 'Athens, Ohio, idiot.' Course, then he asked me today if that was c-c-close t-to where I lived.

"I'm from Idaho. That's like t-twenty-six hundred miles away from Ohio. So, maybe if Forrest becomes p-p-President, he could do something about the education in this country?"

He scratched his chin, trying to think of something else to say.

"Oh, um, it would have been nice if he'd waited ffforty-five minutes to make his speech or done it half an hour earlier. Then it wouldn't have interfered with our show. I heard a b-bunch of zombies invaded his community in p-Pensa c-Cola last year. You'd think with that and the movies he's done, he'd want folks to know about fighting zombies. Ah, who knows? Maybe his p-press agent makes all those arrangements. Still, it would've been nice. Neeta and the rest of the team work real hard to put these shows t-together. I hope you'll all catch it on the reruns. They told everyone how to keep their houses safe, you know?

"I'm from a really small town, and fffolks are always asking my mom which episode is best. Well, it's not the most exciting, but I think everybody ought to watch this one. I'm calling Mom to tell her to t-te-tell folks that, too.

"I mean, the other episodes are neat and all, but this one c-could save your life."

He paused, and not having anything else to say, signed off. Then he went to get some iced tea and call his mom. He'd tell her about the video, too. She'd be proud that he'd spoken so long.

Lawyer Larry had advised the cast against going to Bergie's funeral. "Presence there could be interpreted as an admission of guilt," he'd warned.

At two o'clock that afternoon, Neeta dressed in a black suit dress and high heels. She left behind the traditional black spray pack and instead grabbed up the new hat with veil she'd bought after Lawyer Larry's "advice." She would have to catch a bus to the cemetery; anyone would recognize her van with its logo of a woman stepping on a cockroach and holding a zombie head in one hand.

When she stepped outside, however, she found Spud lounging against his Ford F450. He opened the door for her.

"Who's g-gu-going to recognize me in a suit?" he asked.

The Truly Eternal Rest funeral home was nestled on a hill, with the cemetery stretched out around it on three sides. Neeta nodded approvingly at the location. One of the few cemeteries to have the resources and wherewithal to exhume all of its "residents" and sever their spines before they could return from the dead, it had profited from its foresight. The engraving on the large granite sign proudly declared "Zombie Free since 2023!"

Some hundred people crowded into the chapel. Neeta and Spud took standing spots against the back wall. Atop the closed casket, the funeral directors had set his surfboard, its surface crowded with flowers and family pictures, surfing trophies and other memorabilia. The preacher talked about "shooting that great tube in the sky." His younger sister talked about him teaching her to surf, her voice so quiet people stifled their sobs to hear her. His uncle talked about his laid back, happy-go-lucky attitude and how they'd rebuilt his Pacer.

No one mentioned his time on the show or his desire to be an exterminator.

When the funeral ended, Neeta and Spud ducked out the back rather than greet the family. Several others had done this, too—to catch a socially unacceptable smoke during the one occasion when people might sympathize, to head back to work, or to get a seat near the gravesite. Away from the need for a tearful, respectful silence, they chattered freely.

"Closed casket," one grunted within earshot of Neeta. "Guess that proves it, then. The exterminator woman really did cut off his head."

Neeta froze.

The guy beside him swore. "I heard Maude didn't believe it until she actually viewed the body. Bob said she passed out right there in the morgue. Said they were going to press charges, get her for murder, but police said they couldn't. Once you're bitten by a zombie, you're considered worse than dead."

The first man puffed out a blast of smoke. "So, sue her pretty ass."

"Can't. Show's lawyer's got documents Bergie signed absolving them of responsibility. Then he said that if they wanted to sue, they had to sue the show, not the girl." He leaned toward his friend confidentially, yet still speaking loudly enough for people nearby to hear. "Maude and Bob aren't saying, but I think he gave them a fat settlement to keep them quiet."

Neeta grabbed Spud by the elbow. "Let's go."

Once in the car, she leaned her head against the back of the seat. Her hat tilted forward. The veil tickled her chin, but even if she thought it was safe to remove it, she didn't have the will.

Spud asked. "You okay?"

She took a moment to make sure she could speak with a steady voice. "Drive me to Studio Law Associates, please?"

At the law firm, Neeta strode past the receptionist before she could protest and charged into Lawyer Larry's office. Spud followed with a shrug. The lawyer glanced up from his computer, took in their black attire, and waved off the apologetic receptionist.

"I specifically advised you against attending the funeral."

"Did you pay off the family?" Neeta demanded.

He leaned forward, setting his elbows on his desk. He clasped his hands over his laptop. "Didn't you yourself say they deserved compensation?"

"Did you make it sound like hush money?"

He set his chin on his hands.

"Was that the only way to protect your precious studio?" she persisted.

He stared at her.

She stared back. She'd looked undeath in the eyes hundreds of times. She was not going to fold before some pompous, calculating lawyer.

Suddenly, he didn't seem so pompous. He just looked hurt. And old.

"Neeta, we both know you can't afford another lawsuit," he said.

Then he reopened his laptop and focused on the screen. "Now, if that's all, I have a lot of work to do."

Shaken for the second time that day, Neeta stormed out.

Dear Mr. and Mrs. Eidelberg,

Neeta leaned back and wiped her eyes with her sleeve. In the trash can beside her desk, four sympathy cards with tear stains and scratched out lines lay torn up among used tissues. This was the last one she'd bought; she had to get it right.

I'm so sorry for your loss. I've never had a son die, but I have lost many people I love, so I know some of the pain. I'm writing to explain in hopes that this might ease some of yours.

My mother was a zombie exterminator. Jerry Lee was her partner. I called him Uncle Lee. Aunt XiaXia used to take care of me when they were on runs; I grew up with their kids. They used to take me everywhere—Disneyland, Universal Studios. We were all going to visit Taiwan to see his family. Then he was ambushed on an extermination call. There were too many zombies. Mom drove them off, but not in time. He died begging her to take care of XiaXia and the kids.

We didn't understand about zombie-ism enough then. We buried him intact and went on with our lives. I was twelve.

Two months later, Aunt XiaXia called us, frantic. A zombie was attacking their house. Uncle Lee had come back and had returned to the ones he had loved most. He'd have killed them—and brought them back—if Mom hadn't re-killed him first.

Bergie was a sweet boy. He talked a lot about all of you, but especially of his sister Gwendolyn. He told us many times how, when this was all over, he was going to take her on a tour of the gnarliest waves on the west coast.

That's why I did what I did. If I could have saved him, I would have, please believe that. But since I couldn't, the best thing I could do for him was make sure he didn't come back to hurt those he loved most.

Bergie died because he wanted to learn to protect those he loved, and he wanted to be a hero to his little sister. Be proud of him.

Neeta dropped the pen and pushed away from the desk. Then she brought her knees to her chest and curled in tight.

She stayed like that until Hollerman came to get her for the late-night 21-spout fumigation of Bergie's grave. She didn't think his family would understand, but he deserved the honor, and she would see that he got it.

Chapter 5

"Good morning, L.A! You are listening to the Brian and Cassie Morning Show on K-RTH 101, the station that rocks California bigger than the Quake of 2-8! Listen to us on Nano-Dee at 101.573! And have we got a treat for you today, right, Cassie?"

"Oh, yeah! Can I tell them?"

"Aw, I want to tell...Oh, okay, but I introduce them!"

"Today we have in the studio the entire remaining cast of *Zombie Death Extreme*! Yay! Wooo! Say, 'Helloness!' everybody!"

"OOH-Rah!"

"Hi."

"Er, helloness?"

"Oh, gawd, I'm so excited to be here!"

"Shuddap, Roscoe. Hey, all."

"H-he-hello."

"So, sitting with us, we have the contestants: Gordon Makepeace. LaCenta Dane. Roscoe Glaser."

"A pleasure, always, Brian!"

"Nasir Haq Qalzai—did I get that right?"

"Oh, yes. Very good!"

"And of course, Spud"

"Spud! How'd you get that name, Spud?"

"Uh, my real name's P-p-pip-pippin Fffrost. I'm from Idaho. Someone here th-thought it was funny. It's easier to say."

"Oh, but it's a great name, right Cassie?"

"I just love to say it. Spud! Spud!"

"Down, girl! We can't forget the star of the show, the master exterminator herself, Neeta Lyffe!"

Canned applause and wolf whistles.

"Hi, Brian, Cassie. Thanks for having us here."

"No problem. We love the show, right Cass?"

"Absolute-a-tively! But I really think last week's was the best yet. I mean, who knew you could defend yourself with stuff you had lying around? Seriously, you can repel zombies with reruns of *The Simpsons Move to South Park*?"

"Or distract them. It varies by zombie. That's really why we wanted to do that show. I think it's probably the most important one of the series. Incidentally, you can find a list of items on the Lyffe Undeath Exterminations or ZERD websites."

"That's great! We have just a minute before weather and traffic, and we'll get you that website. Or find the link on our PeopleSpace account. First, though…I don't want to be a downer, but I've got to ask you. You've had a lousy run of luck lately, Neeta: your mother died, you got sued, now this thing with Eidelberg—"

"—oh, yeah, poor Bergie! He was such a hottie, too—"

"—so why do you do it? What makes you want to keep fighting zombies day after day?"

"I… Well, someone has to do it. People will die otherwise. Die and come back. I know what I'm doing, and not to be conceited, I am good at it. I've re-killed possibly 40 zombies in my career so far. I don't think I could live with myself if I didn't do what I could."

"Wow. That's so…wowsers."

"Yeah. You're amazing, Neeta. I mean that. I'm glad you're out there protecting us.

"We'll be back to talk more with Neeta and her trainees after K-RTH's own Roger Tellerman gives us the low-down on the low front coming our way. Roger, please! Give us some cool news."

Dave turned down the volume and looked at his assistant, Sharon, who was studying her DoDroid intently.

"Well?" he demanded. His foot tapped the accelerator of his 2041 Jaguar impatiently, making it lurch. Watching Sharon, he unconsciously edged the car to crowd the white line.

A red GovMo Bailout passed them on the right, the driver yelling obscenities through his closed window. As usual, Dave noticed but pretended not to.

Sharon spared him a glance and a grin. "Chitter hits, forum posts, K-Earth PeopleSpace activity all exceeding expectations. I don't think we need to call in the plants at all."

"Brilliant! Call the limo, have him take them someplace special for lunch afterward. Take them to The Pantry—that's always amusing."

He stomped on the gas, gaining on the car in front of him until the automatic proximity alarm sounded. He changed lanes without looking, causing another alarm as well as silent fist-shaking from a different motorist. Sharon concentrated on texting the limo and making lunch reservations for six at Rochelle's.

"You know, I think Neeta could be our most popular show host yet. Wonder if we could sign her on for a second season. Maybe go on location. I hear Louisiana is crawling with undead."

On the radio, Roscoe had started to wax poetic about chopping the undead with Neeta.

"You like Cajun, Sharon, baby?" Dave asked over the proximity alarm as he cut someone off to get to his exit.

Sharon nodded, but opened a job search app. Bunnies. Maybe she could find some kind of work with bunnies.

In the back booth of Rochelle's, the cast *of Zombie Death Extreme* dined and chatted like old friends.

Spud called for another bottle of wine—it was on Dave's tab—and poured for everyone. Neeta set her hand over her cup.

"One's my limit," she said.

"Come on, Neeta, loosen up!" LaCenta said. She'd already polished off her third glass, plus a margarita, and motioned for Spud to pour her another.

"I don't 'get loose.'"

"Oh, yeah?" Roscoe challenged. "Then explain your reply to that John caller."

LaCenta shrieked and leaned against Roscoe, slapping his shoulder with delight. Spud snorted, and even Nasir looked amused at the memory.

When the station took listener calls for the group, "John" had called in with a rather explicit proposition for Neeta. Everyone had gasped protests and Brian had moved to cut him off, when Neeta stopped him.

"Tell me, John," she asked sweetly, "can you field strip a BelchingDragon M2-7 flamethrower, clear the petrol and ignition lines and get it back together in time to stop a shambling horde of undead?"

Silence.

"John?" Brian prompted.

"Uh, no."

"Sorry. A girl's got to have her standards."

"That was classic!" LaCenta shrieked, causing other diners to turn their heads toward the table in annoyance. "'A girl's gotta have her standards!' You put him down good, that's all I'm saying!"

"I could do it," Gordon grumped, causing the whole table to bust out laughing. "What?"

Roscoe waved his hand dismissively. "Oh, boyfriend, you ain't got a chance, anyway. Not after what I saw in the lobby."

The table went silent, eyes on Neeta.

She felt her face get hot and tried to hide it by taking a sip of wine. "Oh, well, Brian asked me out."

Roscoe jumped in, "And she didn't make it easy, either. I thought I was going to have to *intervene*. Oh, I am serious! He came on so smooth, asking her if he needed to know how to field strip a flamethrower, too. And she asked him if he was thinking of becoming an exterminator!"

LaCenta spat out her drink. Spud handed her a napkin.

"Can't we call that 'playful banter'?" Neeta asked, her face again burning.

"Oh, girl, I would have, honest to gawd, if it weren't for the blank look you gave him when he said, 'No, but I'm thinking of asking one to dinner.' I mean, honestly— how long has it been?"

Neeta reached for her ice water and didn't reply. Fortunately, the food came then, sparing her the need.

By the time the limo arrived to take them all home, Neeta had acquiesced to a second glass of wine and was enjoying a warm mellow glow. She leaned back in the plush leather seats—"rich, Corinthian leather" Roscoe had intoned in a joke no one remembered the origin of anymore, but with a rounding of his vowels that set LaCenta into fits of giggles. LaCenta was propped sloppily between Roscoe and Spud.

"You know, you're all right," she told Roscoe. "Too bad you're gay."

"Oh, honey. I'm not gay. I'm just not particular."

She shrieked with mirth, but Gordon moved his legs just a bit farther from Roscoe's. He and Nasir were talking in low serious tones about the zombie situation in Afghanistan. Spud glanced past the rocking and knee-slapping LaCenta at them, obviously wishing he were there, yet helped steady the drunken girl when she nearly slid off the "Corinthian leather" seats. He caught Neeta's eye and shrugged.

These are good people, she thought.

"I wish I could give each one of you a million," she said.

Roscoe pulled LaCenta back in her seat and turned to wag a finger at her. "Now, none of that. There's only one winner. That's the rules!"

"I wouldn't shay mo to a nillion, but if all I get is the training for free and job when I'm done, I'll be happy, that's all I'm shaying." LaCenta piped in. "Not that I'm giving up, nossir. I'm going to whoop all your asses, and then kick zombie butt besides."

"Not mine," Spud said.

"Girl, you've got a long, hard fight if you think you're gonna reach my beautiful white booty, much less whoop it."

Neeta felt a catch in her throat. "Just...be careful. Do what I say and don't take chances..."

"Oh, gawd, don't you get melancholy on us! You'll make Placenta here cry."

LaCenta swung at him, but without malice.

Neeta took a deep breath and released it slowly. Roscoe had it right: People died hard in this business; no point getting melancholy about it. Part of the job, right? Instead, she let herself enjoy the moment and feel the pride she had in her plebes.

The limo disgorged her at her two-bedroom cottage with the large airline-hangar style shed that marked her home and office. She waved at everyone as the car drove off, then turned to see Ted sitting on her porch, polishing the flamethrower he held cradled in his arms.

The sight stopped her dead in her tracks. Her head swam with a vision of the two of them field-stripping the tool. He'd lean his bare chest up against her back, arms reaching around her to remove the nozzle from the hose, the Righteous Brothers singing *Unchained Melody* in the background.

She shook herself. What kind of wine was that?

She stormed up the steps, ignoring the singers crooning in her mind. He looked up at her with that rakish grin, and suddenly the day felt too warm for her T-shirt and jeans.

"Enjoy your interview at the radio station?"

"You didn't hear it?" She couldn't stop looking at his hands caressing the nozzle. Bobby Hatfield singing about hungering.

He shrugged, not apologetic at all. "Had to go do some location work. I was in the field all day."

"What are you doing here?" she demanded more harshly than she'd intended.

"Time for my first lesson." He swung the nozzle like a guitar, and Neeta felt a bass playing to her heartbeat.

…and time can do so much…

"That's a BelchingDragon M2-7." She couldn't believe how rough her voice sounded. She couldn't believe she'd managed to talk at all.

If he noticed, he was as good at ignoring it as Dave. "Yep! Bought her the day after you agreed to tutor me."

I need your love…

Shut up! She snapped at the ghost of Bobby. Lessons! *Get with the game, girl!*

"Have you read the manual?" she demanded.

He rolled his eyes. "Have I read the manual?" he scoffed.

She made him read the manual while she changed into work clothes and splashed her face with a lot of icy cold water.

Roscoe straightened the leopard-skin patterned cover on his chair and flopped into it twice to be sure he had just the right posture. He moved just enough to turn on the video recorder.

"Hi, everybody! Just got back from our interview and the most *exquisite* lunch with the others. I just want to start by saying thanks to K-RTH's Brian and Cassie for a fabulous time. I love you both, you know it, and I'd do either of you, anytime!"

He covered his mouth with both hands for a moment. "Did I say that? Oh, honeys, it's the wine talking, I'm sure. Not that it isn't true—*in vino veritas!*—but you know I don't normally talk so base. Just a little tipsy, and my tongue is loose."

Then he winked like the cad his viewers knew he was. "Of course, not as loose as LaCenta's! If only you could have heard the things she said on the limo ride home. But I'm going to leave you in suspense. Beg me, and I might tell!"

He switched off the camera and chuckled. That would bump his comment hits, and Dave loved those numbers high!

LaCenta slammed her finger onto the Video On key. She didn't bother to check her face and hair. She knew how awful she looked, and she didn't care. Her brother had called her out of a sound sleep to tell her about Roscoe's little blog game. Two can play that.

"I know you all probably seen what that blabber-boy Roscoe said about me on his blog. Let me set the record straight: all I said was I was gonna whoop his skinny white ass, and everyone else's. Then I'm taking my chainsaw and my spray bottle and I'm whooping zombie ass.

"'Loose tongue.'" She snorted. "Only thing I'm gonna loose are zombie heads from zombie necks, that's all I'm saying."

She jabbed the off button and dragged herself back to bed. Oh, was she hung over!

BrainDeadHead:
Subject: WTF? Neeta, sued?!
I just heard that somebody is suing Neeta?! What's that all about?! It's a joke, right?!
MANIC_MIND:
No joke, Brain. You can read about it on my blog: <u>Exterminator Saves Lawyer's Skin; Lawyer Skins Exterminator</u>. It's grim, man.
Trolll:
Figures she's on a reality TV show, if she's so in-competent at her job. We're only halfway into the season and somones died all ready. I wouldn't hire her—setting fire to people's houses. Should've arrested her for arson!
LimbCollector:
Don't be an idiot, Trolll. You obviously have no idea what you're talking about. In fact, she took out six zombies single-handedly. The seventh was on fire. It might have staggered around the yard if weren't for some idiot filming him on a cell phone and yelling, "Look this way!" Then another idiot threw alcohol on it.

I heard the idiots in Congress want to require that individual bottles of alcohol have "Caution: Contents Flammable" written on it.

Neeta is hard core and awesome. She can protect my place, anytime!

Oh, and activate spellcheck! You look like an idiot even more than you are.
MANIC_MIND:
You're just surrounded by idiots, aren't you, LimbCollector?
LimbCollector:
Just you and me, MANIC. And I'm not so sure about you, LOL.
Trolll:
Who're you calling idiot, *hole? Fact is, Neeta got called to do a job, and instead she damaged the back half of his house, terrified his partygoers—who were clients in his business—and generally botched the job! Just cause you think she's awesome doesn't mean she's right.

And I notices you didn't say anything about poor Bergie. Can't argue that, can you?

And people should be warned about alcohol! Obviously, not everyone knows its flammable. It's a safety issue!
Rigormortis:
"*hole" LOL. Are you on a GPC Anti-AI, by any chance? Incidentally, people die on reality TV. That's why it's real. Anybody remember Nintendo Live? What, they lost three players to the Frogger challenge?
Decapitator3000:
Those were real people? OMG :O
You know, I'm glad Katie bowed out. I don't think she had what it takes. She would have been next to go in the wrong way. And 20,000 dollars is nothing to sneeze at.

That stinks about Neeta, though. Is there any way we can help her?

LimbCollector:

How about we send that idiot lawyer a broken vat of pickled herring?

Decapitator3000:

Lutefisk! With Special Sauce!

BrainDeadHead:

500,000 dollars?! He sued her for FIVE-FREAKING-HUNDRED THOUSAND DOLLARS?!?!?!?!? For a little yardwork, a retractable awning and some paint?!

LOL on the GPC Anti-AI, by the way. Government never should have bought out that computer company. Did you know the guy used the profits to make his own orbiting hotel? I want a reality TV show on that!

Trolll:

It's not just the damage, stupid. He was having a party for his clients. She traumatized them and now he's loosing business. Its obvious none of you have any idea how the real world works, so go back to watching your stupid TV.

I wouldn't feel to sorry for Neeta, either. She's probably raking in the dough on this show. Wonder if she gets Bergie's cut?

Spla77r64:

Sorry, got to chime in with Trolll here. I caught parts of the trial on TV. He did show that he lost a significant number of clients after the incident. Loss of clients=loss of income. I know she was doing her job the best she could, but she should have had more help, contained them faster, something. It was a botched job.

MANIC_MIND:

Seems to me he's losing clients (not loosing, btw) because they're questioning the judgment of a man who would serve pickled beets and blue cheese dressing at an outdoor party on a hot summer's day when he lives so close to a cemetery. Not to mention the fact that he actually thought his electric fence would keep them out. He's lucky they hadn't invaded his home earlier, like at night when his family was sleeping. Besides, don't you think the zombie invasion was traumatizing enough? It would certainly turn me away!

Spla77r, it's easy to armchair-quarterback. If you followed the trial, you'd know she was the first to answer the 9-1-1 call, which didn't come until after they crossed his fence, even though people saw them approaching long beforehand. By the time support arrived, she had taken them on, single-handedly.

Like someone said, hard core.
BrainDeadHead:
Trolll, know what you can do with your real world?! If I were Neeta, I wouldn't pay.

<Trolll response deleted by administrator>

BrainDeadHead:
That's what she said, Troll! :P
MANIC_MIND:
Update on Lawsuit Man. He's rebuilding his pool! Look here for the before and projected "after" pictures. Swimming in Injustice.
LimbCollector:
That's wacked! I'm ordering the pickled herring!
likemineliving:
We had GPC computers in our comp sci lab. It was great! We learned so much about computer repair!
Rigormortis:
LOL, @likemine. Never thought of that.
Katieforthewin!:
Hey! I saw that Katie is going to be on the Evening Show tomorrow. #can'twait

This really stinks with Neeta, but what can we do?
StudlyWithSwords:

Hi, guys. Roscoe here. Oh, gawd (sp!) it's so good to see such an outpouring of love in this forum. I thought I'd give you some inside scoop: rumor has it, the lawyers are not only holding her home hostage but also her license to re-kill if she misses even one payment! I think she could actually stand losing her house—believe me, it's not much. I've seen it—but zombie extermination is Who She Is!

As for the money she's making on this show; trust one who knows. It ain't as much as you'd think. The million goes to the winner; the rest of us get peanuts. And that take-away money Katie got? Neeta had to help pay for it, is what Ted (the gorgeous cameraman—so wish you could see him!) told me.

Anyway, if you love Neeta as much as we do, and you really want to help, here's what you can do...

Chapter 6

Notes for: *The Zombie Syndrome*

A Documentary

By Gary Opkast

Episode: Zombie Hot Spots

Need a graphic here—perhaps the world with the earliest known zombie spots marked, then adding the next spots until it shows the progression of the phenomenon over the earth?

NARRATOR

Whether it began with a single contagion, was the result of a planned attack, or is simply a natural if horrific evolution, the zombie syndrome has spread throughout the world. However, that does not mean zombies are evenly spread across the globe.

Scene of a busy city—can get news footage of a zombie shuffling? Scan some vids of homeless areas—might be something that will pass.

NARRATOR

High population areas are, of course, statistically more likely to have a higher zombie population, but that is not always the case. Key political states like Iowa and Massachusetts see an increase in uprisings, especially during Presidential campaigns and primary elections.

ALISTAIR PENDRAGON, FEDERAL

ELECTION COMMISSION

It's a real problem, I tell you. I mean, recounts used to be a fairly rare deal, Florida being the exception, but now, we have to hold them on a regular basis. We're working to institute procedures for screening out undead, but some people in a certain party are blocking it. Think it's a "violation of civil rights." What rights? They're dead!

Flip through different scenes as NARRATOR describes. Food Processing centers, restaurants, fast food dumpsters. Definitely use that "Funniest Home Videos" clip with the zombie getting cut in half by the dumpster lid as he leans in after a Happy Meal.

NARRATOR

Zombies also seem attracted to certain areas, particularly those associated with strong odors. Pickling facilities… Homes and restaurants with kimchi on the menu…and anywhere "secret sauce" is left to spoil.

DR. HANSEN

We're not really sure why the undead are drawn to such smells. We do know that the hind brain is the most intact in the zombiefied, and that the sense of smell is tied to our primitive mind. Of course, the receptor cells of the olfactory epithelium are degraded from the decaying process; in other words, they can't smell much. So, strong scents that might once have been considered unfavorable would appeal on a primal level.

Cut to the mattress-shaped building of the Bedder Rest mattress factory and showroom.

NARRATOR

Another primal appeal seems to be a place for comfortable sleep. Mattress factories and warehouses in particular have a problem with zombies. One of the most famous, the Bedder Rest Mattress Center of Burbank, has long been a problem—or has it?

May 15, 2022: The first zombie was discovered by the morning shift in the pillowtop testing room. Former employee Mortimer Parsons, three months' dead, was thought to merely be returning to the place he felt most drawn to in life. However, as the months went on, more and more zombies—some identified as having been buried up to a hundred miles away—migrated to the manufacturing plant. In 2025, amid lawsuits, indictments for negligence and hefty fines for environmental insensitivity, Bedder Rest, Inc. went bankrupt, and its owner and CEO, William Somna, committed suicide. Two weeks later, Somna's grave was found dug up from the inside. Has he returned to the place that was his life—and death?

Twenty years later, the Bedder Rest Mattress Center continues to stand and to draw zombies. Is it a threat? Or a useful containment area?

DR. HANSEN

The Bedder Rest Mattress Center is what we call a "roach motel." For the most part, zombies that enter are content to remain in the factory itself.

Cut to footage of a surveillance camera on a small robot inside the factory showing zombies sleeping, shuffling, picking off each other's skin…

VOICEOVER DR. HANSEN

Inside, they stay docile unless something arouses them. A significant smell, the presence of a living creature…

Footage of a horde piling on a rat, ripping at it and each other in a feeding frenzy.

VOICEOVER DR. HANSEN

Or something perceived as a threat—and that can mean just about anything unusual.

Footage from the surveillance cameras of the robot being nabbed and torn to shreds.

DR. HANSEN

Bedder Rest and other mattress factories have given us an opportunity to study zombies in unique ways. But will this help us exterminate them? Myself, I'd rather coat the place in napalm, but that's a personal opinion, mind.

NARRATOR

And why hasn't it been "coated in napalm"?

(Clip from press conference, 2028)

BUDGET COMMITTEE CHAIRPERSON TANYA CARRELL

The Bedder Rest Mattress Factory is known by the state of California to contain hazardous materials of an undead nature. However, the fact of the matter is, they aren't doing anything. They check in, but they don't check out. Meanwhile, setting the place ablaze poses serious budgetary, logistical, and environmental issues. Rest assured, we are studying the situation to determine the best and safest course of action. In the meantime, we are carefully monitoring the issue, and there's no present threat to the population.

BURBANK POLICE CHIEF FRIDAY ACKROID

It's a menace—a disaster waiting to happen. We have patrols—uniformed officers and exterminators—keeping an eye on the place. Anything steps out, we squish it fast. But we know more are sneaking in there somehow. If they can sneak in, they can get out. They're just waiting for the right motivation.

NEETA LYFFE

I patrolled Roach Motel for a month as part of my certification. We had a couple of incidents—once they came after some poor bum too drunk to know what he was stumbling into. We even captured some for ZERD. All part of the job. So, yeah, it has its uses. Still, if I had my way, we'd have the National Guard bomb it from the air. Totally raze the place—only way to be sure.

"Oh, gawd, Neeta! You can't make us do this again! It's too cruel!"

Neeta regarded her plebes with narrowed eyes. Roscoe begged with theatrical expression; Gordon squared his shoulders, ready to "embrace the suck–OOH-Rah!" Spud cast down his eyes, resigned. Behind them, LaCenta rolled her eyes at Nasir, who shrugged in reply.

Neeta spoke with the sweetness of a Rottweiler in a tutu. "Oh, I'm sorry. Did you think this was all glamour, guts and glory?"

"G-guts, mostly," Spud muttered.

Neeta ignored him. "Or did you think that I'd cut you some slack because we 'bonded' over lunch?"

"Oh, Neeta…"

"This is serious business, people, and I expect you to take it seriously."

She reached behind her and picked up the stack of practice tests. She held them before her like a fan as she addressed the three men squirming in their ill-fitting student desks. "There's more to extermination than chopping off heads or splashing around cleaner."

"Chapstick?" Spud offered. This time, Gordon growled.

Neeta slapped a test on Spud's desk but gave him a slight grin. Now that he was finally loosening up around them, he was starting to show a sense of humor. She liked it.

"You cannot become a Zombie Exterminator without becoming an exterminator. You need both licenses— your re-kill and the general certification. You three failed that test." She paused to glare at them. "You will not fail again."

Roscoe sighed and opened up his practice test. "We should at least have a cameraman filming some of this. Let people see the dull grind."

From the classroom door, Ted said, "I'll see what I can do. Neeta, can I pull you away for a few minutes? Dave is on a ledge."

"Let him jump."

Ted shrugged in that easy-going way of his. "He'll take your challenge with him."

Neeta sighed and looked heavenward. She did believe in heaven; not to would have sacrificed her sanity. Sometimes, though, she wondered if heaven believed in her. "Let's go."

They found Dave on the set, shaking his head and waving his arms pessimistically as he circled a zombie. A few steps away, his assistant was cooing at her DoDroid, a beatific expression on her face.

"Barry!" Neeta cried, and broke from Ted's side.

At the sound of its name, the animatronic creature raised its lolling head and with a low moan, shambled toward Neeta, its arms outstretched. They embraced in a sloppy hug.

Laughing, she waved at the technician off-stage. "Zeek! Who else did you bring?"

Zeek returned the wave. He stuck his iBrick back in its carry-all and pushed the sound diffuser mike away from his mouth. "Just Barry for the testing, but tomorrow, we'll bring some Janes, Xaviars and a couple of Virginias as back up. We got a maggot team out collecting fresh supplies."

"Perfect!"

"It is not perfect," Dave countered. He put his hands to his head as if trying to physically contain his "negative vibes." "Neeta, this isn't working for me. Where's the suspense? Where's the danger? Zombie piñata? It sounds like a comedy, not reality TV."

Neeta bit back an angry retort. They'd gone through this for hours at the last meeting. "Dave, I'm not pitting my plebes unprotected against actual pests until they are better prepared."

"I know, I know! But...look at it!"

Barry lolled its head toward Dave, slack jawed. Something green spilled out of its mouth.

"Dave, these are the same animatronics we use in training. The ones I wanted to use in the warehouse. Remember the warehouse? Barry could have gnawed on

Eidelberg to his heart's content and he'd be around to laugh about it today."

"Like I said then—he'd have been laughing about it *during* the challenge. For the cameras! There's no danger here—no immediacy."

Zeek said, "What if we don't tell them they're fake?"

Neeta shook her head. "I'm not doing that to my plebes. It's too soon."

Sharon glanced up from her phone. "The audience isn't ready, either. Current polls indicate that another uncontained live zombie challenge could result in a loss of up to twenty-three percent of current viewership."

"And potential for new viewers?" Dave demanded.

She pressed a button on her DoDroid. "Fifteen." She glanced to make sure he didn't have another question, pressed another button and was soon grinning delightedly and twitching her nose at something on her screen.

Zeek started moving Barry around the room, pacing him, making him whirl and lunge.

"See?" Neeta told Dave. "Not worth it. Trust me, Dave, if you want freaky, get effects in—dark sets, fog, strobing lights. It will get pretty darn freaky. But this isn't about danger—this is about handling the gross side. I don't know if you noticed, but despite everything else that happened in that warehouse, I saw plebes flinching."

"Katie's gone."

"Gordon. Great with the blood and guts, but did you see how he backed away from the maggot nest? He bumped into me, while I was wielding a *chainsaw*, Dave. And that's after I've spent weeks making them stick their hands and feet into gross things. I've been preparing them for this challenge, Dave, because it's one they need."

His face hardened into stubbornness. He didn't care what they needed. She had to change gears fast.

"And it's one we need for the show! You said it yourself, Tuesday!" Mimicking his behavior from that day, she draped an arm around him and waved her arm expansively before them. "One exterminator. Three Zombies. Seven Thousand in Cash! Who has the guts to break the Zombie Piñata?"

Barry dropped into a slack-armed bow. Zeek went over to it and peeled back its shirt, making some adjustments to the spine. Then he grasped it by the ears to make sure it had its head on straight.

Neeta felt Dave relax. "It has been a good commercial."

Sharon spoke up. "Making a real impact with the college demographic."

"That's right! You don't want to give them a death downer—but something exciting and fun with enough gross to appeal to the kids…"

"All right!" He threw up his hands. "It's not like we have time to change plans, anyway. It's just missing something…an emotional element… No, no! You're right! Go back to your plebes. I'll work it. I'll work it." Suddenly, his focus narrowed on Zeek, who was pulling at the skin on Barry's forehead. A keen look crossed Dave's face. "In fact…"

His voice trailed off, and with a shooing motion toward Neeta, he approached the technician.

Neeta sighed. Should she go after him? Nah—as long as he didn't bring anything "live" in, they should be fine.

Zeek and his crew had been training exterminators for a decade. He knew his business. Still, Ted had called her in here.

Remembering Ted for the first time, she glanced around, but didn't see him. No matter; maybe he'd grabbed his camera to go film her test-takers. Dave was waving his arms in that manic way that said he was onto something. Maybe she had better—

Her phone rang.

"Neeta."

"You are indeed-a just what I need-a," Brian's warm, familiar voice answered. "Sorry, bet you hear that a lot."

She laughed, causing heads to turn her way. Dave glared in his *Why are you still here?* way. She hurried out the exit and into the hall. "Not since high school." *And from some old guys who want me to spray their homes.* She squashed that thought. "What's up?"

"Just wanted to be sure we were still on for tonight."

"Why wouldn't we be?"

"Okay, good. Listen unless you have other ideas, I thought we'd play this easy. First dates, you know."

She tried to remember the last time she'd had a date at all, much less a first one. "Got something in mind?"

"Well, I saw on your *ZDE* bio that you majored in Art Appreciation, so how about dinner and a trip to the J. Paul Getty Museum?"

She felt a warm flush move over her. When was the last time she'd been to a museum? Too long. And on a date? "I…That sounds lovely."

He laughed. "Sorry, but that's not a phrase I ever expected to hear you say. Kind of…gentle."

"'Feminine, you mean?" she teased. "I do have a feminine side, you know."

"Yeah?" he teased back. "I'm looking forward to exploring all your many sides, Neeta Lyffe. Five o'clock, then."

She was still smiling when she entered the classroom.

Katie clipped on her microphone as the make-up lady blended the last bit of blush with expert strokes of a brush. Relaxed and smiling, Katie knew she hadn't looked this good since her audition video. In fact, she looked better. Her zombie hacker had weighed twice that of the katana she'd black-belted in; six weeks of training with it had given definition to her arms. First thing she'd purchased with her prize money was one of her own; she may not hack zombies with it, but she could use it in her new career.

Which, she shivered with excitement, started tonight! The Roy Speegleman theme song played, marking the return from the commercial break, and Roy shared a zombie joke and started into his introduction.

"But we all know zombies aren't a laughing matter. That's why I don't make them guests on the show." A pause for the rimshot. "But tonight, we do have a very special guest that I'm sure you'll come to associate with zombie defense. If you've been following *Zombie Death Extreme*—and who isn't?—you'll know her. Now you'll get to know her better. She's a tough lady with a heart of gold, and she's a knock-out besides…Katie Haskell!"

The make-up lady backed away, and Katie strode out and across the stage, careful to remember the model's walk that made her kicky skirt swish fetchingly. She stopped mid-stage, pulled her sword from the sheath behind her back and did some showy swings and twirls, eating up the applause. Then she did the quick hop-up to the stage just like she'd seen the New York Governor do last year. When Roy pulled her in for a hug, she didn't resist; he wouldn't get handsy in front of the cameras like he had offstage.

She removed the sheath and set her sword next to her as she sat down.

"So!" Roy said. "You are off the show! Let's look at those tender last moments..."

They played a clip from her last episode. How did Dave get a close-up of the burning envelope? She wondered, then decided he must have re-shot it afterward. She said her tearful goodbye—wow, in the firelight, even her crying looked good! Then LaCenta said, "One liability gone!"

Katie felt a warming in her heart when the audience started booing that nasty witch. She refused to believe they were just following the cue cards two assistants held up at the base of the stage.

"Wow, that had to hurt," Roy said.

One of the writers had warned her he was going to address this.

"It did, Roy, it really did. But not nearly as much as watching poor Bergie go down under a horde of ravenous zombies. I meant what I told the others; I can't watch another person die like that. It's just too much." She stopped and took a breath. No tears here. Right before the show, she'd puffed a nasal spray that was guaranteed to dry the tear ducts and contract the pores in her face. She'd had to plop in eye drops every couple of minutes and her face felt prickly, but it was worth it.

"But I also meant what I said. I want to help people, and zombie defense is the most important issue of the 40s. That's why I'm applying my experiences to education."

"Your new website," Roy concluded. "Can we get that on the screen for our viewers?"

She looked to the camera, knowing they were splitting the screen for her and her site. "I didn't put my prize money into tissues," she said, echoing LaCenta's post-episode blog. "I've designed an educational website to teach about zombie defense. You'll find basic information, downloadable brochures, links to local trauma centers... We're working now on an interactive game to teach the children the basics of zombie defense."

Downstage, an assistant held up a hand. Two minutes left. She moved into her practiced lead-in.

"We're also training what we call 'defensucators' who will travel across the country promoting zombie defense awareness, and we plan to lobby Congress to revisit current legislation in order to let zombie exterminators like Neeta Lyffe do their job effectively."

As people cheered, she turned to Roy for the next question—the one that was going to make her career.

"We? So, you're not in this alone?"

"No one's alone when it comes to zombie defense, Roy. That's why I've teamed up with B to Z Household Products." She leaned forward, hands folded as if in prayer, a trick she'd learned from Dave.

"One thing Neeta taught us is that people need to realize that they can find anti-zombie weaponry right in their own supply cabinet. B to Z wants to make every American empowered in the fight against zombies—" She sat back and smiled brightly. "—and against the more common threats of bacteria and flu virus! From cleaning your bath to repelling that zombie, B to Z is a name you can trust!"

LaCenta smirked into the camera. "Look, I know some people choke on tests, but come on! This isn't geometry. If the instructions on the label say, 'Use no more than three times a year,' then you don't mark that you can use it four times if you alternate it with something else. It's just common sense. I mean, Nasir passed it first try and it's not even in his native language!

"And before you all start getting down on me, I ain't dissing Nasir. He's a smart guy. My point is, can you imagine taking a test in Arabic or whatever? But he passed our test—he pwned those other guys, that's all I'm saying. Did they even study? Pfft! Roscoe was probably posing for a self-published calendar of himself or something. Anyway..."

She stepped back from the camera to show off her sequined tank, tight black skirt and high heels. "We're getting the night off while the losers have to study. I am going out with my girls and I'm gonna forget all about undead and find me a live man—and you know what I mean. Chit me a photo. Maybe I'll tell you where we are."

Neeta was still digging through her drawers for eyeliner when the doorbell rang.

"Coming!" she hollered as she pawed through the mess of bottled foundation, powdered blush and other artifacts that hinted at a social life she'd never really had. She found the mascara, pulled it open. It was dry.

The doorbell rang again.

With a huff of resignation, she tossed the tube into the trash and hurried to the door.

Brian's eyes widened as he looked her up and down. "Wow! You look terrific!"

She found herself blushing and shy—something she hadn't felt since high school, maybe. She toyed with the embroidered edge of her tunic. "Um, thanks," she stammered. "It's borrowed."

After their class, Roscoe had dragged her over to the wardrobe department, where he'd cajoled Colleen, the wardrobe supervisor, a good friend of his, to let her borrow something for her special date. She'd had to push off his suggestions, which ran, in her opinion, from racy to tramp. The wardrobe mistress, seeing her plight, pulled out a peacock blue silk pantsuit with colorful embroidered flowers. A couple of temporary alterations and it fit her perfectly. Fortunately, her mother had collected sexy shoes, and she'd held on to the ones that fit. The black strappy heels with gold filigree worked perfectly. Her short hair didn't need much, but she'd gelled it so that it was fashionably messy rather than just a mess.

"Well, don't give it back!" he said and held out his arm, elbow crooked. "Ready?"

"As I'll ever be!" she said and enjoying the flutter in her throat that came from pleasure rather than fear for once, she took his arm and let him escort her to his car.

They spent their first hour at the museum showing off to each other until it became obvious what they were doing, and they calmed down into a friendly appreciation of each other's knowledge. They ate dinner in the café, where they agreed not to talk about work and ended up discussing their favorite childhood cartoons. Afterward, they strolled through the gardens hand-in-hand, staying long enough to enjoy the sunset.

She didn't let him into her house, but when he kissed her at the door, she didn't want the night to end.

He pulled away from her gently. "Hey, what's wrong?"

She blinked and realized her lashes were heavy with tears.

"I'm sorry!" she said, scrubbing at them with the heel of her hand and glad she hadn't put on mascara, after all. "I have no idea where that came from."

He eased her hand away from her face and brushed his thumb over her cheek. "You don't have to be strong all the time, you know."

She smiled at him and pulled him close for another kiss, but she was thinking, *Yes, yes, I do.*

It's the only way to keep the demons at bay.

Chapter 7

Notes from *The Zombie Syndrome*

A Documentary

By Gary Opkast

Episode: Zombie Myths

DR HANSEN

One of the really fascinating things about zombie studies, in my opinion, is the fact that so many of our cultural myths are true—or at least partially true. It's almost as if somewhere in our past, we have experienced a similar zombie syndrome, and while the facts of the phenomenon are gone from the history books, they remain in our mythology.

Film clip of voodoo ritual creating a zombie.

NARRATOR

Are the myths of zombies the result of a more primitive civilization coping with the unknown, or merely
the fruits of an active human imagination with an interest in the macabre? Whatever the answer, myths
change and evolve, and even the most common are
not always completely true. In this segment of *The
Zombie Syndrome*, we will cover Zombie Myths:
Busted and Confirmed.

Film clip of slow-moving group of zombies—perhaps Night of the Living Dead? Lettering over clip: Myth One: Zombies are slow to move
and slow to react.

NARRATOR

The shambling horde. One of the standby myths of
zombies. But how true is it?

Footage from ZERD: Zombies released separately into a large area.

DR. HANSEN

Actually, for the most part, the shambling horde
myth is true. We find that when we release them into
a large area, they will wander, gather, then begin to
move back and forth across the room. Not unlike
goldfish, really. (laughs) At ZERD, we have some
film footage of the phenomenon as our screen
saver. You know, once you get past the fact that
they are the living dead, it's kind of relaxing to
watch.

Footage from tour of computer monitor with a screensaver of zombies
pacing and scrabbling from one side of the screen to another, with a

little cartoon brain hovering just past their reach. (Be sure to note Ted Hacker for the clip in the credits.)

Footage of ZERD: Athletic-looking zombie running on a track. Focus on timer and speed counter at the bottom.

                    NARRATOR
          Of course, one should not always count on being
          able to outrun a zombie.

                    DR. HANSEN
          We have clocked zombies running up to fifteen
          miles an hour—that's a four-minute mile—and since
          they no longer experience fatigue, they can keep
          the pace. In that case, the best you can hope for is
          that they trip or a foot falls off to slow them down.
          Now these are usually zombies who were runners in
          their living years, but since people are seldom bur-
          ied in their athletic gear, it's kind of hard to tell.

Footage from movie of human ducking the swinging arms of a zombie.

                    NARRATOR
          …and the idea that they are slow to react? You can't
          count on it, as Darwin Award Winner Henry Ste-
          phens demonstrated.

ISAAC STAPLES, DARWIN AWARDS CHAIRMAN, in his office. Pan
room of different news articles of people dying stupid deaths, focus
on "Man, 19, loses game of zombie tag; returns on the other side."
As STAPLES speaks, segue over to video footage of 2019 AFEHV
Winner.

STAPLES

Stephens and a couple of his frat brothers got drunk and decided it would make a great entry for America's Funniest Extreme Home Videos, the Danger Edition if they filmed themselves playing tag with zombies. After eating a garlic-and-anchovy pizza, they donned necklaces made from used sweat socks that they stole from the university football team and headed to the local cemetery, danced on a few graves, and managed to wake the dead in true frat fashion.

Stephens' partner in the game, Ed Grisson, developed stomach cramps and bowed out, saving his life. Shortly thereafter, Stephens tagged a zombie on the shoulder and dashed away—but not fast enough. The zombie, former quarterback for the University of Colorado, tackled him and bit his neck through the sweat socks. Stephens lost the game of tag, but he did win the 2019 Darwin Awards for using his stupidity to remove himself from the gene pool.

DR. HANSEN

When it comes right down to it, the best way to win a race with a zombie is simply not to enter into one with it. If you are being chased, use your brains. Run past a foul-smelling area; chances are, you'll distract it. Get to a higher area—a fire escape or high branches. Zombies, we've found, can't jump and do not climb easily. Throw distracters its way. And if you have a phone, call 9-1-1.

NARRATOR

Stay tuned as the Mythbusters 2030 team works with ZERD to dispel that age-old myth: Are brains a zombie culinary delicacy?

"Good morning, LA! You are listening to the Morning Show with Brian St. James and Cassie Delastraude. Cassie, what celebrity gossip do you have for us today?"

"Helloness! I think that's your job today, Brian. Didn't you go out with reality TV's hottest hostess, Neeta Lyffe?"

Wolf whistles. Zombie moaning, "Braaaaiiinns!"

"Hey—no way. We don't discuss our private lives on the air."

"Oh-oh! You know that means it was *that* good or *that* bad. You seem to have all your limbs intact, but let us know for sure: good or bad?"

Laughter.

"Neeta, if you're listening, I had a terrific time last night. This song's for you: 'You Really Got a Hold on Me' by none other than the Zombies."

Neeta stood on a small hill of trash at the Los Angeles County Landfill/Environmental Reclamation Center. She glared down at her plebes, but the pinched expression on her face had more to do with the fetid odor rising from the pile beneath her feet. When Dave said, "I can give you gross, baby!" he hadn't been kidding. She only hoped her eyes didn't start streaming.

At the base of the hill, her plebes did their best not to react to the smells. Roscoe and LaCenta unconsciously mimicked each other by holding scarves up to their faces. Gordon stood with squared shoulders and a steeled expression, but Neeta caught him scanning the area for grubs when he thought she wasn't looking. Spud had his lips mashed together to keep from retching. Nasir watched Neeta, seemingly unaware of the filth around him. Dave had pulled him aside before the shooting. She didn't know the details of their heated argument, but she was betting he'd just earned himself another bonus for his act.

"All right, plebes," she started. "Last week you had it easy. Controlled situations. Nice, clean working environment. But we all know that there's nothing tidy about zombies. That's why today we're—"

Her phone started belting out "Sweet Springtime" by Acoustic Blender.

"Cut!" Dave screamed through his gas mask.

Immediately, her plebes bucked over, gasping, coughing and begging her to get rid of whoever was calling.

She snatched up the phone just as a gusty breeze sent a new malodorous bouquet her way.

"Yes?" she gasped.

"Hey, it's Brian. Uh…did I catch you at a bad time?"

Spud had dashed behind another hill. She thought she could hear vomiting noises. "We're…filming," she said, exhaling just as much as necessary to get the words out.

"Say no more! I was just wondering if you'd heard my morning show?"

How was she supposed to answer and still "say no more?" "No, sorry. Listen, can I call you back?"

"She'll call you later!" screeched LaCenta, who then buried her head into her shirt. Roscoe was gagging too hard to make a smart remark.

"Oh, sure! Sorry. I just wanted you to know I had a great time, and I hope we can do it again soon."

Neeta inhaled shallowly through her sleeve. "Sounds great. I'll call you."

"Okay, great. Are you sure everything's all right…?"

She hung up without answering and tossed her phone to Sharon. Gas-masked make-up people were swarming around her plebes. One dashed up to her, wiped her face and eyes, patted on new powder, and spritzed New-Breeze AntiStench all around her. She shook her head to eradicate the last few minutes from her mind, then tried to remember her last pose. Behind the camera, Ted placed one hand on his hip, fist balled up, and she mimicked the gesture. He gave her a thumbs-up.

"Start with, 'that's why today,'" Dave instructed. "Action!"

"That's why today, we've set up a challenge to test your ability to handle gross."

"So, we just have to stand here for an hour?" LaCenta snarled. Roscoe snorted, and immediately regretted it as he had to inhale again.

"Actually, I have something a little more intense in mind."

Zeek, knowing his cue, made Barry crest the hill behind Neeta.

Roscoe and LaCenta screamed. Spud gasped and froze. Nasir and Gordon, however, started to charge up the hill.

Neeta held up her hand. Barry stopped, as did the others. "Easy, plebes. This is Barry. He's a training zombie."

Directed by Zeek, Barry grasped the ends of his T-shirt and pulled it straight, so all could see his caption: **Sanitized for your protection**.

"These robots are remotely controlled and look, act, and smell very much like the real thing. If you slice them, they will spill body parts. Cut an artery, it will spurt. They are loaded with maggots, spiders and roaches. In other words, all the disgusting grossness you can expect from your average undead.

"They are also loaded with several thousand dollars."

Suddenly, everyone stilled, intent on her, oblivious to the smell.

She grinned and pulled out her zombie sword. The heavy but razor-sharp blade glinted in the sunlight. "They say one exterminator can take on three zombies if he or she is good. Today, you're going to prove how good you are. We have for each of you three Zombietronix training drones like Barry here. Each has one, two, or four thousand dollars trapped inside it. Your job is to get in close, slice them—"

She spun suddenly on Barry and sliced off his head and shoulder. It slid off and hit the ground with a meaty thunk. She reached inside its torso. She heard Spud retching again.

"—and pull the money out of their bodies."

She yanked out a blood-and-guts covered baggie and shook off the maggots in Gordon's direction. Ted focused in on his face. She hoped the camera could capture that shade of green.

"However, you will lose five hundred dollars for each time a zombie manages to grab, scratch or knock you down. Compared to what you lose if a zombie scores on you in real life, you're getting off easy.

"Any money you extract, minus penalties, you keep. I suggest you put it to equipment, but if you want to splurge on a spa day after this, I'd say you'd earned it.

"We've set up five training areas. There you will find your equipment and a technician from Zombietronix who will run your zombies. I've also asked exterminators from Hollerman and Company to assist me in evaluating your performances. You will use zombie swords or chainsaws. You will don your standard uniform—and yes, it will be hot. Maybe your own sweat will cut through some of this smell. You will have thirty seconds to bust your zombie piñata before the next enters the scene; a minute for the one after that. You will have five minutes in all to destroy your targets and extract your prizes. And trust me: this is the only time in your career when you will be so handsomely rewarded for your efforts. Enjoy it if you can."

They broke up then, each plebe meeting with their evaluator and a camera crew and moving to a different section of the dump. Neeta chose to stay with Gordon. She felt confident in her ability to predict how the others would react, but Gordon wasn't always predictable. She'd seen him eat a worm in front of Roscoe, but the way he'd almost bumped her into Nasir just to avoid a maggots' nest…

As she expected, he eviscerated his Barrydrone easily enough, but hesitated to reach into its open guts. Only after taking several deep breaths, like a soldier about to run screaming through enemy fire, was he able to plunge his hand in. He took so long that the second zombie scored on him twice before he was able to extract his hand and decapitate it. Losing his thousand dollars to his hesitation, however, taught him a valuable lesson, and he sliced his second zombie in half with a long vertical stoke and plunged his hand in to grab the loot, stuffing it, maggots and all, into his pouch just in time to swing toward the final zombie.

When he saw it, he laughed.

Neeta blinked. Laughed?

"Yeah! Frag the L.T! OOH-Rah!" he shouted and lunged gleefully at the animatronic. Rather than just snapping off its head, however, he first went for the right arm.

"There's your salute!" he hooted.

What was he doing? "Quit playing and focus!" she shouted, but he was already swinging for the head, howling in joy.

She was about to scold him again when she heard La-Centa screaming from her place in the right.

"Moe! No!"

Neeta left Gordon happily dicing his last zombie while rooting through the remains for the money and ran to where LaCenta continued to scream.

She rounded a large pile labeled "organic and semi-biodegradable" waste to find LaCenta standing in front of a decapitated zombie, screaming and crying, her sword tossed carelessly aside, it and money forgotten.

"What's wrong?" Neeta called.

LaCenta whirled, and her face transformed from grief to rage. "You!"

She ran at Neeta and tackled her. She knocked Neeta to the ground, just missing the pile of dirty diapers and tampons, and knocking her head against the hard ground instead. Stunned, Neeta could only twist aside as LaCenta landed a blow on her cheek.

LaCenta screamed obscenities as she swung. "'Enjoy?' This is what you want us to enjoy? You sick—"

"What? What are you talking about?" Neeta managed to bring her arm up to protect her face. LaCenta yanked her hair.

Jason Hollerman grabbed at LaCenta's shoulders to pull her off, but she elbowed him, and he let go. He yelled at the cameraman to stop filming and help. The cameraman, probably listening to Dave, ignored him. Zeek, who was running the animatronics for LaCenta's challenge, shouted to hang on as he pulled off his equipment.

Meanwhile, Neeta tried ineffectively to roll away from the crazed woman pounding on her.

"How you get your thrills, is it? Think it's funny?" LaCenta continued to rave, but now her snarls were mixed with sobs.

Hollerman and Zeek finally managed to pull her off. Neeta scooted away—right into a pile of restaurant waste. Ignoring that her hands were touching the rotting remains of someone's unfinished "biggie size," she pushed herself up.

"Would someone explain what this is all about?" she yelled.

Sheepishly, Zeek picked up the head of one of the zombies. With rotting dark skin and dreadlocks, it wasn't one Neeta had seen before, yet she recognized the face.

From a family photo LaCenta had shown her during their interview.

LaCenta fell to her knees, crying.

Spud looked at his computer screen, his eyes occasionally rising to meet the electronic eye of the video camera.

"I g-guess I don't b-b-blame Neeta. I'm a Christian, so I b-believe that the, um, the soul—that th-hing that makes you a person—leaves at death. So, zombies are..." He shrugged. "Moving meat, I guess. It's not like they're p-people, or even alive. So, I guess that's why I could do this challenge.

"Still, I didn't like it. I mean, did they really have to make it look like m-mo-Mom?"

He looked away and hugged himself. It was several minutes before he realized the camera was still running.

Roscoe hugged himself and moaned. "Oh, gawd! I couldn't do it. Cameron was the love of my life! And when that zombie shambled up wearing that face! Oh, gawd, it even moaned like Cameron! Oh, and dears: Don't blame Neeta. This was a decision made at the top, without her knowledge. I don't think they'll show it, but she was as surprised as LaCenta to see poor Moe's zombie head. Wish I could be a fly on the wall when she confronts them about it!"

Roscoe sighed theatrically, switching back to a melancholy mood. "So, I failed, okay? I lost the four thousand dollars. But let's face it, my dears: if I were to do this job, I'd be part of a team. No way would I ever solo like Neeta. So, if I ever run into an old lover, I'll back up fast and let one of my partners handle it. I mean, I'd do the same for them."

He smirked, his eyes wistful. "Still, didn't they do the most awesome job on that face? Looked a lot like Cam in the mornings."

Nasir looked into his laptop screen and geared himself up for his next try. During his first attempt to blog, he was so shaken, he kept falling into Dari. The second time, he forgot to butcher his English. Finally, he'd written himself a script and practiced it in front of the mirror.

He turned on the camera and shrugged at it.

"But we are told they were being machine. I know mad this the others made—"

He stopped and switched it off. Now, he sounded like Yoda. Stupid challenge. Stupid director.

Stupid million. When the muezzin on his phone app reminded him to pray, he gladly abandoned the blog.

Gordon waved his six thousand dollars at the computer.

"That was fun! I want to do it again! Yeah!"

Neeta shouldered the door from the garage open and staggered under her heavy grocery bags into the kitchen. She just managed not to spill them but bumped her cheek in the process. She yelped in pain at the bruise LaCenta had given her. Not that she could blame the young woman. Stupid Dave and his stupid "emotional tension…"

A knock on the door interrupted her internal rant. With a sigh, she abandoned her groceries and headed to the door, thinking that she really should have splurged on a chicken from the deli. She so did not want to cook…

Brian was standing on the porch, a pizza in one hand, flowers in the other.

Neeta's brows narrowed in confusion. "Did I forget something?"

"No, no, I just thought— Hey! What happened?" He gaped at her face.

Her hand flew up to the dark bruise under her eye. "What, this? Thank Dave for that."

"Your director hit you?"

"What? No! Oh, come on in. It's a long story, and I could use some good pizza."

Brian set the table with paper plates and put the flowers in a vase while she got her groceries put away. Then he dug around her cupboards for wine glasses for their sodas, using a third one to hold an emergency candle he found in a drawer. As they devoured the sausage-and-mushroom pizza, she explained about the challenge and how Dave had convinced Zombietronix to work with the special effects department to make faces that resembled people her plebes knew.

"Man," Brian breathed, shaking his head. "No wonder you were having a bad day when I called."

"What? That was almost an hour before the challenge."

"Oh." He looked into his glass. "So…"

It took her a minute to realize he thought she was upset over his call. She huffed in annoyance. "Brian, we were filming at the landfill. We were all struggling to breathe without gagging."

He brightened. "So, you weren't upset?"

"Only about having to inhale."

He laughed and reached out to squeeze her hand. It was the best thing she'd felt all day. She was suddenly very glad she'd taken a shower at the studio.

"So," he started, his voice low and sultry, "is it true what they say about exterminators?"

She felt herself grow warm—and suspicious. "What do they say?"

Now he laughed at his own joke. "That they're fastidious about keeping their houses clean! Want some help clearing the table?"

Relief stunned her motionless. Then she threw her napkin at him. "You!"

His eyes sparkled, "Why my dear Miss Lyffe, whatever did you think I was implying!"

"Never mind!" She couldn't quite make herself snarl at him. She picked up the pizza box and took it to the counter where she could transfer the leftovers to an airtight container.

"I wish you could have seen your face," he said as he placed the trash into the can and sealed the lid. "Has it been a while?"

She stuck the pizza into the second shelf of the fridge, then turned to take the glasses he held out for her. "It's been never, and it stays never until I've found the man I'll be with the rest of my life. We should be clear about that now."

He raised his brows. "Old-fashioned girl?"

"Practical girl." She met his gaze. They were both still holding the glasses, fingers just touching. She could almost feel a current moving between them.

His skeptical gaze softened. "Well, I hope you're practical enough not to limit our kisses to the front porch. It was drizzling outside when I came over and your roof isn't exactly waterproof.

That's 'cause Twiddle took my savings, so he could replace his awning with a sunroom, she thought, but smiled. "I think I could be persuaded to the couch—if you're good."

"My dear Miss Lyffe, I am very good, indeed."

Later, as they snuggled on the couch, he said, "I've been thinking."

"Really?" She leaned back to look at him. "Guys do that when they're kissing?"

"I'm a DJ. I can multi-task." He pulled her head back down against his shoulder and stroked her hair. "Anyway, I was thinking. What if you came back to my show and told folks what really happened—that it was all Dave's idea to surprise your plebes with zombies that looked like people they knew?"

"Why? What's it matter?"

He paused a moment in his caresses. "Well, people should know you aren't so cruel."

"I don't care what people think. Anyway, how Dave did it stunk, but I don't have a problem with what he did. I just wish he'd have consulted me, so I could have prepared them for it."

"Wait a minute! You're *okay* with what he did?" He pushed away.

She pulled back as well. "Yeah. I just planned to give them a week or two for prep and do it as a challenge. It's so soon after Bergie, and usually you get some desensitization training."

"Desensitization? Against lopping the head off your little brother?"

Neeta crossed her arms. "Brian, what part of this are you not getting? That wasn't her little brother. Even if it had been the real deal, that wasn't her little brother. That was a zombie! Reanimated, mindless dead flesh. Cockroaches have more right to live. It's not a being, anymore. It's a thing. If they want to do this job, they have to understand that."

"Well, it didn't look like a thing to them. It looked like someone they loved."

"And would you let a dog attack you just because it reminded you of your childhood pet? Or what if I made an assassin bot that looked like me. If you knew it was an assassin boy, would you let it near you, just because it happened to look like me?"

Brian crossed his arms, unconsciously mimicking her. "That's not a good example."

"You're right! Because zombies don't really look like their former selves. They look like decaying corpses. You can't talk to them. You can't appeal to their hearts. You can't bring them back! But do you know the most common last words of a zombie attack victim? 'Honey, it's me.' I don't want my plebes dying with those words on their lips."

Brian went silent. Neeta leaned back against the other corner of the couch and waited. She wasn't going to back down. This is who she was, and he'd either accept it or leave now.

Finally, he sighed, and she felt herself relax. He held out his arm, and she returned to where she'd been nestled against his side.

"I just don't think you should let people think of you as so hard-hearted, especially your plebes."

For a moment, she didn't answer, but enjoyed his sweet concern, not to mention how nice his hand felt ruffling her short hair. "Don't worry. Roscoe figured it out, and if Dave is King of Reality TV, Roscoe is the Crown Prince of Publicity. He'll get the story straight."

"And Dave?"

Neeta snuggled closer, grinning. "I've got plans for Dave."

Chapter 8

TrollI:
Subj: National Weekly: *Zombie Death Extreme* Host unstable, abusive, say contestants
<u>See the article here.</u>

Can't say I'm surprised. Still think she's so hot now?
Rigormortis:
Oh, look! The troll is back! And he's spelling! Get rid of the Redundancy, by any chance? Or did you just take typing lessons?!

At any rate, before you go blasting news from the tabloids (Do you really believe Woody Forrest is getting campaign advice from Ted Kennedy's ghost? That's in that issue, too!), maybe you should check out Roscoe Dane's video blog. He's certain she didn't even know about it. He's even got some of the actual video footage from the episode—the stuff they didn't show. Look at Neeta's face—she had no idea they'd pulled that stunt. My opinion—this was a practical joke gone bad.

You want abusive? What about what LaCenta did to Neeta? I knew the woman was a {word deleted by server}, but that was extreme! She should be kicked off the show!

Trolll:
It's Tro 1 1 1, ONE-ONE-ONE. And it's none of your business what kind of computer I have.

I saw the blog. Roscoe is a kiss-up. My opinion stands. She destroyed sum guy's home, got another guy killed, and know she's taking it out on the survivors by making them slice the heads off their own family members to win money. It's sick!

BrainDeadHead:
Then don't watch.

Trolll:
I don't. I'm trying to make you idiots understand what a {word deleted by server} this show is and how stupid you are for watching it.

Something ought to be done about Neeta before she gets someone else killed. Oh, wait—she already has! She should be in jail for negligence or something.

LimbCollector:
I did something! I sent that lawyer some picked her-rings!

BrainDeadHead:
ROFL! You go, LC!

MochaMomma:
I thought the whole episode was awful—gross and cruel. The way she grabbed that poor girl by the shoulders and told her her brother was meat and nothing more!

MANIC_MIND:
Tro ONE-ONE-ONE: If it's none of our business what kind of computer you have, why is it your business what shows we watch? Get off the forum and go do something worthwhile with your life.

LimbCollector: Please tell me you're joking. That's not going to help her!

Momma: Zombies are meat. The person that was, is no more. Like Neeta said on the show: if you forget that, you will die...and come back.

Re-DeadMan:
My uncle's best friend was almost killed by a zombie. It was his old girlfriend. Uncle had to drag him into the car to get away. Not saying what Neeta did was right, but you can't think of zombies as people you know.

Rigormortis:
Are you people reading? Neeta didn't know. Roscoe said so on his blog. <u>Here's the link again</u>.

Incidentally, I used the address Roscoe gave us in <u>WTF?! Neeta sued?!</u> thread and sent her something. Got a thank you from the studio. Anybody else? Anybody know if Neeta's getting the stuff?

Neeta walked into the staff meeting carrying a stack of tabloids in one hand and her chainsaw in the other.

Dave grinned at her in that oblivious-to-all-but-himself way of his. He waved his arms toward the screen that showed a graph chart, its line on the rise. "Neeta, baby! Have a seat! We are so on! Have you seen the latest viewer stats?"

He applauded, and the others around the table joined in.

Neeta tossed the tabloids onto the table, fired up the chainsaw and slashed the blade across the screen. The chain blade ripped through the stats, the screen and the wall.

The room went silent, save for a tiny "eep!" from Gary.

"Okay," Dave said, taking a seemingly casual step back. "I see that you're upset..."

Neeta pressed the kill switch and spun toward Dave. The chain stopped its angry rotations as the blade came inches from his chin.

"Tell me, Dave, do you know how many zombie exterminators have had psychiatric care after lopping off the heads of a former loved one?"

"Uh…" He turned his eyes toward Sharon, but she seemed happily focused on her DoDroid. In fact, she was making twitchy sounds.

"About half of what it used to be. Do you know why, Dave? Because we prepare them as trainees. We give them skills to cope. Do you see where I'm going with this Dave?" She gave him her best crazed serial killer look. She'd rented The Shining over the weekend and studied Jack Nicholson's expression to get it just right.

"Neeta, let's be rational about this…"

"Oh, I don't need to be." She jerked her head toward the table, where the tabloids had spilled to show their headline: "Unstable Host of *Zombie Death Extreme* Teaches Trainees to Kill Family Members. 'They're Just Meat!!!'"

"Funny how liberating it is to have half the world thinking you're a serial killer in the making. If I decide to remove your scheming mind from the rest of your backbiting body, I think I have a good shot at an insanity plea, don't you agree, Eugene?"

"My name's—" The lawyer started automatically, then coughed. "A good case, actually."

She winked at him, then gave her attention to the director. She used the flat of the chainsaw blade to tip his chin up to meet her eyes. She'd worn her mom's platform, high-heeled boots just for the occasion. "So, here's what we're going to do, Dave. You're going to let me decide the challenges. You're going to discuss any and all changes with me. You're not going to do anything without my approval. You will not so much as add in a sneeze without my approval. Got it?"

She held his gaze for a moment, then dropped them toward her right hand. As he unwittingly followed her gaze, she caressed the trigger with her index finger. He gulped.

"We'll do it your way. But the ratings..."

"...will be what they will be. Got it?" She chucked his chin gently with the flat of the blade.

"Wha-whatever you say, Neeta!"

"Good. I'm glad we had this little talk." She relaxed her eyes from their strained, too-open expression and lowered her chainsaw. Then she sat down at her usual place, smiling as if nothing had happened. She dropped the chainsaw in front of her on the table and leaned back into her seat.

"Oh, hey, help yourselves to a copy," she told the stunned crew. "I got enough for everyone."

Ted reached over and grabbed one. "Nice likeness," he said, grinning at the cover bearing a doctored photo of her in a bloody, torn T-shirt and jeans, hair wild, eyes wilder, bearing a butcher knife in one hand.

"Thanks! There's an even better one of LaCenta beating the crap out of me. Wonder where they got that still?" Her eyes drifted toward the cameraman who had been filming LaCenta's challenge, and her hand stroked her chainsaw.

He paled and ducked his eyes.

Neeta smirked. He wouldn't be sharing any more candids, no matter how anonymously. "So, I was thinking for our next challenge, we take this show on the road. Split them up in pairs and team them up with licensed exterminators on 9-1-1 patrols. You should get some action for the show, plus a nice human angle, and they'll be working with professionals. I already talked to the guys who helped evaluate and they're game. What do you think?"

Everyone practically bounded out of their chairs to agree, except for Sharon, who continued to coo at her DoDroid. When Neeta glanced her way, however, the executive assistant gave her a smile and a wink.

After what Neeta thought was a very productive meeting, the lawyer approached her as the others left. "Miss Lyffe, may I see you in my studio office?"

With a philosophical shrug, she followed him into the office in a small bungalow just off the set. Unlike his lush, Hollywood office, this one was small, utilitarian, and crowded. A large blue mailbag slumped in the only chair.

That was fine. She didn't intend to stick around. "You going to legally chide me on my behavior toward Dave?" she demanded.

"Not at all." He unbuttoned his suit coat, which he wore despite the heat, and settled into the chair behind his cheap desk. "Dave has crossed the line a few too many times. You, however, are the only one to have ever brought him back at the point of a chainsaw."

"Chainsaws don't have points."

"But I do have a point for bringing you here. These have come for you the past couple of weeks." He indicated the mail bag.

She grinned like a cat that ate the canary—if the canary gave the cat indigestion. "Hate mail. Great. Thanks for bringing it to my attention, Eugene."

Eugene cleared his throat. "Not quite. There is hate mail—I can forward it to your home if you wish, save any death threats which are automatically forwarded to the police, of course."

"Death threats?"

"Don't worry until we tell you to. You're actually quite well thought-of. At any rate, these are of a different caliber. Go on."

Neeta reached into the bag and pulled out an envelope. "It's opened."

"Of course, we screen all mail. It was in your contract, if you recall."

Not answering, she shoved the mailbag off the chair and sat, feet resting on the bag.

Inside was a letter and a child's drawing of a stick-figure Neeta lopping body parts off squiggly zombies. It was signed in all caps: Justin, age 5. Neeta snorted and showed the picture to Eugene, who nodded before turning his attention to his computer. She read the mother's note.

Dear Neeta,

Four years ago, I lost my husband to zombie attack. When he came back, I almost lost Justin and my own life.

I heard about the lawsuit. It stinks—they obviously don't understand the danger they were in. I'm sorry. I'd like to help. It's not much, but it's all I can afford right now.

You keep lopping off heads and don't let anyone tell you different!

Patricia Whilte, aka Rigormortis on the ZDE forum

Paper-clipped to the note was a five-dollar bill.

"Uh, Eugene..."

"There's approximately $8000 in that mail bag alone, and I don't think it will be the only one. If you wish, I can establish a non-profit fan organization."

"I can't take this money! Besides, I'm not giving Twiddle the satisfaction of having someone else bankroll his new sunroom. Can we just pass it on to the Exterminators' Survivors Fund?"

Eugene smiled. "I thought you might suggest as much. I'll make the arrangements. Do you wish to read the letters?"

She looked at the mailbag. It was huge—and just the first? She looked back at the picture lying open in her lap.

Take the accolades where you can, Mom used to say.

"Yeah, I would. If that's all right..."

"I already have an intern sorting out the cash and sending the usual replies and cast photo on behalf of the studio. The one you opened is the only one with actual cash in it. She's made a note of each donation on the envelope in case you wish to personally reply."

She gaped. "How long will that take?"

"Depends on whether you have help, I suppose."

Maybe she should ask Roscoe. He must deal with this. Or maybe Brian...

The door banged open and Dave bounded into the room, Sharon and Ted close behind. "They told me you were in here! I knew something was brewing!" His wild, enthusiastic gaze moved from the lawyer to Neeta to the bag at her feet. "Eugene! Is that fan mail? For our Neeta? Yes! I knew there was something! This is perfect for our weekly website candid! Is this all? No? Of course not—Neeta's a star!"

His gaze turned inward to some vision in his mind. He snapped his fingers. "Sharon, baby. Gather up this mail. Call the stage crew. I want the lounge setup—let's add a large coffee table to scatter the letters with careful abandon—careful, not careless. These are adoring fans! Then, stacks of thank you cards, pens, pictures of the cast—you know the drill. Call our plebes. They need to be here an hour or two early. Ted, block the scenes. I'm going to want emotions: tender, heartfelt feelings of gratitude. This will be a real bonding moment!"

Neeta frowned. "You don't think you're wrecking the 'tender, heartfelt' of the moment? I'd really rather look these over in private."

Dave spread his hands, "Neeta, baby! Moments like this are meant to be shared!"

Notes from *The Zombie Syndrome*

A Documentary

By Gary Opkast

Episode: Zombies—Dead or Alive

News footage of the 2027 protests—focus on the signs "Zombies are people too!" or "Don't re-kill my son!"

HANNA NADALMAN, RE-GRIEF COUNSELOR
AND AUTHOR OF *NO LONGER THE ONE YOU
LOVE: THE TRUTH ON DEATH AND THE UN-
DEAD*

The classic first stage of grief is denial. We don't want to let go of the people we love, no matter what the circumstances. So, when the dead started returning, of course it was natural to believe it was some kind of miracle—and you have to remember, the popular literature of the time, from Twilight to Generation Undead, made what were once classic embodiments of evil seem very human, even romantic. But in reality, that's a fatal assumption.

NARRATOR

Unfortunately, zombies will occasionally show characteristics in death that they held in life, which can influence their loved ones. The classic case is that of Jebediah Gump of Winston Lake, Tennessee. Three days after his burial, Gump showed up at his home, let himself into the trailer he had shared with his wife, Josie, and sat down in front of the television.

2021 Interview of JOSIE taken by local news station. Josie, 30-something, wore leopard patterned blouse over straining black sweats. Her dishwater blonde hair was dyed brassy copper.

JOSIE

Well, I woke up and he was just there. So, you know, I got him a beer and it's just like he'd never, never.... I'm sorry, I...

She paused to dab at her nose with a lace kerchief.

REPORTER

So, has he told you what it was like? To die and come back?

JOSIE (wiping eyes)

Oh, he weren't never much of a talker. Now, he just grunts when the channel needs changing or he wants another beer. But, well, between you and me, it has changed him. He's a lot gentler. There's no— well, you know—but I figure death takes a lot out of a guy.

REPORTER

What about the smell?

JOSIE

Now, listen here! I had been in mourning, and Jeb has special needs now. If I can't keep up with the housework, that's none of your damn business!

REPORTER

No! I meant -

Camera angle goes nuts as Josie manhandles both reporter and cameraman out. Last scene is diagonal angle of her on the four-board porch shaking her fist and shouting obscenities. End before the dogs start mauling the reporter.

Various shots of tabloids and magazines with Josie on the cover.

NARRATOR

While the world watched on at a respectable dis-tance, the Gump house seemed to function as normal. Josie even claimed to family and friends that now that Jebediah didn't eat and didn't seem to mind cheaper beer, she was actually better off financially. Then came the fateful phone call.

(Need some kind of stills to go with the radio show.)

DR. WILSON

You're talking to Dr. Wilson. Who's this?

JOSIE

(sniffles. Reruns of Jerry Springer in the background) Josie Gump, doctor.

DR. WILSON

The Josie Gump? Wow! How can I help you, Josie? Things not going so well with Jebediah?

JOSIE

Well, I know I shouldn't complain, and I really am grateful to have him back. A house needs a man, if you know what I mean. But all he does is sit there and stare at the TV. Night and day, day and night.

DR. WILSON

Have you told him how you feel?

JOSIE

And it's grunt for a beer, and grunt for another. And I don't even know where they all go. Literally, Doctor. He never, never gets up from that chair.

DR. WILSON

Have you talked to him, Josie?

JOSIE

And when that reporter talked about a smell, I thought he was criticizing me. He was trying to tell

me about Jeb, and I sicced the dogs on him. I feel
so bad about what Buford did to his...

DR. WILSON

Josie! Have you talked to him?

JOSIE

The reporter? I sent him a nice card at the hospital.

DR. WILSON

Jebediah, dear. Have you told Jebediah how his behavior makes you feel?

JOSIE

You don't think I tried? All he does is watch TV. He
don't even look at me, anymore.

DR. WILSON

You have to make him look at you, Josie. Didn't you
turn his head once?

JOSIE

I'm not that pretty anymore.

DR. WILSON

Every woman is beautiful to the man who married
her. Get yourself dolled up, Josie. Get dolled up,
turn off the television and remind him that you're his
woman and you need—no, you deserve—his attention, too.

JOSIE

Welllll, I thought you might say that, so I got pertied
up before I called.

DR. WILSON

> Go, Josie. Set the phone down so we can hear what
> happens. I promise to hang up if it gets too...atten-
> tive.

JOSIE giggles.

Sounds of heels clacking on linoleum. Josie purring Jebediah's name. A flat male grunt. The television sound suddenly stops. The grunt turned to an inhuman bellow.

DR. WILSON

> Josie?

JOSIE

> Now don't get so mad! I just want a little of your—
> no! no!

DR. WILSON

> Josie! (slightly muffled) Lulu, call 9-1-1!

Sounds of things crashing, dogs barking.

JOSIE

> You're not the man I married! You're not even a
> man! You're a corpse! You lied to me for the last
> time!

Shotgun blasts.

NARRATOR

> Through a miracle and the heroic effort of her toy
> poodle, Pinkie, Josie Gump made it out of her trailer
> alive and uninfected. She went on the talk-show cir-
> cuit telling everyone about her experiences.

Footage from Josie at the *Evening Show*—the one where she's all cleaned up—her hair straight and sandy brown, wearing a tailored pink suit.

It was wishful thinking. I wanted Jeb back, so I didn't question it. I didn't question a lot in those days. Maybe his returning and my near-undeath experience was the best thing to ever happen to me. I dunno. But this I do know: No matter how much they act like the people you loved, that's not them. When somebody dies, that's it. What comes back, ain't human.

"Drunk!" the group had called as Neeta flashed up a clip of a man staggering down an alley. She switched videos.

"Zombie!"

Switch.

"Stroke victim?" LaCenta asked as the others puzzled over the video of a man leaning against a hospital wall and dragging himself along with twitching steps.

"Yes! Very good LaCenta!" Neeta beamed at her.

Gordon snorted. "Come on, Neeta! When are we going to confuse a zombie with a stroke victim?"

Neeta sighed. "April 21st, 2023. Paul Moran, exterminator in Queens, answered a call at a hospital. Zombies don't always come out of the ground, as you know, and some had risen from the morgue, still dressed in hospital gowns. Fortunately, Moran always fired off a shot of 409 before following up with more lethal means."

Gordon replied with a shake of his head, but he paid closer attention to the clips until Dave came to get them for the filming.

"Oh, my gawd! Neeta, Neeta, you got a letter from Josie Gump!"

Roscoe hopped up from the casually lumpy couch someone had dug up from the props room and walked over to the Queen Anne chair where Neeta slouched, her feet propped up on the mailbag. Dave had loved that casual pose she'd had in the lawyer's office and had the props department bring the mailbag onto the set and switch out chairs until they found one that met with his "vision." While he'd fussed over the sets, she'd spent time with her plebes going over the undead identification procedures they would need to know for their license to re-kill.

Roscoe handed her the envelope and leaned over the back of her chair to read, careful not to tear the child's drawing that one of the stage crew had pinned to the cushioned wing of Neeta's chair. "Josie Gump! I so admire that woman!" He crooned happily deep in his throat.

"She did a lot to deflate the 'Zombies are people, too' movement," Neeta agreed.

"So true! And the transformation she underwent after her experience with that Jebediah corpse? It was like watching a daffodil bloom." He sighed, then shook herself. "So, what does she say?"

The others looked up from their letters to listen. They'd rehearsed this "spontaneous scene," and Dave had made Neeta read the letter aloud so many times, she had it memorized. "Dear Miss Neeta," she started.

Perhaps you will not remember me, as you were quite young when I joined your mother in her fight against so-called zombie rights. I do remember what a capable girl you were even then. It makes me proud to see the young woman you've become, and I know your mother would be proud, too.

As I continue my work as a re-grief counselor to those who have encountered their deceased loved ones come back, I still find too many who want to believe there was still something of the person they loved trapped in that mobile corpse. (For that is what they are—mobile corpses—and no sense mincing words.) It's heart-breaking to see, not because these poor dears have lost hope, but that the hope was false to begin with. Having lived with false hope for most of my marriage and for weeks afterward, I know how easy it is to cling to, and how hard to let go. Still, how freeing to be rid of false hope and to rediscover what's real.

But I do go on! I just wanted to let you know in your difficult time that what you are doing is both right and good. You teach your "plebes;" you teach your viewers. May your show help those with fears to release their fears and those with false hopes to find true hope.

Cordially yours,
Josie Lynn Taylor Gump

"No truer words," Roscoe sighed, his hand on his heart.

LaCenta glared past the camera. "Doesn't make what you did to us right, Dave, that's all I'm saying!"

"Cut!" Dave snarled.

Chapter 9

Neeta paced between the two rows of her full-suited plebes as they worked through the martial arts form her mother had adapted to zombie work. Their clubs made sure, deliberate moves before them, and she felt a spark of pride. When they'd first started, some couldn't keep their basher up through a single routine; now, they were finishing their third run and she thought they could make it through one more.

She reached the end of her row, still calling out commands in a steady rhythm, and started back to the front. Suddenly, she swung her right-hand stick toward La-Centa's head, and the left hand-stick toward Gordon a moment later.

Both broke routine to block them with their clubs.

"Excellent!" she said. "Situational awareness! It's very important to keep aware of surroundings, to pay attention to that peripheral vision. Too many people die—and not just from zombies—because they only pay attention to what's ahead of them."

"It'd be easier without the helmet," Roscoe puffed.

"A helmet with a faceplate is an exterminator's best friend," Neeta chided.

"Thought that was the chainsaw!" Roscoe teased.

"Cleaning products!" Gordon added. He ducked to avoid Neeta's switch.

"Flamethrower!" Ted chimed in from the corner where he was running the cameramen and film crew through the routine himself, using his camera in place of the club.

Neeta gave up. "See? And you thought an exterminator's life was lonely!"

Naturally, her cell phone picked that moment to play Brian's ring tone.

"Break!" Roscoe cheered.

"Once more through the routine, then break! Ted, whack them if they get out of line." She tossed him her switches. He caught them, cackling demonically.

She answered the call just before it switched to voice mail. "Hi, Brian!"

"Oh, good! You're there! Is this a bad time? You're not shooting, are you?"

"No, just making diamonds out of coal." She moved the phone from her face to holler, "Keep that arm up, Spud!"

"The p-pressure," he shouted loud enough for Brian to hear. Ted whacked him on the back of the head. Roscoe snickered.

"Focus!" She turned back to the phone. "I have a couple of minutes before pandemonium. Was there something you needed?"

"Well, Disney, Cartoon Network, and Nickelodeon are teaming up for a big concert to help fund research for global cooling…"

Neeta groaned. "Oh, you don't really believe that, do you? All the weather tracking stations moved their temperature sensors off the blacktop and away from the front of hot-air vents. Of course, the mean temperatures have dropped. "

In 2024, a charismatic woman named Ann Guildhaus won the Presidency because, among other things, she promised to put an end to global warming. As soon as she was in office, she had directed the NOAA to enforce its regulations for positioning temperature sensing stations, removing them from areas known to radiate heat and putting them in protective boxes that didn't hold in heat, but rather kept the box's internal temperature the same as the temperature around it. The Guildhaus Initiative cost the government $100 million and employed 5000 people across the 50 states. By mid-tern, the results were in: The mean temperature of the United States was slowly decreasing.

By 2028, the initiative had completed, and the mean temperature had dropped three degrees overall. The opposing party declared that Guildhaus Initiative had created a Global Cooling Emergency in the United States, and their candidate won on the promise of preventing a Global Winter. As soon as he was in office, he created an investigative committee to study the Global Cooling Emergency, which in turn appropriated studies. The Global Winter Accountability and Negation Operations (GWANO) initiative cost the government $400 million dollars, employed about 1000 specialists in five key states and by the end of President Standish's term, came to the conclusion that America's industries and use of artificial chemicals and fossil fuels had caused the problem. He was elected to a second term to enact legislation to help solve the crisis.

Meanwhile, the rest of the world had also begun changing their temperature tracking stations. As recorded temperatures decreased, the UN blamed the United States for starting an "environmental pandemic." The nations proposed to punish America with several billion dollars in fines and enact economic sanctions, which the United States vetoed.

Neeta's mom had told her that zombies were easier to understand than politicians.

Brian sighed, but with good humor. "You're missing the point! All the cartoons we talked about our first date? Those bands are going to be there, singing their theme songs! Miley Cyrus, Echo and the Bunnymen…"

"They Mite B Robots?" Neeta asked.

"Yep! And Sashimi Ice. "

"I loved that one! 'Throw the card/Fight another world,'" she sang.

"Bowling for Soup is opening."

An uncharacteristic squeal escaped Neeta's mouth. "Bowling for Soup? I loved *Phineas and Ferb*!"

Roscoe dropped his club and pulled off his helmet. "Are you talking about the 'Jackets for the World' tour?"

"So! I can get us tickets—front row—and backstage passes!"

"When? When?" She bounced on her toes, and in her excitement, ignored the group as they either dropped their weapons to gather around her or simply dropped onto the floor, panting.

"Friday!" Brian said.

She groaned. "We have patrol duty that night!"

"You can't change it?"

Roscoe leaned toward the phone. "Did you say, 'backstage passes'?" Neeta shoved him away.

"I can't," she said. "We're filming. Hollerman already agreed to take LaCenta and Nasir and a cameraman with them that night. The Cuthberts have Spud and another cameraman. I'm taking 9-1-1 duty with Roscoe and Gordon and Ted. A lot of people already made their plans, and there's a full moon."

"Oh, please!" Roscoe yanked the phone from her hands.

"You are so losing the big picture here," he snarled at her, then turned his back. "Hello, Brian? Roscoe, love, how are you and that delicious Cassie? Good, good to hear. So, about this concert. Oh, I am so with you! It's a can't-miss opportunity! Honestly, the only real question here is can you swing three more passes?"

"What?" Neeta yelled. "Roscoe, we have work that night!" She lunged for the phone, but Roscoe jinked and evaded.

"You have got to get past this martyrdom kick, girl. Ted?" he called. "A little help?"

Ted grabbed her by the arms.

Roscoe grinned and turned his back on them. "So, Brian, didn't I hear that Sashimi Ice had a concert canceled in Nagasaki because of zombies? He did? You do? Will he say something, you think?"

Neeta struggled and snarled, but Ted held fast. "I want to see They Mite B Robots," he told her.

"Fabulous!" Roscoe was saying into the phone. "So, I will make this gold with Dave, and you talk to whoever it is that can make a little camera action happen back-stage. Oh, gawd, it was the best day in the world when you asked Neeta out! Yes, yes, she is. Do you want to say 'goodbye'?" He held out the phone, a smug smile on his lips.

Ted released her, and she snatched back her phone. "Brian?"

"Don't worry, honey! Roscoe's got a brilliant mind when it comes to this sort of thing. I'll call you after work in a couple of hours—or shall I just show up at your doorstep with pizza again?"

The memory of that evening softened away her protests. "How about Thai? I can only do pizza once in a while."

"I know just the place. Seven?"

"Sounds great!" She hung up, face smiling so hard she could feel it to her hairline.

"Well, can I make it happen or can I make it happen?" Roscoe purred.

She busied herself with putting her phone back in her pocket, and when she looked up again, her face had composed itself into something stoic and dangerous.

"Why are all of you out of formation?" she demanded.

They glared at her, stunned.

"Get in line!"

They scrambled into their places, fumbling with chin straps and getting proper grips on their weapons. Ted gave her one of her switches back, winking, and took the other to whip the camera crew into place.

"We'll discuss this later," she told Roscoe, but she knew from his smug expression that he'd seen through her tough act.

Not that she intended to drop it, anyway. "All right! Form Two. Take two steps away from the person beside you. Watch where you swing. Ready. Cut right! Step. Block left. Swing down. Watch that blade—remember Heisman!"

Notes from *The Zombie Syndrome*

A Documentary

By Gary Opkast

Episode: Zombie Behavior

NARRATOR

...and of course, they are more active when the
moon is full.

Clips from various horror movie scenes with the full moon prominent in the background: Werewolf, Dracula...Get the iconic scenes—high drama, low action.

NARRATOR

There's always been something about the full moon
that calls to the human senses. It speaks of mystery,
of romance. It calls to the living...and the undead.

NEETA LYFFE

(start clip at the shrug—she's so cute when she shrugs and leans against the arm of her chair.)

> Yeah, I do get more calls on full-moon nights—one or two more. That's what—20, 25 percent increase? Thing is, people are out more. Most of my extra calls come from couples out parking. (laughs) One time, though, I did get a call from this guy…I can't be sure, but I think he was about to break into someone's house when the previous owner, deceased, decided to come home. He saved that family's life, though, got to give him that.

> DR. HANSEN

> There actually is some evidence—not just anecdotal—that there is a lunar influence upon zombie-ism. However, it's not biological, but cultural. In other words, cultures that still harbor the idea that a full moon does influence human behavior see greater zombie activity during those times. This is terribly exciting for us at ZERD—but not just at ZERD! The implications are…phenomenal! Proof that cultural icons not only subvert the conscious mind but embed themselves so firmly into the human psyche that when all that's left are a few misfiring neurons, as in the case of zombie-ism, those cultural icons are the ones running the show.

Roscoe grabbed Neeta's arm and squealed like a fangirl. "Oh gawd, isn't this amazing? We are surrounded by the cultural icons of our generation!"

Roscoe spread his arms dramatically and spun to take in the "cultural icons," most of whom ignored him, more interested in having a pre-gig snack or working out some last-minute detail with one of the stage crew. A member of Cassidy's Fall nudged his buddy and pointed their way, rolling his eyes. Gordon caught the look and hissed at Roscoe.

"You're making a scene!"

"Oh, gawd, Sergeant Straight. What do you think this is all about?" He turned to the two snickering band members and posed. They turned their backs on him.

Roscoe snorted and called them something nasty, but without much malice.

Gordon clenched his fists and pulled his neck into his shoulders, as if trying to shrink his six-foot-four frame.

Meanwhile, Ted grinned like a kid in a candy store.

Neeta told them, "Just remember that if that phone rings, we're gone. Got it?"

Roscoe tossed his head. "Yes, Mother! Honestly, Brian, can't you loosen her up?"

Brian smiled and put an arm around her waist. "I think it may be a long-term project. However, I think I know what might help. Ready to meet Sashimi Ice?"

"Really?" she said. "Right now?"

Her crew laughed, and Brian with them. "I love when your eyes light up like that," he said, kissing her cheek. "He's been wanting to meet you. For one thing, he wants to thank you for the extra security."

Neeta laughed. Earlier that day, she'd combed the theater and surrounding area, assessing it for zombie threat and setting out a few "traps"—trip alarms that would warn authorities of an undead shambler. "All part of the job. Thanks for arranging for me to get paid."

Roscoe sighed and let go of her arm with a pat. "Such modesty. Between you and me, girlfriend, if it were anyone else, I'd vomit. I would. But you just wear humility so well. Now run along and enjoy your time with Sashimi Ice. Meanwhile, I think Gordon here wants to meet Indira from They Mite B Robots."

Gordon pulled his gaze away from a woman in steampunk grunge pulling her garter into place. "So, that's really her? She's even more beautiful in person."

Roscoe leaned toward Gordon and crooned in a conspiratorial whisper. "And I hear she likes Marines."

"You shitting me?"

Roscoe tossed his head. "Maybe—but we'll never know until you meet her, right? I wonder if she remembers me from the Governor's Ball? Oh, who cares? I remember her! Come on, I'll introduce you. Semper fi and all that."

He pushed into the crowds with a now-tall-standing Gordon in tow. Ted, small camera at his side, hesitated. Neeta could almost see him imagining the choices before him: serious interview between Neeta and an international star, or meet his favorite band and possibly get something for the blooper reel.

"Brian?" Neeta set her head on his shoulder and spoke into his ear. "Think we can meet They Mite B Robots after the show?"

Brian had also been watching Ted's angst. "As long as Gordon and Roscoe don't screw things up."

Neeta linked one arm through Brian's and the other around Ted's. "Well, let's not waste any more time, then!"

They found Sashimi Ice, aka Kyun Bae, in his dressing room, texting with his wife while playing Battlespace Online. While they waited for him to post a battle interrupt command and sign off with his wife, Ted spoke to his publicist and private guard about a good camera angle. They greeted each other with bows and gushing compliments, then did it again with Ted filming.

"You speak Korean!" he exclaimed when she greeted him.

"Some. My best friend is half Korean, but I'm rusty," she replied, then switched to English. "We loved your music. We would play 'White Lamppost' for hours."

He laughed. "I was very young then. But after Nagasaki…" He looked away, toward the spray bottle of Raid that she'd sent ahead as a gift.

"Who was it?" Neeta asked.

"Uncle. Very…tight…in the business. He got me my contract to sing for television—the *Battlespace Roaring Mutant Pre-Adolescent Ninja Armadillos.*"

"BROMPANAs was a cool show. I'm sorry about your uncle, and that you had to see him like that."

"He was part of a larger horde. Twelve died that night. Three came back, I am told. It has been many years since I could sing again." Then his eyes lost their faraway look and he straightened and faced her.

"But now, I am on a comeback tour. I have a new album, *Sunrise in VR*." He spoke to his publicist, who handed a thumb drive to each of them with a bow.

Neeta clicked on the cover button and a picture of Bae wearing a VR headset came into view. A Pacific sunrise colored the lenses of the headset.

"This is great! Thank you!"

"I have more! Thanks—and a favor. Your work is very important, Neeta. Please, I would honor you tonight. You come on stage. I will sing a special song for you."

"Me?" For a moment, she just blinked. She looked over at Brian, who grinned, then back to Bae. "Wow. I—but not just me, right? I have a team."

"Yes, yes. All of them. Very important work. I am just a singer. But you—always risking your life…"

As if on cue, Neeta's pocket shouted, "Hey! 9-1-1, Neeta!"

With a moan more suited to Roscoe, she snatched her phone out of her pocket and went from gushing fangirl to zombie exterminator. "Lyffe Undeath Exterminations…okay…where? Elysian Park's pretty big, can they be more specific? And they're certain this is a zombie? Okay. Call in the police, just in case. The woman—she's in her home now? Tell her to lock the doors, turn the TV on, and gather as many insecticides and cleaning supplies… You've got it. Great. We're on the way."

She hung up and pressed Roscoe's number. "It's Neeta. Is Gordon with you? Well, snag him and meet us at the truck ASAP. We've got a dead one."

She hung up and bowed low to Kyun Bae. "Bae, it was such a pleasure to meet you. I'm sorry, but…"

"Please! Go! But be very careful."

She kissed Brian on the cheek. "Be back if we can."

She and Ted dashed out of the room.

Neeta stopped the van at the police roadblock and rolled down the window. The policeman stepped out of his car, made a careful look around, then ran up to her. A small bottle of wasp spray bounced against his leg from where it hung off his belt. He started a little when Ted twisted around Neeta to point a camera at him.

"Ignore him. What's the situation?" she asked.

"We found couple of lovers parking, no one out in the woods that we know of. Got a few more units making sure the rest of the park and surrounding neighborhood is cleared out."

"Any sign of the zombie?"

He shook his head. "We haven't actively looked, though. Been more concerned with getting people out and securing the area."

"Appreciate it. There's nothing worse than civilians"—she cast a dark look at Ted—"getting in the way."

The officer pulled out a map and pointed to a picnic area. "Last sighting was here. Lots of dense overgrowth, very hilly. Snakes'll be more active in the cooler temperatures. Watch your step. Good luck." The policeman went to move the barrier and touched two fingers to his brow in salute as they drove by.

"Civilian?" Ted protested as they drove up the hill. "Bet I have more training than that guy!"

"Remember it when we come across that zombie." She pulled the van into the parking area, ignoring the barely visible lines, and shoved the gearshift into park.

She kept the engine running. She turned her head toward the back where Roscoe and Gordon sat in the jump seats. "Spotlight in the bench."

They passed her the handheld light and leaned over the front seats as she held it out the window and shined it into the playground beyond. The light cut a bright line upon the trees and equipment. They strained their eyes for signs of movement.

"Think it left?" Roscoe asked. He sounded almost hopeful.

"Why would it be here, anyway?" Gordon asked.

Neeta twisted the light to a right angle to the windshield, then started a sweep back. "Depends on the zombie," she said. "Fond memories. Habit. Suicides return to the place they died."

"Maybe it was heading to Dodger's Stadium?" Ted suggested.

"Or the police academy," Gordon added.

"Gawd, I hope not!" Roscoe said. "Those poor officers, having to shoot someone they might have known. We all know how traumatic that can be!"

Gordon shrugged. "As long as they go for the head, right, Neeta?"

"They've been trained," she said. "All right. I'm not seeing anything. We'll—"

"There!" Gordon called. "Ten o'clock."

She jerked the light back to that position and caught a movement several yards into the trees. She thought she saw scraggly hair.

She pulled out her phone and pointed it in that direction, then read off the compass directions to the others. She spoke while still casing the area with the light. "All right, plebes. Full gear, weapon of choice—nonflammable, Ted. We're not setting LA's oldest park on fire."

Ted groaned, but just for show.

"Supersoakers are loaded. Everyone grab one. Spray first, and if it continues to approach, use weapons."

"Come on, Neeta!" Gordon started.

Neeta turned her head to cut him off with a glare. "We don't know that what we saw is undead. We also don't know if it's the only one. Never assume. Remember the videos; watch the signs. We spread out, ten-fifteen feet between, move in if you have to as we get deeper into the brush. We keep in sight of each other. Full moon is going to help, but watch those shadows. What do you do if you see something?"

"Spray, then weapons," the three chorused; Gordon, in a reluctant growl.

"Good. It's me, Ted, Roscoe, Gordon. Ted, when we're in the woods, stow the camera until after we've neutralized the threat. Dave will have to be satisfied with helmet cams."

"Set them to night vision, then," Ted said.

"Let's go." Neeta scanned the area once more with her light, just in case it had approached while she'd been briefing them. Then she pushed open her door and got out, hurrying to the back of the van. She didn't intend to wait for Ted to get there before gearing up, but he beat her to the back and had the camera ready when Roscoe swung open the doors and Gordon tossed her the supersoaker. She slung it over her shoulder and accepted the chainsaw. She handed Ted an aluminum-handled ax with a titanium head.

"Be careful with that; it was a graduation present," she told him.

Roscoe hopped out, holding his zombie basher like a ninja and winking at the camera, while Gordon jumped down, bearing a chainsaw.

Neeta took a look at the tight set of his jaw. "Ted, turn off the camera."

"What? Uh, yeah, sure. Off."

"Roscoe, Ted, keep watch." Neeta stepped up until she was nose-to nose with the veteran Marine. "Gordon, this is not Korea. Got it?"

"What do you know about Korea?" he demanded.

"I know this isn't it. Keep your head in the game. Got it?"

For a moment, he bared his teeth, ready to snarl. Then he shut his eyes, took a breath and released it slowly. "Walk in the park, Neeta."

She slapped his shoulder. "Walk in the park, Gordon."

They made their way quickly through the open area, Neeta growling when Ted paused to get some video of the moon through the crisscross of tent poles that were preset along the park. A breeze rustled the trees, sounding like the surf. A low moan broke the tranquility. Neeta glanced at her plebes, but none hesitated.

When they reached the tangle of bushes at the base of the hill, Roscoe groaned.

"Can't we draw it out? I am so not wearing the right shoes for this."

"You're in a rubber suit," Gordon retorted.

"And I suppose you hike in galoshes all the time? What about the snakes? I hate snakes."

"Quit whining!"

Neeta scanned the area, clicking her tongue as she thought. Roscoe's wardrobe complaint aside, she didn't like the terrain, either. Anything could hide under all that vegetation, and with the wind gusting, she couldn't tell if the movement of the bushes was natural or undead. As she reported their position to the police, she reached into the pocket on the leg of her pants and pulled out four small canisters. She passed one to each of them.

"Combination antihistamine and air freshener," she told them over their helmet mikes, then added for the cameras. "Low concentration of antihist, so it's legal. It's not enough to incapacitate the zombies, but if there are any hiding, it will bring them out—and probably make them mad."

"Uh, do we want to bring them out if it will make them mad?" Roscoe asked.

"Make up your mind." Gordon sighed. He hefted his chainsaw.

"I like the idea better than an ambush," Neeta answered. "The wind's in our favor tonight. Throw as far as you can. We want to drive them down to us. Gordon, put that down. We spray first.

"Don't fire until you see the scabs. We don't want to waste ammo, especially if there's more than one. If we look like we're getting overwhelmed, we make an orderly retreat back to the van. Got it?

"Okay, then. Throw on three. Roscoe, throw toward eleven o'clock. Ted, one o'clock. Gordon, three o'clock. Ready? Pull the pin. One. Two. Three!"

"Five!" Ted yelled as he threw his high up the hill.

Roscoe had a weaker arm; his only went half as far as Ted's. However, no sooner had his landed when something rose from the bushes and started to shamble toward them.

"Here it comes!" Gordon yelled and fired up his chainsaw. He stepped forward.

"Spray, Gordon! Hold your position!" Neeta yelled.

Something was wrong. This zombie was paying way too much attention to the ground. It stepped around a bush instead of just plowing through it. And the way the moonlight reflected off its head...

Then the wind gusted a cloud of gas its way and its hands went to its eyes as it started cussing.

No.

As *he* started cussing!

"Oh, no! Stand down!"

But Gordon was rushing forward.

"Gordon, no!" Neeta dropped her chainsaw and raced toward the man, who was now stumbling and swearing and trying to protect his eyes. Fortunately, she was closer and got between him and Gordon before he could bring the chainsaw to bear.

"Gordon, he's alive!" she managed to shout before the wind brought another cloud of gas their way and she, too, started gasping and swearing.

"It's pulling its face off!" Gordon gasped out.

"It's—" she broke off coughing. "It's a mask!"

"What?"

The "zombie" raised his hands. "I'm not a zombie! I'm alive! Please don't hurt me!" Then he, too, buckled over in a coughing fit as another cloud of gas wafted their way.

Gordon used the chainsaw to clear them a path and they staggered upwind to the clearing, where Roscoe and Ted hurried to meet them. Though her eyes were streaming, she could see that they were keeping formation, supersoakers up and watching the area around them. She wanted to praise them, but her lungs had other ideas for the air they took in.

I'm going to be smelling Mountain Fresh Spring for a week, she thought.

"Van," she gasped out, snagging their imposter with one hand and scooping up her chainsaw with the other. As they walked, Roscoe used his walkie-talkie to let the police know the zombie threat was a hoax and asked for a squad car to meet them.

By the time they'd crossed the flat parkland to the van, everyone was breathing a little easier. Roscoe yanked open the van doors and hopped into the back. Neeta let Gordon pull off his helmet first, then handed him their impersonator while she yanked off hers. She tossed it up to Roscoe to stow. Ted passed up his helmet and ax and pulled out the camera. Gordon kept hold of his chainsaw.

The zombie impersonator was still partly buckled over. "My eyes!" he cried.

"Take off that mask," Neeta ordered. She helped him wash his eyes with bottled water.

"Better," he said after they'd gone through two bottles. He wiped his face with the towel Roscoe handed him from the truck, then looked at each of them slowly, beaming. "I cannot believe I did it! You're the real deal, aren't you? *Zombie Death Extreme*! You're Roscoe. And Gordon. And…" He skipped over Ted, and when he came to Neeta, his voice fell into a reverent hush.

"You're Neeta Lyffe! My friends are going to freak! I knew this would work. Yes!" He pumped his arms in victory.

"You did this...to meet us?" Disbelief made Neeta's voice a raspy whisper.

"Bet your redeath, I did! And it worked. Neeta, I am your greatest fan."

He gazed at her with wide star-struck eyes, and she fervently hoped she hadn't looked at Bae that way.

"Who *are* you?"

"Tony! Tony Morales!" He grabbed her hand and began to pump it. "I'm the most active member of the *ZDE* fan club at Moorpark College. You probably remember my name. I run the *ZDE* fan website—the unofficial one—and the PeopleSpace fan page. And of course, I've written you after every episode! I mean, I had no idea what I wanted to do with my life, but when I saw your show, I knew my calling."

Gordon glared at him with raised brows and a turned lip. "You want to be a zombie exterminator."

"Guts and glory, man! Oooraw. That's why after each show, I send you my analysis of what everyone did wrong. Figured I could get that inside track before the next season's auditions."

"Next season?" She didn't think she was going to survive this season, and people were thinking she'd do this show again? "Why don't you take a certification program?"

"Parents won't pay for it. Besides, why would I want to waste my time with all that academics when I could learn as I work? I'm really a kinetic learner after all. I practice every day with my weed whacker—well, you know, when I'm not busy with the *Zombie Death Extreme* Unofficial Fan Blog or stuff."

"You still have to—"

"And you're Neeta Lyffe! Why would I want to learn from anyone else? You are so awesome and hotter in person."

"What were you doing in a zombie costume?" she shouted.

"Well, you didn't answer my letters, so I wasn't sure you'd gotten them. And I didn't want to wait until auditions. I mean, I'm 26 soon, and I'll be off my parent's health care and lose my government starter adult allowance, so I really need to know I'll have something to fall back on. Besides, when I heard on the commercials that you were on 9-1-1 duty this week, and that your boyfriend was going to take you to the Coats for Kids concert or whatever, I knew exactly how to get your attention."

He paused and grinned. "Worked real well, too, didn't it?"

Once again that night, she found herself blinking and speechless, but for a completely different reason. Was that how people thought of her now—as a celebrity with an exciting job? Despite her best efforts, did they really see extermination like some kind of…adventure show?

I just wanted to pay my bills. She glanced at the hillside where just a few wisps of antihistamine gas chased across the brush like ghosts. *I just blew $400 on a clueless fanboy…*

"Neeta," Roscoe called. "The police will be here in a couple of minutes. They're going back to let folks know it was a false alarm."

She started to tremble.

"Neeta?" Ted walked up behind her, camera down, and grasped her shoulder. "You okay?"

"Wow! I made an impression!" Fanboy Tony preened.

Neeta whirled and ran at Tony, slamming him against the side of the van.

"Impression? What about the impression you made on the people who live around here? There are lots of elderly and young families. Thanks to you, they got roused out of their homes!"

"They're coming back."

"Frightened out of their minds!"

"Oh, come on. It wasn't real. They're all safe. No harm done."

Was this kid for real? "You caused a false 9-1-1 call to be made. You pulled a half-dozen police officers off their normal patrols—not to mention me and my crew. What if there had been a real sighting while we were dorking around with you?"

"That wasn't so likely."

"Do you know the penalty for what you've done?"

Now, his expression melted into confusion. "I figured once you understood my motives…"

Her lips curled back in a snarl. "You thought wrong. This is not just a show. This is real life, and until you're ready to deal with that, don't even think about dealing with the undead." She shoved him once more before releasing him.

"I…" he started, then fell silent as she turned her back on him and stalked over to the open back of the van to shuck her hazmat suit. Ted, she noticed, abstractly, had filmed the whole thing.

Good.

Gordon gave her a sympathetic shrug as he walked past her and went to stand guard over their fan.

"And don't ever say 'OOH-Rah!' unless you earn the right and can pronounce it correctly," the veteran Marine growled at him.

Neeta had sent Ted and Gordon to try to find the canisters when they heard a car coming up the hill.

Roscoe sighed. "The police. Finally! Maybe we can get back to the concert before it ends!"

Tony spoke up. "Neeta? Would you autograph my mask? You owe me that much."

"You've got to be kidding!" Roscoe laughed in disbelief.

"No, wait!" Neeta stepped forward. "Toss over the mask."

He smiled eagerly and yanked it from his pocket. As it arched through the air, she fired up the chainsaw and swung. When the teeth bit into the rubber, she cut the power so that the slower moving chain mangled the mask.

Tony screeched.

"That cost $150 dollars!"

Neeta peeled it off the chain and dropped it on the ground. He fell to his knees and cradled it in his hands. The flayed zombie face fell in limp strips. He looked up, made vague protests.

"Next time you think about playing zombie, consider that that could have been your real face." Neeta snarled.

After the police had taken their statements and driven off with their fanboy, they climbed into the van. Neeta rested her head against the steering wheel.

"Neeta?" Roscoe asked. "Everything okay?"

"I don't want to be a celebrity," she murmured. "I don't want to be famous. I just want to be able to do my job and maybe raise some awareness…"

"But you're doing that! Oh, gawd, Neeta, don't let the Tonys of the world get to you!"

"He's an idiot." Gordon chimed in.

"How many people are like that, though? How many people watch this show and just think it's…what? Fun?"

"Not as many as are watching at and learning," Ted told her. "Come on. Remember all those letters?"

"I suppose…"

"Hey." Roscoe leaned across the back of the seat and gripped her shoulder. "Let's go back to the concert. Maybe we can still hear Sashimi Ice sing—and Gordon needs to get a certain bass guitarist's phone number."

"Bae!" Neeta jammed her keys into the ignition and started the car with a roar. "We were invited to go on stage with Sashimi Ice!"

Roscoe shrieked. "Drive, girl, drive! We are not letting some wannabe ruin our night!"

Her tires spat gravel as she tore out of the parking lot.

The helmet camera flickered to life, revealing rows of dilapidated or abandoned buildings in a Los Angeles warehouse district, sharply defined in blacks and grays.

"Is this thing on?" LaCenta asked. "You reading, Shogun?"

Shogun, the cameraman for their team, replied. "Yeah. Looks great. Nasir, you're fine, too. Go get it, guys. Wish I could say I'd like to join you, but that'd be a lie."

LaCenta laughed. "Don't you worry, Shogun. We'd rather have you safe in the truck, anyway."

She turned her head and the camera panned swiftly until it focused on Jason Hoffman, with whom they were riding patrol. His exterminator's suit bore a zombie being splatted by a giant flyswatter. His helmet had the same logo along with his name in letters that looked silver to the night-vision camera of LaCenta's helmet.

LaCenta asked, "Okay, Jace, what's the plan?"

Hoffman pointed with his chainsaw. "Police saw the zombie heading down this alley. It might just be passing through. Thing is, there are other dangers in this area. Lots of gang activity, drug dealing, etc. We stick together. We see something…questionable, remember: Our first duty is saving lives from the zombie. We tell them to clear out and find a populated area. Got it?"

"I understand," Nasir said.

"Got it," LaCenta said. "So, we're not splitting up?"

He shook his head. "And if we run into trouble, defend yourself."

LaCenta held out her weapon: a hilt and curved hand guard, with a short, narrow blade. Just a stub of a sword, but when she pressed a button near her thumb, the blade lengthened and widened as the microfilaments extended. Power surged through them, causing the sword to both shed a gentle but lethal light and emit a hum.

"Don't need to tell me twice," she said.

Hoffman smirked. "Let's go re-kill something," He lowered his visor.

They set off then: Hoffman on LaCenta's right, Nasir on her left. They started down the alley, supersoakers in hand. The moon bathed everything in a silver light, and the motion-oriented security lights shed conical brightness as they approached. The effect, combined with the fact that some of the warehouses had been built over a hundred years ago, made LaCenta feel like the heroine in a noir film—a modern and well-armed, but out-of-place heroine.

As they came to dumpsters or breaks between buildings, Hoffman or Nasir would turn and point their soakers toward the darkness, checking, while LaCenta kept an eye in front of them. Sometimes, she'd turn and look behind just in case.

They finished checking the first alley and started down the one on their right, heading back toward the parking lot with the van. They'd made it about halfway there, when LaCenta said, "Guys, there's something on the left!"

They ran forward and caught a hooker earning her pay from a none-too-particular john.

"Oh, that's so gross," LaCenta said. Nasir just cleared his throat and turned to keep an eye on the area ahead of them while Hoffman went to warn them. The woman screamed, and the john whirled on Hoffman. He jumped back, arms up in a show of peaceful intent. He spoke to them in quiet urgent tones. LaCenta turned her attention to the way they'd come, glancing back now and then.

Hoffman offered to hose them down with cleaner. The prostitute agreed with a "Hell, yes, honey!" but the john was arguing that he hadn't gotten his money's worth and he wasn't going to "finish his business covered in Drano."

LaCenta turned her head to see Hoffman raising his huge squirt gun at the girl, who held her arms wide. The man jumped in front of her and they began to scuffle.

"Oh, for pity's sake!" She tossed her head.

The camera caught a ghost of movement.

"LaCenta, watch the rear!" the cameraman shouted. "Something's coming your way!"

She turned and was nearly knocked over by large black man in the high-water skinny jeans and pocket T-shirt that some objectionable teen singing craze had made popular a decade ago. He grabbed her by the shoulders, as much to steady himself as her.

"It's after me! You gotta stop it! He wan' snack my brains!"

"Spray me! Spray me!" The john started shrieking.

"Let her go!" Nasir turned and interposed himself between LaCenta and the man, shoving him back.

"Man, you gotta believe me! He's following me!"

The prostitute started to scream and ran down the alley, her boots clunking heavily on the sidewalk and echoing off the corrugated steel of the warehouse walls.

Nasir said, "You're bleeding! Were you bit?"

"We've gotta zone!"

"Were you bit?"

The man started to swear. "He's coming! Man, you gotta download me."

"I load!" LaCenta shouted to be heard above the noise. "Now shut down 'fore he bead us!"

The man took a great swallow of air and nodded.

"Level. Now, he snack you?"

"I... Chained me, I think. Smash me good on a wall. Brownout, but I romanced him ninja and peeled."

"What?" Nasir demanded.

"Zombie smacked him into a wall. He hit his head, almost blacked out, but doesn't think the zombie had time to bite him. He knocked it down and ran."

Hoffman appeared at their side. "They took off, hopefully toward their cars." He paused to let out a long puff of air, a sign that he'd tried to chase them before giving up and running back. "I'm getting too old. Which way'd you see the zombie?"

The man pointed down the alley and to the right.

"OK. LaCenta, since you speak GangstaWoW, you get him back to the van. Find out anything you can from him and report to us. Check him over for zombie scat. You know how to do that, right? Good girl. Nasir and I'll go after the zombie."

LaCenta grabbed her charge by the arm. "Come on. Let's zone to our van, get you checked."

"But the zombie! He—"

She pulled the sword off her belt and activated it, then shut it down, but kept a hold of it. "Zombie ain't got nuthin' on me, baby."

She pulled him toward the van while her partners moved off in the opposite direction. Her charge shuffled along, and not just because his pants were too tight. He glanced fearfully into every corner and dark crevice, which she appreciated, but paused before each darkness, which she did not.

After yanking him into action for the fourth time, she said, "I'm LaCenta."

"Rips."

"We're almost to the van, Rips. End of the alley, cross the parking lot. We take that at a run. Copy? What're you doing out here, anyway? Never mind. Not my business, right?" She spat that last.

"He shouldn't have come back."

LaCenta stopped, turned to face him. The camera wouldn't show it, but he was pale and shaking slightly. His eyes were wide.

"Liberty said we done it right. Back of the neck."

"Liberty was fighting the zombie?" she asked.

He shook his head. "Liberty home…" Suddenly, he swore and squeezed his fingers into his pocket. "Liberty home! Jackson not get me, go for Liberty!"

"Jackson?"

He pulled at the phone in his pocket, moaning in distress as it only moved in inches. "He shouldn't have come back! Your posse gotta tank him!"

"Tank? You been aggro'd?" she shrieked.

"Liberty said we done it right!"

The cell phone popped out of his pocket and clattered to the ground. He crouched for it.

LaCenta backed up and sprayed him with several blasts of her supersoaker.

"What you doing?"

"Saving your life, fool! Zombie aggro you, you stay aggro'd. Stick close and we run." She grabbed him and sprinted out of the alley and across the parking lot. As they ran, she hit the switch for her radio.

"Jace, Nasir. Our man is a target! This zombie is after him personally."

"Spray him now!" Hoffman ordered. "We're coming."

"Done that! Sprayed the trail, but he's been bleeding! We see the van. "

She slowed as she saw the cameraman pounding on the window and pointing behind them.

"LaCenta!" Shogun's voice sounded in her earpiece. "Behind you!"

LaCenta released her grip. "Zone the van!"

As soon as he released her and ran, she primed her supersoaker and spun, spraying a protective circle around herself. Then she slung the squirt gun behind her and activated her sword, scanning the parking lot for her target. She saw it shuffling quickly past a half-collapsed warehouse forty yards away.

She stood directly between it and the van.

The moonlight shone on the tall, thin zombie, giving its pale limbs an even more sickly glow. As it passed under a lamppost, LaCenta saw that its pleated shorts and once pressed polo shirt were crusted with drying mud. Seaweed hung from its shoulders and sand coated its boat shoes. Its head lolled oddly and bounced as it moved. It dragged one side of its body, more like a stroke victim, and it moved its head only with an effort of shoulders and trunk.

When it saw Rips, it let out an odd, strangled scream and shambled forward faster than LaCenta had imagined. She gripped her borrowed sword in both hands, braced her feet as much to keep herself from running as to ensure her balance, and waited.

Ten yards.

Over her helmet, she heard Shogun shrieking, "Where'd he go? Where'd he go?" but she ignored him. If Rips were smart, he'd duck under the van and pound on the door on the other side. She didn't think he'd be smart. No matter.

Three yards...

If it had been daylight, she could have seen the zombie's face, but the angle of its head cloaked its expression in shadow. Didn't matter: its breathy screams spoke of outrage and murder. LaCenta shivered but didn't let her eyes move from its form.

She heard the police siren, but ignored that, too.

Almost there...

As she'd expected, it skirted past her circle, barely taking in its or her presence. As it brushed past, she turned to track it, swinging the sword high. She saw its back and swung down hard with a cry of her own.

She barely felt the resistance as electrified monofilaments sliced though skin, bones, muscles and nerve. In fact, it took her by surprise as the blade exited the front of its neck and she nearly stumbled.

It moved forward another step, then crumpled, the head sliding from the body as it fell.

"Now, it's over," LaCenta said. "But what was its problem?"

Carefully, sword still at the ready, she used the toe of her boot to push the body onto its back. Even waterlogged, she could see the small holes in its chest.

LaCenta swore.

"LaCenta!" Hoffman called. "Are you all right?"

"Where's that kid?" She scanned the lot, saw him heading back toward the alley. She started to run. "Nab him! Don't let him get away!"

Nasir ran toward him. The police car raced toward the alley, too.

Hoffman, however, was heading toward her. "What about the zombie?"

"Never mind that! It's done. Get the kid!"

"Why?" Hoffman started.

The police car made it to the alley and blocked it. As the policemen jumped out, Rips changed direction, heading straight toward Nasir, then jinking away as he saw the exterminator. Nasir made a flying tackle and knocked him to the ground.

Rips swung and kicked as Nasir grabbed his arms, twisting them behind his back and leaning, pressing down with all his weight.

Rips jerked his head back to break Nasir's nose with the back of his head. It impacted against the exterminator's helmet.

The gang member groaned and fell still.

LaCenta and Hoffman caught up to them just as the police did.

"What's going on?" the officer demanded.

"That boy's a murderer!" LaCenta declared. "That's his victim over there."

"Are you certain?" the officer asked, though he pulled out his handcuffs.

Rips protested groggily. "Not me, man. Liberty. I was kiting. He said we done it right. Thing aggro'd me. Almost killed me. Liberty said we done it right, and it came back to kill me!"

The policeman looked from LaCenta to Rips, then shook his head. "You have the right to remain silent," he started as he took Nasir's place and handcuffed the gang member.

His partner turned to LaCenta.

"Good work back there," the female officer said, jerking her head toward the now-truly-dead corpse. "All things considered, I think we'll need to call city morgue on this one."

Hoffman bowed his head. "Best news I've heard all night. I'm glad to have you clean up the mess."

She snorted. "We sure this area's clear? No more undead? 'K. I'm going to need to get your statements. The guy in the van, too…"

Her voice trailed off as she looked toward Hoffman's van.

The cameraman had rolled down the window and was being noisily sick out of it.

Hoffman groaned. "You'd better have missed the interior!" he shouted.

Spud sat in the jump seat of A to Z Exterminations next to Lacey Cuthbert, holding the slim young woman's wrist while she leaned in the opposite direction and made a little hum of pleasure. Across from them, the cameraman, Jake, shared a bemused look with Spud as he filmed her stretching exercises.

In the front, Gregory Cuthbert spoke to the police over the phone. The dispatcher had just reported to them about LaCenta's and Nasir's success not only in taking down a zombie but also a potential murderer. Now the driver, Boris Cuthbert, was griping about how dead Burbank was.

"It's going to get more dead if you don't turn on that webcam while you're talking on the phone," the dispatcher chided.

Studies had shown that "hands free" cell phone use while driving did nothing to reduce the number of accidents, and of course, the introduction of automotive video phones, which put the person's face on the GPS screen, only added to the problem. A study by UC-Berkley showed that the real problem was not that the driver wasn't holding onto the wheel, but that he or she was having a conversation with someone who was not also in the car and watching traffic. The real problem, it asserted, was the lack of a second person to yell, "Watch out!" as the distracted driver failed to see, for example, the garbage truck moving into the intersection.

Two years after the study went public, the State of California required that all cell phone users have a second webcam facing traffic. That way, the person talking to the driver could see the street ahead and call out warnings if necessary. California hadn't seen a decrease in traffic accidents yet—though experts asserted they needed to wait a few years until people were "used to the technology;" however, the use of cell phones while driving had decreased significantly, especially among married couples.

"Sweetness, you know I love you better when you don't watch me drive," Boris retorted.

"Oh, that's so much better!" Lacey hummed. She set her heel on Jake's seat, then bent down, shrugging out of the shoulder belt so she could touch her nose to her knee. "That LaCenta has got it together. But don't you two worry. We got something special planned for tonight. She leaned her head up to wink at the camera, then switched legs.

Boris and the dispatcher finished their repartee about his driving. "Well, I'm hanging up then before I get in trouble for not turning you in. I'll give the kids a kiss for you when I get home, but I don't think I'll wait up. Been a long night. You doing a ZERD run?"

"Yeah. Not much else going on. Gotta give our star here some royal treatment."

"Maybe I won't sleep until you're home then. Be safe, all right?"

"Always. Too much to come home to."

"Love you. Now uncover that webcam. I'm sending Torrenson out there to keep an eye on things, and you know how he is!"

Spud waited until he'd heard the click of the phone and saw Boris reach over and remove the bandana he'd tossed over the camera. "What's a ZERD run, sssir?"

He barked a laugh. "Neeta not mentioned those yet?"

Lacey Cuthbert rolled her shoulders. "Told you, brother, that she's saving it for her final exam."

She turned to Spud as she crossed her arm in front of her and used the other hand to push the elbow. "Where do you think ZERD gets its lab rats? It's not like zombies leave their bodies to science."

"Why not?" Jake asked.

Lacey rolled her eyes and followed the motion by rolling her entire head. "Come on! Who expects to become the living dead? Can you imagine how much trouble it would be to keep a bunch of corpses on ice, hoping for that one in a thousand to rise up? Much more effective to hire some bodysnatchers."

"Wait a minute! We're going to capture some *zombies*?" Jake's camera fell onto his lap with a thump.

"Karl will meet us at the Bedder Rest Mattress Factory with the truck. ZERD has a very nice cage for us to use—heavy plexiglass on wheels. Airtight. Zombies don't need air, you know. Plus, there are some nifty little devices in case we miss one or they get too frisky.

"You do know that Bedder Rest is like Zombie Central for the Los Angeles area, right? We send in some remote cameras into the outlying areas, find a few who aren't with the herd, and bring them in."

"How do we g-get them into the c-c-cage?" Spud asked.

Lacey rotated her ankles, then leaned down to pull the laces of her running shoes tight. She twisted her head toward him to wink. "With bait, of course."

The Bedder Rest Mattress Center was a long, two-story building designed to look like a pillow-top mattress when seen from above by the drivers on West Burbank. It took up over half the roughly oblong cement slab between South Front and the I-5 exit, with its back to South Front and the high walls that braced the hill on which Burbank ran. The parking lot faced the sloping three-lane exit to I-5. Once, its entering and exiting delivery trucks had been a menace to traffic. Now a different menace lay behind the eight-foot chain link fence and razor wire.

Boris switched off the headlights as he turned off the exit and into the open gate. They pulled into the factory parking lot next to Karl's truck—a short semi, nondescript except for the multitude of warning triangles indicating hazardous materials.

"Everybody out," Boris said. "And stay quiet. We don't want to attract any attention until we want to attract attention."

They donned their protective suits, except for Lacey, who grabbed a spray can and a liquid-filled plastic bag from the trunk next to her seat. Spud looked at the cameraman, who nodded and gave him and Lacey a lopsided grin. Everyone grabbed gear and exited the van.

Boris led them past the truck. The rear doors were opened wide, and the attached elevator lift was resting on the asphalt. About a hundred yards away, in the shadow cast by the rising street, a man in a yellow Hazmat suit was hunched over some controls. They walked in silence until they got near him. Lacey moved to one side, set down her flamethrower and began spraying herself with the can she'd carried.

Boris broke the silence in a hushed tone just above a whisper, the kind of voice used in theaters or funeral homes. "How's it going, Karl?"

The man in yellow grunted.

Jake trained his camera on them, backing up into the shadows to get a better angle. He stopped abruptly when he backed into something.

"Careful!" Lacey hissed. "That cage is expensive!"

"Didn't see it!" Jake's voice registered surprise.

Spud hadn't seen it himself until just then, either. The glass was so clear that it barely showed up in the dim light, except for a faint outline of a rectangular cube where the sides and ceiling met. Spud followed one edge toward the front.

Now that he knew what to look for, he could see that the side facing the factory had its doors flung open at wide angles, like corral doors to direct cattle into the pen.

Lacey tapped him on the shoulder and pointed to the other end. "There's a small door on the back that closes in nothin' flat. Now, both of you, stay quiet and listen. Here's how this goes down: Boris and Karl are using a crawler remote to find a small, isolated cell of zombies near a door. I'll go in and draw them out."

Neither Spud nor Jake spoke, but even in the dark, their expressions said it all.

Lacey rolled her eyes. "We're not stupid. I was state champ in track three years running—and I'm even faster when something undead is at my back. This spray on stuff?"

She scratched hard at her skin. A thin line of something curled under her nails, but her skin remained unmolested.

"It's like liquid Kevlar. They won't be able to claw me on the fly. Fire retardant, too, so if I need to, I can roast the place and keep running. The guys at ZERD are geniuses. I could have their babies!

"So, I come tearing out of there like a bat out of hell with the demons on my tail and run right for the trap. I dash in the big door, out the small; the small door slams shut. They follow me in, get trapped, and we got ourselves a delivery!

"Your job, Pippin, my man, is to keep any strays for escaping—either corral them or destroy them. Karl will swing the doors shut, and we keep a covering fire while we get to the van in case any others come after the first group. Jake, probably the safest place for you is right past the small door. We've got bots with cameras hanging off the walls by the entrance, so you don't need to worry about that. You can catch me in my moment of glory, then run with us to the van."

"How many times have you done this?" Jake asked in a strangled voice.

"Five. One more run, and Boris's mortgage is paid."

Boris came up from behind. He spoke softly. "We've also scrapped more than that because the conditions weren't perfect. Lacey may be an adrenalin junkie, but I don't want anyone thinking I'm risking her life to pay my bills, got it?"

"Um, you are risking her life," Spud pointed out.

Lacey punched him. "*I'm* risking my life. And you want to tell me this is any different from signing up to fight in a war? These vermin need to get taken out, and we need better ways to do that. I'm no brainiac, but I'm fast and wily, and this is how I can help. Boris, you find a spot yet?"

She started bouncing on her toes and shaking her wrists and arms to loosen them up. Boris turned his back to them and held his pad up, so they could all see the screen. In what once passed for a reception area, a half dozen undead lazed about. The Coke machine was spilled onto its side, and mattresses either half-made or half-destroyed rested on it and around. Two zombies lay on one, arms and legs tangled together. In fact, Spud counted five legs. The extra leg's owner sat on the sagging sofa, methodically slicing at its forearm with a torn soda can.

Two other zombies sat on the floor, leaning against the machine. One kept pushing its head upright, only to have it sag again. The other was slapping at something on the floor. The final zombie lolled in a corner chair like a discarded rag doll.

"Friday night in Zombieville," Lacey said.

"They don't look like much," Jake said.

"They're not motivated yet," Boris replied grimly. He worked the touchpad, and the scene retreated and shifted as their bugbot slunk out of its spot near the doorway and scanned the hall.

"Karl's been watching the area for about twenty minutes and nothing has shown up. Finish getting ready while we give it one last sweep."

"Got it, big brother."

While he looked intently at the screen, his finger on the touchpad to guide their surveillance bot, she guided Jake to a spot well into the shadows. Spud followed. She pulled a thin can of energy drink and downed it in a series of quick, heavy swallows. She tossed it to Spud.

"Hold that for me. Don't want to litter on international TV."

He glanced at the Bottom's-Up logo. "My mom loves this stuff."

"The Energize is great for quick rush if you drink it fast enough. Now for the *piece de resistance*." She picked up the plastic bag of liquid and read its label in a fake British accent.

"O-positive. Yes, a favorite among the discerning undead."

"Wait!" Jake gasped. "That's blood?"

"Keep your voice down!" she hissed. "Of course, it's blood. I told you they need motivation."

She tore the plastic, then poured about half on her shoulders and chest.

She handed the bag to Spud. "Do my back?"

Wordlessly, he took the bag and poured it messily over her clothes.

"Is that really necessary?" Jake asked, though he filmed the whole thing.

"It is if I don't want to get too close to them. First time, I went in clean. Had to get real close and aggressive. Never been so scared in my life."

"You scared now?"

"Sure. It's part of the rush!" She took the bag from him and tossed it into the cage. Spud noticed that Karl had placed some packets of hamburger in the corners.

Lacey went back to her routine of stretching and shaking, speeded up slightly from adrenaline and the energy drink.

Boris walked up to her. "Clear all the way down the hall. We should go now. It's a straight shot in, room on the left."

"I remember it. This should be easy."

"You sound d-disappointed," Spud pointed out.

Lacey shrugged, then rolled her shoulders quickly. "Well, I was hoping for some excitement for the cameras. Gotta show up LaCenta for you—get you some points for the game, right?"

Spud shrugged, then stood still, a counterpoint to her restless energy. "Don't want to w-win if it costs anyone a life."

Lacey stopped her bouncy movements. "That is so sweet!"

She took his face in her hands and kissed him full on the mouth.

She pulled away before he could react, and still smiling directly at him, donned the clear helmet her brother gave her. She did a quick sound check on her mike, gave them a thumb's up, then trotted off toward the entrance.

Spud stared after her, blinking.

Boris whacked him with the nozzle of his flame thrower. "Wake up, Romeo. You get that side. Flame anything that veers from the path."

Spud nodded and took a position to the right of the open doors. He watched Lacey pull open what was once the employee entrance and move in, leaving the door braced open. He decided he'd blog about her: how she was brave and funny.

And a great kisser, he thought, but he wouldn't mention that. It wouldn't be seemly. Besides, his mom watched that blog.

"Ew," Lacey's voice came over the headsets. "There're guts all over. Fresh, too. Better tell Monica to have them check Missing Persons. If I see a wallet or something…"

"Leave it and concentrate on the mission," Boris cut her off sharply.

"In and out," Karl said.

Lacey sighed. "Got it. Coming to the door. Ew. Okay…"

Spud winced when she suddenly called out, "Who ordered bait to go?"

Then he heard roaring, panting and a half-elated shriek.

Lacey's slim form erupted from the doorway, followed only steps later by a slower, shambling horde. The carefree manner had disappeared, and she ran full out, increasing the space between her and her pursuers.

Suddenly, her foot slipped out from under her and she fell headfirst onto the cement of the parking lot.

"Lacey!" Karl bellowed.

Spud didn't even think. He ran toward her. He caught a glimpse of Boris running her way, too, but he quickly outstripped the older, slower man. As Lacey scrambled to her feet, shrieking in earnest, Spud stood beside her and let loose with the flamethrower.

"No!" Lacey whacked down on the nozzle with her hand. The flames struck the ground feet in front of the zombies. They jumped back. "We can salvage this!"

"Run!" he yelled at her. He let off another bout of flame. It struck the ragdoll zombie, who had forged ahead of the group. The others swarmed past it.

Lacey grabbed his arm. "You, too. Head for the cage! Go!"

He released the flame thrower, grabbed her hand and ran. Lacey was crying and limping, and he pulled her along, ignoring how the flamethrower bounced against his leg.

"Go, go, go!" Gregory yelled.

Behind them, five zombies moaned, and another screamed as the flames consumed him.

They rushed into the cage, Lacey again slipping as her blood-and-gore encrusted soles struck the slick Plexiglas. Spud pushed her in front of him and through the small door. He thought he felt something pull at his suit, but it didn't catch.

Then he was through.

The small door slammed shut faster than he could track. The large doors swung closed not a second later. The lack of groanings assaulted Spud's ears with its silence.

Lacey all but fell onto Jake, her face contorted with pain and she breathed in high-pitched gasps.

"Get her in the van!" Boris yelled. "Keys are in the ignition. Don't wait—we'll go in the truck."

Spud went to pick her up, but Boris grabbed his shoulder. "Not you! We've got company. We cover them, got it?"

Spud looked past the exterminator at more zombies pouring out of the entrance. They moved slowly, unsure of their purpose. They looked at the exterminators, dazed, processing.

Jake wrapped Lacey's arm over his shoulder and together they ran toward the van, with Greg following to protect them. Karl already had the cage moving. Boris and Spud took positions between them and the zombies and waited.

"Wait until they make a move," Boris warned. "Our goal tonight is to get the goods and get out. Everything else is gravy."

A zombie with a tremendous belly jerked his head up. Its head twisted clockwise as it took in Spud and Boris, the cage, then Lacey and Jake. It held up a flabby arm, one finger pointing.

"Gra-vy!" it groaned, and the entire horde started toward the fleeing duo.

Boris swore. "Covering fire! Measured bursts. I'll get in the cab, start her up. You cover Karl and the cage."

"How many…"

"Don't count. Just shoot!"

Spud let loose on the large zombie, who seemed to be the leader. As it went up in flames, the rest simply parted around him.

He heard the van door slam and the engine start.

Boris grabbed a grenade from his belt, an actual pine-apple-style grenade. He pulled the pin, counted "one-two" and threw it.

A loud boom and a flash of light came from the center of the zombies, followed by the meaty slap of flesh hitting the pavement.

The swarm stopped, turned inward and as one, began to pounce on the victims, ripping and feasting on their flayed bodies.

Spud swallowed hard.

"Truck, now!" Boris shouted.

Boris dashed into the cab. Spud closed the distance between him and Karl. The older exterminator had driven the cage onto the elevator ramp and had clipped the restraining straps into place. He started it rising as Spud sprayed fire on one zombie that broke from the feeding frenzy.

"You! In back. No time!" Karl didn't wait but jumped into the back himself. He looked back long enough to make sure Spud had followed him in, then pounded on the wall.

The acceleration made Spud stagger. He slammed into the Plexiglas cage.

A zombie flung itself toward him, smacking the other side of the wall, mouth open in a savage but soundless scream.

Spud's scream echoed in the trailer as he flung himself backward, falling on his behind and scrambling back, crablike. If he hadn't lost his grip on the flamethrower, he would have set it off on the cage.

Karl laughed. He operated the controls, and the cage moved forward into the truck. He slipped between the cage and a wall, banging on the glass as he did, and reached out of the moving truck to pull the doors closed. Then he returned to sit by Spud's side.

"Seventy-five thousand dollars, there. Thirty-five for business. Ten for each of us. Good night's work. Lacey, you okay?" He directed the last into his headset.

Lacey, her voice high and tight, answered. "I pulled something in my leg, and I think I broke my wrist. I don't know which hurts worse." She swore.

"Lacey," Boris' voice came over the line, calm but firm. "I know you're hurting, but we've got to tell the police."

"I know. I called Monica on the radio. They're sending a Z-Mat crew and calling in Neeta to contain the mess. I'm sorry. Stupid guts got in the treads of my shoes. Ow! Gregory wants to take me to the emergency room."

"Yes, little sis. Go. There shouldn't be much left at the factory. As soon as I find a quiet place to pull over, I'll let Karl drive and we'll get a cab and meet you there."

"No. Go help. Our mess." She paused, and they could hear her breathing through her teeth.

After a moment, she asked. "Hey, Pip on the line?"

"Here, Lacey," he replied.

"Thanks. You saved my life, you know. Maybe I should have your babies."

Karl laughed as Spud felt his face heat. He hoped Jake was not recording the conversation. He didn't know what he'd tell his mom.

Chapter 10

Notes from *The Zombie Syndrome*

A Documentary

By Gary Opkast

Episode: Zombie Reality Meets Zombie Culture

CASSIDY MALONE clip from the special features DVD for the anniversary release of *Unwashed Unholies Six: Houston, We Have Cluster!* She sits in an office chair, one leg resting against the arm, elbow braced on the knee. Goes very well with the SWAT-style outfit and bandoliers from the movie. She still fits them perfectly. She runs her hand through graying hair as she speaks.

CASSIDY MALONE

You know, when we did these movies, they were just

fun. None of us ever thought that people would ever

really rise up from the dead. I remember scenes

where we'd have to do take after take because I'd laugh so hard... I'd laugh every time I watched the movie, too. But after I saw a zombie attack on the news—well, it wasn't funny anymore.

NARRATOR

In the late 2000s and early 2000-teens, zombies shambled their way into popular culture. Movies like *Zombieland*, books like *Pride and Prejudice and Zombies*, games like *Zombie Fluxx*, and even zombie plushies and action figures, made zombies fun.

Cut to DR. ROURK POTTER, PhD, in front of the Horror Movie Hall of Fame's Zombie exhibit.

DR. ROURK POTTER, PhD

By 2014, zombies had taken their place as a modern cultural icon. While there were some attempts to make zombies a romantic figure—*Blue Moon* comes to mind—for the most part, they took on a harmless, even comedic role or became the embodiment of evil. The cult classic, the anthology *The Zombie Cookbook*, illustrates this quite readily. In fact, this is part-and-parcel with the emergence of vampires as sensitive, romantic creatures rather than bloodthirsty parasites.

As with so many trends of the twentieth and twenty-first centuries, it began in America, which was reeling from the shock of 9-11, the tragedy of an ongoing war in Iraq, the bureaucratic fiasco of universal health care reform—which reminds me, I have an appointment in 15 minutes; I'm over the cold, but it took two weeks to get in, so I'm not wasting it... Where was I? (NOTE to self: Cut that aside)

And let's not forget Tiger Woods. America was reeling—losing confidence in its government, its security, its celebrities. There was a feeling of powerlessness, and with the rising awareness of the fragility of the individual's self-esteem and the penalties for expressing racial, social, gender, and choice-based prejudice, people needed a new outlet. Yes, there was Internet trolling, of course, but that does not translate well into groups and with the enactment of Godwin's Law with its subsequent fines and jail time, it became a dangerous way of releasing frustrations.

As a result, the Living Dead became the perfect scapegoat—you could mock them, hurt them, even drop a piano on them and not feel guilty. They aren't sexy, which made them all the more attractive, if you will, as a scapegoat. We all knew they were fake, and there was no wishful thinking that they weren't.

They are the politically safe group to abuse. And because of that, they took on a safe, almost cuddly aspect in the minds of Joe and Jane Public.

NARRATOR

Of course, all of that would change when zombie
fantasy became zombie reality.

FADE IN to parade of masked figures shambling past the Stone-
hedge Unitarian Resting Place cemetery—"zombies" in latex masks
and wearing long-sleeved T-shirts with their state flag.

NARRATOR

Even as late as 2028, years after the outbreaks of
actual zombie-ism were common knowledge, people continued to "celebrate the zombie." Zombie
crawls, like this one in New England, still happened
across the country.

In October of that year, five states banded together
for what was supposed to be the largest zombie
crawl in history. They'd hoped to make the record
books, but made history for an entirely different reason, as actual zombies joined the parade.

Cell phone video of the zombies clawing their way out of the graves.
Be sure to clean up the voiceover of the owner gushing over how
creative some people got about joining in.

NARRATOR

Some actually joined in the parade, and for a while,
were lost in the crowd. Those that were hungrier attacked the parade goers. However, as they had
risen just as the New York City zombie brigade was
passing the cemetery, the attack didn't go quite as
expected.

She made herself a mushroom-and-tomato omelet and strong coffee, and ate it on the back porch. Bookkeeping today, but tomorrow, the garden, she decided as she ate and looked out over the wild disarray of plants that had somehow flourished, albeit messily, despite her neglect. Her mother had had the green thumb. She'd really like to hire a landscaper; here in LA, they didn't cost much, but right now, she needed to save every penny she could.

When the lawsuit's paid, she promised the tangled grape vines and overgrown roses, and went in to wash her dishes before heading to her business office to tackle the paperwork.

Half an hour later, she was regretting her decision.

She set another bill into the "next payday" pile, then grimaced as she realized she'd already put that bill off twice. She got online and made a token payment, noted it on the bill, then returned it to the pile. She was a good customer, and she'd explained her situation to the sales rep the last time he'd taken her order. Besides, she wasn't using a lot of pesticides lately.

Nonetheless, her hands shook as she balled them into fists. She hated being late on her bills!

"Maybe I shouldn't take a vacation," she told the spreadsheet on her computer. "I have four days. I could get some exterminating jobs. Roaches and ants might be a refreshing change."

A knock on the door interrupted her one-sided conversation.

"Hey! Customer!" she told it and, shucking the haori, she tossed on a T-shirt with her logo over the pocket and went to answer.

Through the peephole, she saw a dapper gentleman in an expensive suit that said, "I expect air conditioning." He held a briefcase in one hand and was texting on his phone with the other.

Not customer. In fact, he looked like a Lawyer Larry.

She opened the door enough to speak through it. "Yes?" she asked. She managed to keep the suspicious tone out of her voice, but no way was she going to ask how she could help him.

"Ms. Lyffe? I represent Mort Bottums."

"I'm...sorry?"

She grimaced. Perhaps that wasn't the best choice of words. Before she could say anything to rectify her error, however, he forced a smile and continued.

"Yes, Mortimer Bottums? From Bottums-Up Diet Drinks? 'We minimize your gluteus maximus'?"

"Okay." Now she wasn't sorry; she was just confused.

Lawyer Larry cleared his throat in the uncomfortable silence. "Ms. Lyffe, we at BUDD watch your show faithfully. Mr. Bottums in particular. He believes you have a most stunning figure."

Neeta felt her face twist. A year ago, she couldn't get a date—now she was getting propositioned by proxy?

"Er...may I come in?"

"No."

"This isn't your place of business?"

"Do you have a pest problem?"

He paused, obviously thrown off-kilter. Which was fine by Neeta—she was, too.

He pocketed his phone, looked at his shoes while he rocked back on his heels. Again, he cleared his throat and met her eyes. "Ms. Lyffe, I'm here to make you a very lucrative offer."

"What do you want killed?"

"No, no."

"Re-killed?"

He shouted, "Nothing like that! We want you to be our next BUDDy!"

"What?"

He sighed and rubbed his eyes with one hand. "May I please come in and explain?"

She stepped aside.

"Thank you," he said as he brushed past her.

"Be warned. I have plenty of lethal weapons within easy reach."

"Err...Noted."

Once they'd settled on opposite sides of her desk, he opened up his suitcase and pulled out a portfolio. The cover held a collage of different celebrities—most of whom Neeta remembered only from childhood or sort-of recognized from her infrequent television watching. All held a bottle of "Bottums-Up" in one hand and pointed to their perfect waists with the other.

"Larry" jumped into his business pitch. "We at BUDD have always dedicated ourselves to creating high-quality, nutritious drinks that not only help you cut calories but burn fat."

"I'm not on a diet."

"We have several lines: Minimize. Stabilize..."

"I'm not getting fat."

"No! Not at all! Like Mr. Bottums said, you're quite fit. Stunning, even. That's what he said. Exact words."

"Look, Mister...."

"Call me 'Lawrence.'"

"You're kidding?"

His face clouded. "No. Why?"

She sighed. She was starting to feel sorry for the guy, but the piles of bills she'd shoved into a drawer stifled the impulse. "Listen, Larry. I don't care what your boss thinks of my figure. Could you just come to the point?"

He smirked and relaxed. "Of course. Ms. Lyffe, we want you to represent our newest line of drinks—Longevitize."

He leaned forward and flipped through the pages of the portfolio. Neeta caught glimpses of celebrities in before-and-after shots, famous athletes in uniform drinking "Bottum's up" or bearing fruit-colored "milk mustaches," the doctor from Real ER-Nottingham standing in front of a nutrition pyramid made of Bottums-Up cans.

With a satisfied "ah!" that sounded staged to Neeta, he pointed to the page that had a still of Neeta from the Obstacle Course episode. She stood in front of the course she'd just run herself. The dummies all bore red marks in the kill zones and her chainsaw dripped red paint. It'd been one of her best runs—did it in one take, too.

They'd photo-shopped the picture so that her hair looked less sweaty and her body more so. They also smoothed out her tan and airbrushed out the blotches she knew she got on her face after exercising. She wished she looked that good.

On the lower right was a bottle of BUDD and a DoDroid screen with a schedule:

9 pm–11 pm. Take out the undead
Midnight–7 am. Sleep satisfied
7 am–9 am. Chainsaw workout
9:15 Longevitize

"This is just a concept, of course," Larry started before she could raise an objection. "We envision a full spectrum: after the workout—Longevitize. Done with the undead—time to Longevitize. Some less gimmicky ones after we've established your identity…"

"I have an identity!"

"Yes, of course," he backpedaled. "You're Neeta Lyffe, Zombie Exterminator! I mean, your identity as Neeta Lyffe, Zombie Exterminator—*and BUDDy!*"

Not sure if she was flattered or horrified, she flipped through the rest of the photos. All were concocted from the show except one: a photo of her and Brian on their first date.

"Where did you get this?"

The wine glasses had been replaced with bottles of Longevitize. The caption read: *What's more desirable in a romance than Longevity?*

Larry smiled. "Like it? We're considering asking Brian St. James to be our male BUDDy. Think he'll go for it?"

"Who said I was going for it? You honestly think I'm going to endorse a product I don't even use?"

"No, no. Of course not. You're a woman of integrity. Naturally, we'll supply you with BUDD products for the duration of your contract."

"What contract?"

Smiling as if she'd already agreed, he slapped an iDoIt on her desk and pushed it her way.

She stood and reached to shove it back—then her eye caught the dollar figure on the screen.

"We're not asking for a commitment right away," he said into her silence. "We understand that you need to finish your season of *Zombie Death Extreme*. Mr. Bottums himself is quite anxious to see what you plan for the final challenge. However, we know that others must be clamoring for your talents. Please, just consider it?"

He tapped the small computer. "There's all the information. Contract, sample campaigns, testimonies from other BUDDies, the works. I'll contact you again in a couple of weeks. I'll just let myself out."

She waited until she heard her door shut before slouching in her chair. In her mind, she could hear her bills arguing with her pride.

She stood and made a beeline for the shed where she kept her gardening tools before they won.

Dear Mom,

You're going to be seeing a deposit for $9,000 in our account. It's my share from capturing some zombies for research. Kind of a long story, but you'll see it on TV. I kept some of it for myself. I know you said to enjoy California while I can, and since we got a week off of filming, I'm going to go do some things with friends. I'll tell you more later and send postcards.

A knock on the door interrupted Spud's flow of thought, and he hurriedly typed in "Love, Pippin" and sent out the e-mail, then ran to the apartment door.

His heart actually skipped just a little as Lacey, a cast on her arm and a brace on her leg, smiled at him. "Ready to go? Boris is in the car. Hope you don't mind a chaperone."

"No, that's fine." He reached back to grab his jacket and camera.

She turned slowly and holding the banister in a tight grip, hobbled down the stairs.

"Are you sure you're up to it?" he asked as he hurried to her side. He resisted the urge to grab her elbow but stayed ready to help.

She made an annoyed sound. "It's whale watching— sit and look, right? I'll be fine. Besides, I haven't gotten to do this since I was a kid. You've no idea the 'pity me' act I put up for my brothers to get them to agree to this. What about you? Sure you're up to having my brothers chaperoning?"

"Ch-chaperoning? I, uh…" Spud froze on the steps. Did they think this was a date? Didn't they approve? Or did they think he was going to take some kind of advantage?

"I thought we were just g-going together as ffffriends. I mean, not that I wouldn't w-want to-to—that is, I don't want to b-be forward or anything, and if they d-don't approve—or, or if you aren't interested, I'm not t-trying to imply that you're interested, I just…uh."

Lacey burst out laughing so hard, she buckled over. "Oh, my gosh! I think that's the most words I've heard come out of your mouth at one time. You must like me, huh?"

He felt his face redden. Why did he always have to act like an idiot around girls he liked? Back home in Middletown, Idaho, his nickname wasn't "Spud." It was

"Stammer" for the way he got tongue-tied. He'd finally given up talking to girls, especially girls he liked.

But he did like Lacey—a lot. He hadn't been able to stop thinking about her since the night they'd gone zombie hunting together.

She was still looking at him, and her amused smile made his heart feel too big for his chest.

I'm not in Idaho; I don't have to be "Stammer."

He met her smirk with a warm, serious smile. "Well, yes. Yes, I do, Lacey. Very much."

He felt a small rush as he watched her expression gentle, and her cheeks take a slight pink tinge. She held out her casted arm and let him help her down the stairs.

"So, maybe after we all see the whales, we send my brothers home?"

"I'd like that very much, too."

"I cannot believe my sister is a hero," Jamal said as he hitched his chair to the table. He gave LaCenta a big, proud grin as his mother set a plate of enchiladas in front of him. He swiped the Tabasco sauce from their little brother, who yelped in protest.

"Your sister has been a hero since you were little," their mother retorted. She squeezed LaCenta's shoulder as she passed by on the way back to the kitchen.

"Momma, let me help you," LaCenta called to her.

"Oh, no! You are the guest of honor today," she called back. "People have been calling me non-stop since they saw you on the news. 'Was that really your LaCenta going after zombies and murderers?' I swear some of them must have thought you were acting all this time."

"I don't know what the fuss is," LaCenta said. "Police do it all the time, that's all I'm saying."

"Yeah," Jamal said, "but you set a zombie after him. That's core."

"Fuze core," Moe added and let out a pleased snort. "Tell you what—nobody gonna mess with me, having you for a sister."

LaCenta leaned across the table and pinned her youngest brother with her glare. "I don't want you in a position where anybody has reason to mess with you, got that? Those days are over. You learn a lesson from that re-animated corpse!"

Moe backed up in his chair, arms out in surrender. "Chill! I learned my lesson before that kid corpsified, remember?"

The long scar across his dark forearm shone palely in witness.

LaCenta sat back down. "Okay. As long as you don't forget. You don't need no gang to make you a man."

Their mother came in and set a plate in front of LaCenta before sitting down with one of her own. "And we are all the family we need," she added.

"Besides," Jamal chimed in, "When LaCenta wins that million, she'll set us up for life."

LaCenta made a rude noise. "With a million? After the IRS takes its share, there ain't gonna be much left— and it's going to my business and your college."

Jamal's head bobbed in gratitude, but their little brother groaned. "I don't need no college. I'm going into the Marines. Semper Fi, man. Hey, LaCenta. Think you can hook me up with that Gordon dude?"

LaCenta rolled her eyes and dug into her lunch. "That loser? You don't seriously want to be like him?"

Dear Mr. Makepeace,

You are cool. You are tough. When I grow up, I want to be tough and cool like you. U-rah!

Gordon paused in opening his refrigerator to read the hand-scrawled note again. That lawyer Eugene had given it to him, along with a photo of a five-year-old boy playing with an action figure of him taking out zombies. OK, so the action figure had been WWF Ken with a mottled green pattern painted on his skin and his hair cut off, and the zombies, broken and dirty remnants of the action figures from Stranger Things in College, but it was the thought that counted. Though he wouldn't mind having had the Millie Bobby Brown figure on his side.

Been too long, he told himself and pulled open the door. Too long with no action and too much reading. He needed a beer before he could tackle the next chapter.

Someone knocked primly on his door, so he grabbed a beer and went to answer it, thinking that it'd better not be that gay neighbor of his again.

He yanked open the door just as Roscoe was raising his hand for another knock.

"Same diff," he said aloud.

"What?" Roscoe asked.

"Nothing. What do you want?"

Roscoe was looking at the beer in his hand. "Please tell me you aren't intending to get drunk alone. On that."

"I'm studying," he growled. "Been studying all day. This is my first, if you must know."

"Well, we can't have that." Roscoe brushed past him, snatching the beer from his hands and putting it back into the refrigerator. Only when Nasir followed did Gordon realize he'd been hanging out in the hallway. *Have to work on that situational awareness.*

"I refuse to let you waste your evening on swill," Roscoe said. "Go put on something presentable. Something that says, 'chick magnet.'" Pawing through his refrigerator with one hand, Roscoe waved in Gordon's general direction with the other.

"What? I'm studying."

"Yeah? Tell me the last three things you read."

Gordon paused, his mind blank. "I hate you."

Roscoe shut the door and brushed off his hands. "You need a study break and some real action."

Gordon snorted. "What would you know about action?"

Roscoe tossed his head. "Please! That little party at the concert? Tourist stuff. I've been working Hollywood for 20 years. I know all the places, all the people. We don't have work tomorrow and there's no taps for you tonight, Marine."

Gordon crossed his arms. "Out of the goodness of your heart you're taking us along on your party prowl? I think you just want to keep us from studying, see us fail."

Nasir cleared his throat in a reminder that he had passed all the practice tests.

Roscoe just shook his head at Gordon as if he were a dimwit. "You really don't get how this works, do you? I don't give a crap who wins, and I'm not in this to win.

You think I want to spend my life wearing industrial-strength rubber and cleaning up decaying body parts? I'm the gadfly. The antagonist. I get paid to be the jerk everyone loves to hate and likes to see fall short in the end. And I'm going to come out of this show better off than even the winner. Nothing personal; it's what I do."

"So, you're the jerk." Gordon understood that much. "Why do you want to take us clubbing?"

Roscoe sighed theatrically. "Oh, gawd. I really have to spell this out? I like you guys. I have total respect for what you're trying to do. And in my own joie de vivre way, I'm trying to thank you for wanting to lay your lives on the line."

Now Nasir stepped beside Gordon, copying his crossed arms and skeptical gaze.

Roscoe gaped at them in the picture of innocence. "Is it too much to believe I consider you friends? I thought we really bonded this season…"

Still, they glared.

Roscoe wilted. "Oh, honestly! You're what's hot in Hollywood. And everyone knows I've got the in with the *ZDE* cast. But that does not mean you can't take advantage! This is Hollywood—decadent Rome of the modern world. And when in Rome…" He raised his eyebrows suggestively.

Gordon traded glances with Nasir. "Something that says 'chick magnet'? BDU pants and black muscle shirt?"

Roscoe put his hand over his heart. "A classic."

He headed toward his bedroom, stopped, and turned around. "I want to shave my head. Won't take long."

"Fine, fine. We'll call Spud again. He's not answering his phone." Roscoe pulled out his phone.

"Calling Neeta, too?"

Roscoe laughed. "You poor naïve fool. I'm sure our Brian has plenty of plans for Neeta's night off."

Neeta stuck the key in her lock, but had a hard time getting the door open. The lock had been sticky for a few months now, and it didn't help that Brian was cuddled up so close to her.

"Brian, I'm telling you, it's not a good idea," she said, but she was smiling, and she knew it came through in her voice. She couldn't help it: dinner had been wonderful, the movie romantic, and she was way too aware of his hand on the small of her back.

"Come on," he nudged back her hair to whisper in her ear. "You know you want to."

She turned her head away, pretending to concentrate on the doorknob. "No, I don't."

"You could use it."

"Oh! Well, thank you!" She shook the door, then realized she'd forgotten the deadbolt. What was with her? She was really thinking about cuddling on the porch swing...

"Neeta, I'm serious," Brian persisted. "Don't you trust me?"

"It's not that." She unlocked the deadbolt, gave the doorknob twist while pushing against the door with her shoulder. Brian took the opportunity to lean in closer. She avoided his eyes.

"Don't tell me you've always done it yourself?"

She shoved on the door. Why wouldn't he let up? Why did he have to be so cute? "No, but that's different. Mom hired a professional."

"So, you don't think I'm good enough?"

The door pushed open suddenly, causing her to stumble away from him. She caught her balance and whirled toward him.

"Brian, for the last time: I don't want your help with my bookkeeping!"

He crossed his arms and leaned on the threshold, his expression a mix of anger and hurt. "I just want to help you."

"I know, I know! And I really appreciated you helping me with the garden, and dinner was fantastic, but…Can we just leave it at that? I have a system; it's under control; I just need to catch up." She met his eyes, but when his expression didn't change, she sighed, turned to set her purse on the side table and flopped onto the couch. She crossed her legs, which she knew looked good in the skirt she wore, and gave him her best pout.

"Are you going to stay mad because I don't want you messing with my system?"

His mouth quirked in a grin, and he shut the door. When he sat down beside her, he spoke seriously. "Is that really it, though? Is it your system, or that you don't want me to see your finances?"

Neeta sighed. Was that what this was about? "Look, Brian. I'm fine. Struggling some, sure, but in this economy…"

"It's not the economy; it's the lawsuit, and we both know it. But the point is, you don't have to struggle. You're a celebrity, Neeta. You can use that."

Suspicion washed over her, cooling whatever attraction she'd been feeling. "What are you talking about?"

"I talked to a gentleman for BUDD."

"Oh, no!" She uncrossed her legs and brought her foot down with a stamp that threatened to break the high heel. "You, too? 'After the undead, Longevitize,'" she sneered.

He held up his hands. "Okay, so it's hokey. But that's part of their image. And did you look at the testimonials from their celebrity representatives? Bottum's Up treats them pretty damn well."

"'Damn' is right. Sell your soul for a diet drink?"

"You're looking at this wrong." He leaned forward. He started to reach for her hands, took in her expression, and pulled back. "It's not your soul. Your name, your image, sure. And you're not 'selling it.' You're lending your name to promote something people want. You know my partner in the morning show, Cassie? Haven't you heard her commercials for the 'Little Pink Pill'?"

Neeta's face twisted. "The one for—"

"For hair loss in women, yes. She's used it; it works; she promotes it. Gets paid for it, too. Is she selling out?"

"No, it's just…" She leaned forward, elbows on knees, head in hands. From the other room, she could hear the bills in her drawer calling, *Listen to him. He just wants to help.*

Brian pressed on, his voice mellow and convincing, "It's a job, like any other job. You don't have to struggle, honey. Deep down, you know that, or you wouldn't be doing what you're doing now."

Neeta peered at him through the side of her eyes. "What do you mean?"

He released a short breath in exasperation. "Come on, Neeta, you are the host of a reality TV show!"

Neeta found herself on her feet, hands clenched into fists at her sides. "That's different! I went on that show to increase awareness of what this job means. I didn't want to be a celebrity, I don't want to be a celebrity, and I don't want to be anyone's BUDDy!"

There was no longer anger in his eyes, only hurt. His voice went very quiet. "Not even mine?"

Rigormortis:
Subject: You think you know someone...
Well, no one was as surprised as me to see LaCenta come out the hero in this week's episode. Though using the victim as bait was pretty cold, even if she did think he was a murderer. See episode summary here if you haven't seen it yet. WARNING: Spoilers.
likemineliving:
Spoilers? Like "using the victim as bait." Thanks, loads.
Rigormortis:
Hey, that's not much more than the commercials said! Trust me, you want to see the episode.
Tro111:
From the summary: "LaCenta single-handedly captures both a zombie and its murderer—using the murderer as bait in the trap."
So, now we're letting the producers act as judge and jury? Whatever happened to innocent until proven guilty? And you sheep just go along with it.

As for what LaCenta did—*of course* it was cold. And convenient. Bet it brought the ratings way up. First she beats up Neeta—and rightfully—now, she's taking the law into her own hands, and winning? Everybody likes a bad girl, right Rigormortis? Bet you're lying around alone in your bed thinking about her right now.
Rigormortis:
How do we get this jerk off the forum? Where's the moderator?

MANIC_MIND:
Okay, I have to agree—the summary does make an assumption, but no one is judging the kid. And he did confess, incidentally. Here's an article in the LA Times. Here's LaCenta's interview about it in ZombieWatch.com. The guy was coated in cleaning products. The zombie would have stopped before he got to him. The cameraman in the truck was probably in more danger. What's happening to him, anyway? I heard he quit.

ZDEMod:
I have contacted Tro111 about proper forum etiquette. However, he has the right to express his opinion. I've not banned him yet.

FYI, Damon Underhill, the cameraman in "To Catch a Murderer," has resigned under amicable terms and is now working at the same studio as inflatable crowd manager for several prime-time shows. He'd like me to pass on his thanks for your concern and let you know that "This kind of non-living people is more my style, LOL."

In the meantime, be sure to watch next week's episode, "The Unlikely Knight." LaCenta was not the only hero that night—and that's all I'll say. No spoilers here!

Also, please keep the plebes of *Zombie Death Extreme* in your thoughts and prayers as they take their certification tests this week.

Chapter 11

Notes from *The Zombie Syndrome*

A Documentary

By Gary Opkast

Episode: The Zombie Exterminator

(Needs clips of zombie exterminators at work—maybe some of the less gross stuff. Check to see if can crib from *So, You Want to be a Zombie Exterminator?* and *Re-Killing for Fun and Profit*.)

NARRATOR

The first confirmed zombie attacks were repelled primarily by policemen and soldiers, but as the problem became more widespread, a new specialization developed: the zombie exterminator. While many ZEs arose from the police and military, the bulk came from actual exterminators who chose to

specialize. Why exterminators? Sociologists and ca-
reer-study experts have asked this question for
years. Ira Butcher believes she has the answer.

Clip: Dressed in a navy suit and dark pumps, IRA BUTCHER sits in
an office chair in front of a wall covered in a collage of people working
at various careers. Across the top, a banner says, "Why We Work."
Short dark hair frames her round face and high forehead, and she
pushes it over her ear as she speaks.

IRA BUTCHER

Extermination in general takes a particular mindset.
You have to be willing to deal with the, well, disgusting things. You have to know how to use chemicals
properly—what's lethal for vermin yet safe for hu-
mans. Following directions is important—take too
many liberties, and you can hurt someone or yourself in this business.

So, the skill set that makes a good exterminator is
also part of the skill set that makes a good zombie
exterminator. Now obviously, there are other important skills—willingness to risk your life, upper
body strength and speed, and a certain mindset
that will allow you to look at what appears on the
surface to be human and see that in fact, it is, as
ZEs say, "just another pest."

NARRATOR

Regulation of zombie exterminators has come under the jurisdiction of the Department of Agriculture.

> Brent Endive, Certification Counselor, explains a lit-
> tle about the exacting process.

BRENT ENDIVE standing at the offices of the County Agricultural Department in Los Angeles. Through the narrow window, you can see
people leaned over desks taking a test. Camera focuses on the room,
then pulls back "through" the window to the door, receding to take in
head-and-shoulders of BRENT as he speaks.

BRENT ENDIVE

> So, certification is really a four-step process. You
> have to apply for the general certification program.
> That's when you take the LIVE scan and we do
> background checks. Standard for any exterminator
> these days. Next you have an initial physical and
> psychological evaluation, which includes a strenu-
> ous test of distance running, sprinting, and wielding
> heavy instruments in a wild random pattern for at
> least ten minutes straight. People often have to re-
> take that last part. Then, of course, comes the
> academic study, culminating and a two-hour multi-
> ple-choice test as you see taking place here. If you
> pass with qualifying marks, you receive a temporary
> permit—not a license yet—to re-kill. After that, you
> may find somewhere to apprentice. In Los Angeles,
> we can help with that. After three months' appren-
> ticeship, we do a second psychological evaluation,
> provided the trainee has not already quit or sought
> mental help on their own.

ENDIVE pauses to release a heavy breath through his lips.

These people go through a lot to keep us safe and
to keep down what could become a contagion. I
have all the respect in the world for them. But no
way would I want their job.

Neeta sighed and shifted position in the conference room chair for the umpteenth time in two hours.

Across the table, Ted made an annoyed sound. "Look, Neeta. If you're going to brood, why not talk about it?"

"Why is it that men always want me to talk about my feelings?" she snapped back.

His entire body twisted in surprise. He pushed out of his chair and grabbed his camera. "I meant talk for the camera about how you feel about the plebes testing."

"Oh!" she reddened.

"You're obviously concerned about it, and Dave's going to ask you to do it, anyway. Why not get it over with, and get some real emotion while we're at it? We do it right, and Dave won't have to tell you how to emote."

"I'm sorry. I thought you meant... No, you're right. Let's do this."

He made a show of hefting the camera onto his shoulder, even though it weighed less than his flamethrower. Then he tilted his head away from it to regard her seriously. "You know, your personal feelings are yours. You want to keep it to yourself, not my business."

"Thanks."

"Until you go postal with that chainsaw, of course. Then my girl and I have to take you out."

"Absolutely." She matched his look until neither could hold it and they burst out laughing together. It felt good.

She waved her hands in the air as if erasing the moment, then ran them over her face. "Okay. Okay! Serious. Concerned."

"Touch of broody. We do it in one take."

"Right." She took a deep breath and released it. He counted from five, using his fingers for two and one, and she looked into the camera as if it were a confidant.

"So, today, they are testing. Standard Applicator license, Branch Four, although LaCenta took the Branch Two last week and takes Branch Three next month. Branch Four concentrates on zombies, of course. Spud will have to retest in Idaho, and Nasir in Afghanistan, as will Gordon wherever he decides to move."

Dave would probably cut some of this, she knew. She was just talking, summing up to get into the groove.

"This is always a difficult time for a teacher, believe it or not, and this is my first—and probably only—class. I hope I taught them enough. I think I did. We've all seen them in action. I'd be glad to have any of them at my side. But it's like my mom used to say, 'The government cares about paperwork, so you do the paperwork. All part of the job.'

"If they blow this test, they can retake it later, of course, but for the show, that's it. They're out. And really, at this point, I'd consider that as much my failure as theirs."

Ted held the camera on her face a moment longer, then turned it off and lowered it. From the doorway, they heard clapping, and turned to see Roscoe, LaCenta and Spud lingering by the open door.

"Oh, gawd, Neeta. You are such a natural at all this. The emotion!" Roscoe enthused as he ran a finger under his eye as if wiping a tear.

LaCenta shouldered roughly past him. "Shut up, Roscoe! She meant it."

Spud swept through in her wake.

"Of course, she did! That tough exterior hides a heart of pure platinum! Gorgeous inside and out. It's been *such* a privilege to work with you."

Neeta felt herself blush but peered at him with suspicious eyes. "So, how did you do on the test?"

Roscoe raised one eyebrow at Ted, who took the cue and started the camera.

Then Roscoe said, "Wait! Wait! Let's start with LaCenta; then I'll make a grand entrance." He ducked back outside, keeping the door open just a crack. He winked mischievously.

Ted turned the camera toward LaCenta, who set her elbows on the table and slumped slightly over them. "Well, I passed, I know that. But I didn't do as well as I could have. Guess I should have spaced the Branches. I just know I got some of the decontamination protocols mixed up. "

Roscoe slammed open the door so that it banged against the interior wall then entered, arms spread theatrically. "Freedom! Oh, gawd, I'll take one of Neeta's workouts to that any day."

"So, you don't think you passed?" LaCenta smirked.

Roscoe settled into a conference chair, resting his feet on the table. He cracked his knuckles then knit his fingers together and placed him behind his head. "*Please*, this is a government test—multiple choice. I filled in dots."

"At random?" Neeta and LaCenta cried together.

"Certainly not! I adapted the pattern found in Melchior Rawling's *Dots on an SAT*. My only regret is that they won't let give me back my score sheet. I'm sure Galletia's would pay a fortune for it."

"You did not!" LaCenta's voice said she believed he did.

He looked at her with the face of innocence that morphed into a good imitation of the superior smirk she'd just given him. "I may as well have. It would have been more challenging."

LaCenta slammed her fists onto the table and pushed out of her chair. "You—" she let out a string of descriptives that would have to be edited out later. "You just think this whole thing is a big joke, don't you? Why are you even doing this?"

Roscoe grinned and studied his fingernails. "You know. The money, the glory, the women—present company excepted, of course. But speaking of glory and women—Spud, how did you do?"

Spud just grinned straight at the camera. "I blew it out of the water. I had motivation."

Roscoe snorted. "Boyfriend, a million dollars will motivate anybody."

Once Gordon and Nasir had come in and officially reported for the camera their impressions of how they did, and Ted had stowed the equipment, Roscoe turned back to Spud.

"All right. Talk. What's this 'motivation' that obviously beats out a million dollars?"

"Yeah," LaCenta added. "And what is with you, anyway? You've been acting differently since we came back from our four-day break. You used to stutter around Neeta and me like Ca-ca-ca Staleman, but you've stopped since we came back."

"Have I?"

"Yes, you have—and stop with that smirk. Look like a damfool who got lucky."

LaCenta tossed her head, dismissing the notion, but the men around the table leaned toward Spud.

He pressed into the back of his chair. "It's not like that."

"What's it like, then?" Roscoe urged.

Nasir, however, cleared his throat. "Perhaps this is not a conversation for mixed company."

Spud's eyes narrowed. "Nothing's happened between me and Lacey I couldn't tell my own mother."

Roscoe hooted. "So, something did happen! No wonder we couldn't reach you to go clubbing."

Spud replied firmly. "We were studying."

Gordon raised a brow. "For four days straight?"

Spud's steady gaze faltered. "There was…the whale watching…"

"And?" Roscoe lilted.

"Dinner."

"And 'study breaks?'" Gordon suggested.

Now Spud reddened. It wasn't that he'd never been kissed by a girl, but he'd never been *kissed* by a girl. He didn't want to share that with these morons. "We… looked at her scrapbooks."

For a moment, they all just blinked. Then Gordon sighed. "Go buy a ring, Spud."

"Oh, gawd." Roscoe snickered confidentially to the audience of his vidblog. "You should have seen the look on that boy's face. 'Get a ring!' The only tragedy is that I didn't think of it first."

He paused, letting his smile grow conniving. "You realize, of course, just how much potential this has? Love is a strong motivator, true enough, but it's a distractor, too. So... How to turn this to an advantage for Roscoe? Oh, darlings, there are so many delicious possibilities! Tell me your favorites in the comment section and if I use it, I'll send you an 'I'd Re-Kill With Roscoe!' T-shirt!"

LaCenta glared at her computer as she recorded her blog.

"Can you believe that Roscoe? He better leave poor Spud alone, or he's gonna find himself distracted by a face full of Raid. That poor boy's been nothing but a sweetheart since auditions, and if he's found the love of his life here, then good for him!"

"Bet he's out pricing diamonds right now," Gordon chortled. "Boy's so whipped!"

Nasir smiled, his eyes a little starry. "Actually, it reminded me of when Badria and I courted. We are no longer being together, but when we were young... Ah! Of course, we were not to having scrapbooks reading..."

Spud gulped as he forced his eyes to meet the lens of the laptop camera. "Uh, m-m-Mom? It was just scrapbooks. Really."

Chapter 12

Neeta turned the corner to her block. It'd been a good day, a normal day. With what Roscoe was calling the "Love Spudisode" airing this week, she'd had time to catch up on some of her regulars. Spraying for ants and checking cracks for roaches or termites wasn't glamorous work, but she liked that a visit from her meant people didn't feel the need to double-check the sugar bowl or cringe when turning on the kitchen light at night.

"Sure, they're just vermin," her mom used to say, "but that's not the point. We make people feel secure in their own homes."

Some days, she missed Mom so much.

Neeta reached up to press the button that would open the chain-link gate into her driveway but paused when her eyes caught a movement on her porch. Someone was messing with her front door!

She parked on the street, then studied the situation. The guy didn't look like the average street thug. He had a light blue polo shirt over Bermuda shorts. That wasn't any gang colors from around her neighborhood. Obsessed *Zombie Death Extreme* fanboy looking for a souvenir? Why couldn't he just take the garden gnome? She hated that thing.

She reached into the back of the van. A super-shot pistol full of roach kill in one hand and a mallet ax in the other, she eased out of her van and made her way to her house. When she got to the edge of her yard, she crouched behind the hedges. She felt incredibly stupid, even as her heart threatened to pound its way out of her chest. Easy, she told herself. You take on the vicious undead; you can handle one live fanboy. Who breaks into a house at three in the afternoon, anyway?

She eased open her gate, wincing at the creak. He didn't even twitch.

Captain Oblivious, apparently, she decided, as she ran the length of her sidewalk.

"Hey!" she yelled as soon as she was within macing distance. If he pulled a gun on her, she'd give him a faceful.

Instead the guy turned, screamed, and slammed himself against the door, hands in the air. "Easy, lady!"

Lady? "Look, if you want something, take the gnome." The words were out of her mouth before she realized it.

"What? No, no! I'm Franklin—with Dorwin Windows and Doors. See?" He pulled at the part of his shirt that had his name stitched above the Dorwin logo. "Your boyfriend sent me."

"Brian? Why?" She lowered the ax she still held aloft, and he sagged with relief.

"Yeah, Brian St. James. He's got it for you bad, Miss. Gloria, our receptionist, said he didn't stop talking about you the whole time he was on the phone."

"Why did he send you to my door?" she demanded.

"He said it doesn't open smoothly, and it was really annoying you, so I'm here to price replacements. Uh, I brought our catalog if you wanted to browse, or you can come into the store."

Annoying her? When did she say she was annoyed? "Um, Frank? Could you hold on for just a few minutes?"

He held up his hands, smiling. "Hey, you're the lady with the ax."

"Right. Sorry about that. I..." She didn't know what to say. Did she actually offer him her garden gnome? She set the mallet ax on the porch railing and stepped out into the yard, pulling out her phone and dialing Brian's number at work. She strolled along the hedge, keeping her back to the porch.

He answered on the first ring. "Neeta, honey! What a surprise. Listen, I'm in the middle of a song."

"I'll be fast. Did you send some door guy to my house?"

"They're there? Great. I wanted it to be a surprise, but that's OK."

It is? No, no it wasn't. "Why would you—?"

"Oh, honey. I saw how annoyed you were at that thing."

"No, I wasn't, I—"

"You don't need to put that tough girl act on for me. Listen, I advertise for these guys all the time. They'll give me a nice deal. That's how it works. Now you just pick whatever you want."

"But I don't want—"

"Let me do something nice for you. Anything you want, okay? Oh, oh! Song's wrapping up. I'll call you later. Anything goes, okay?"

"Brian!"

"We'll talk later. Sorry I can't watch Spud's episode with you. 'K, bye!"

The line went dead.

She forced herself to press the CALL END button gently and calmly return her phone to her pocket. *Whatever I want? How about what I don't want?* She was glad Franklin could not see her face. She took a cleansing breath, careful not to let it out too loudly, and headed back to the porch in what she hoped was a non-threatening manner.

Franklin was examining the top edge of the door but turned when he heard her on the steps. "Let me guess—anything you want, right?"

She shrugged.

"Yeah, Gloria said he made that very clear. Should have heard her sighing about it afterwards. You're a lucky lady."

She supposed she was. Why didn't she feel that way? She leaned against the railing. "Thing is, Franklin, I like my door."

Franklin glanced back at it, then turned a grin to her. "You know, me, too. Solid wood, heavy decorative glass... The peephole on the side is nice—was that added later? Thought so. It looked like custom work. It could use a paint job, maybe a little planing to make it close better?"

That was a compromise she could agree to. "Can you do that? You don't just sell new doors and stuff?"

He shrugged. "Brian St. James says, 'Whatever she wants.' I give you whatever you want. My boss can figure out how to charge him. So, if you could unlock it and show me what it's doing?"

At eight that night, Neeta signed the invoice and closed her "new" door. It was an inviting green and slid shut with a minimum of effort. She had to admit Franklin from Dorwin Doors and Windows had done a great job.

Nonetheless, she turned off her phones and went to bed after watching the Spudisode, where she tossed and turned until she surprised herself by bursting into tears.

BrainDeadHead:
Subject: Whoa! Spud the Stud!
I am so nuked! Did you see Spud in "Unlikely Knight?" And Lacey running up to those zombies and teasing them. That was like some kind of action movie! It wasn't faked, was it?

I know LaCenta caught that murderer and all, but Spud was hero-tesimal, running in front of his fallen damsel and going to face the zombie horde all on his own. I don't think I could have done it.
StudleyWithSwords:
Brain, let me assure you personally. No script. No directors. No retakes. What you saw was pure StudleySpudly. I hate him for it, I really do!
Rigormortis:
Including that deer-in-the-headlights look when Lacey kissed him? You'd think the man had never had a girlfriend in his life. Sweet, though.
StudleyWithSwords:
Totally unscripted…though I'm sure there have been a lot of, shall we say, *private encores* since then. And I

know what you're going to ask next and no, the scrapbook dialogue was not scripted or rehearsed. Last practice, I just said, "scrapbook" and the man turned red.

By the by, fanpeoples. Thanks to all who posted their Mess With Spud ideas on my blog. I especially liked leaving photos of Lacey and Spud around. If only I knew where that last challenge would be! But convincing the director to use Lacey as a damsel in distress? As if! She was a fully qualified exterminator when this show was just a twinkle in the producer's eye!

Tro111:
Give it a rest, Roscoe. You know as well as I that you've got an in with the director. You've been his favorite since Mani-Pedi. We all know you were doing more than his nails.

StudleyWithSwords:
Oh, my gawd! I'm being trolled—by none other than Troy LLame! Boyfriend, are you still upset about Mani-Pedi? Is it my fault I give better foot massages? And your nail art? I mean, sure, flowers are classic, but did you really expect to win with a 5-petal daisy?

Bitterness is sooooo unbecoming.

Tro111:
I don't know what you're talking about. But as far as "massages," I don't think that's the only thing you gave.

And as long as were on the subject, RE: "Studly Spud," are you people that stupid? The one thing this show's lacked is sex. Neeta's an ice queen. Don't believe me; check out the K-RTH morning show. It's obvious Brian ain't getting any. Nasir's too Muslim; LaCenta's too {word deleted by server}. Not even being a war vet is going to make up for Gordon's personality. For that matter, StudleyWithSwords, despite your little "towel blog," you aren't seeing much live action. Losing it, are we?

Let's face it: the only hope the show had was Katie and Spud, and then Katie left like the coward she was. Or maybe they didn't offer her enough to do country boy on camera. Ratings were falling. Dave had to do something. Probably paid Lacey for that kiss. She looked like she'd be a happy {word deleted by server.}

Katieforthewin:
Where's the administrator? Troll, get off this list. You are not welcome!

StudleyWithSwords:
Easy, Katiefor. It's just the envy talking. BTW, did you see Katie's new commercial? Oh, gawd, she's just gorgeous when she isn't screaming or crying! Her new website launched, BTW. Check it out.

BrainDeadHead:
"Getting some?" Look who's talking! Troll, the only action you get is the action you give yourself when you're insulting regular people. Make you feel more like a man?

Katieforthewin:
Makes you less of a person!

Wait a minute? Were you the guy on Mani-Pedi who threw the cuticle softener in that girl's face? You have some nerve coming onto this site!

StudleyWithSwords:
I don't think he's coming on to anything!

BrainDeadHead:
ROFL!

Tro111:
You {word deleted by server}. What would you now? Wasting your worthless lives watching a reality TV show instead of going out and living? Probably none of you have had a {word deleted by server} since Junior Year of college when everyone was too drunk to be discriminatory.

All I'm trying to do is expose how fake and stupid these shows are. Run by ratings and catering to the intellectually lowest common denominator—you.

Grow up, people!

MANIC_MIND:

Well, considering that I'm working on my PhD in chaos theory and climatology, I take umbrage to your statement. Sometimes, people want to have fun. That's what entertainment is, right, fun?

Meanwhile, am I correct in assuming you are a manicurist who was on reality TV? And Junior year—specifically? Sounds like you're speaking from personal experience.

ZDEAdministrator:

Tro111 has been removed from this server.

BrainDeadHead:

Thanks, ZDEA. Thanks, Studly.

StudleyWithSwords:

De nada, Brain! Told you I could get him off. You just have to know how to exploit the weakness. Now, remember, when it comes to audience vote, Roscoe is Re-Kill Man!

ZDEAdministrator:

This thread is being closed and deleted. Please feel free to resume discussing "An Unlikely Knight" here.

Chapter 13

The heady scent of coffee washed over Neeta as she stood at the counter of the studio's Starbucks, and she closed her eyes, breathing it in, hoping to take in some energy by osmosis until the man in front of her was done ordering.

"Ah, the sweet scent of sugar and caffeine!" Ted's voice sounded behind her. "You get your order yet, or are you just sniffing?"

"Venti triple mocha latte," she told the girl behind the counter.

He eyed the package of chocolate-covered espresso beans in her hand. "Are we going to have to lock up the chainsaws today?"

"I can handle it."

"For Dave's sake, I hope so. Here, it's on me." He started to hand the cashier his card.

Neeta slapped his hand down. "No! I can pay for my own *goram* coffee! Why do people keep wanting to do things for me?"

A pocket of silence followed her outburst. Even the gurgle of the espresso machine stilled.

She threw her head back and stared at the ceiling to avoid the looks everyone was giving her. "I'm sorry. I didn't sleep well last night."

"Smacking down the undead alone?"

"No," she moaned, feeling stupid all of a sudden. "Brian had my front door fixed."

"Oooh."

"'Ooooh'?" she mimicked his understanding-but-not-really-understanding tone. "What does that mean?"

The anger in her voice made the couple behind them step back, but Ted just shrugged, unaffected. "Nothing. Just kind of liked how you had to give it a little shove to close it. Felt more, I don't know…"

"Secure." Even as she said it, she felt her eyes and nose sting. She turned her attention to pouring out a handful of espresso beans. She must be tired, ready to cry again over a stupid door.

Ted didn't seem to notice. "Yeah. Something like that. So, okay, then: You treat me. I'll have what's she's having," he told the cashier. "I think I'll need it to keep up with her today."

Neeta almost choked on her espresso beans laughing.

The studio canteen was across the parking lot from the *Zombie Death Extreme* offices. Lattes in hand, they headed to their meeting together. As they passed a line of cars in a row that was marked with a decapitated zombie head, Ted stopped.

"Whoa! Idea! Come on." He led her to a Kia Forte whose copper paint job didn't quite manage to hide the rust. The surfboard strapped to the top gleamed in the sunlight, as if trying to make up for the state of its ride. He handed her his latte, dug in his pocket for his fob and unlocked the passenger side door. Then he bent into the passenger side, searching for something on the floor, tossing wrappers and beach gear into the back.

Neeta leaned against the Nissan Blok parked next to it and admired the view, a bemused grin on her face. "What are you looking for?" she asked.

"You'll see. It's awesome! Ah! Here we go." He pulled out a ball hook and a u-shaped piece of metal and handed the two to her. "Don't say I never gave you anything!"

She set the lattes on top of the Blok and examined the gift. He kicked his door shut, then pointed the fob at it. It chirped in cheery obliviousness to its abuse.

"Isn't this one of those door-stop thingies like you find in hotel rooms?" Neeta asked.

He grabbed the lattes and started walking. "Yeah. It's called a door limiter. I looked it up and everything. Cool, huh?"

"Why do you have one of these in your car?"

"Roscoe took us partying last week."

She waited, but he just sipped his latte as if that explained everything.

"And, what? They were handing these out as party favors?"

Ted chortled, snorting out coffee. "Good one. No, see. Seventh Day Inventists—you know them?"

"The heavy metal band that uses power tools in their music?"

"The very ones! So, they were having this after-gig thing in their hotel and they wanted to try out a work in progress on us, and you know, Manny had the circular saw and he was so wasted... Well, the door was ruined anyway, so when Bob finished with his power drill solo, I just helped myself."

"You stole a door lock."

"Limiter. What a hoot, huh? I mean, everyone was grabbing souvenirs. Had to act fast, or I'd have gotten a splinter or something lame. Roscoe said this happens every time they hold a hotel party. Their manager pays for the damage ahead of time."

She glanced from him to the door lock—door limiter, she told herself. Then she grabbed her latte from him and took a large swallow. Caffeine. She needed caffeine to keep up with this conversation. When she thought she felt a kick, she started again.

"And why are you giving this to me?"

They walked up the two steps to the building, and Ted pulled open the door. A blast of air conditioning caressed his hair as he went in, Neeta following.

"I'm not the knick-knack type."

"So?"

"Well, I sobered up, and I realized I can't use this thing. I'm in an apartment where I can't even put a nail in the wall. I should have gone for the safety procedures sign—I could have had them autograph it and stuck it up with poster tape. Live and learn."

"But why are you giving this to *me?*"

He shrugged. "You own a door."

Dave lurked around the corner and watched as Neeta and Ted entered the conference room. Neeta was shaking her head and snickering as she shoved something into the pocket of loose long vest that she wore over a tank top and shorts. She pushed open the door easily and sailed in, clearly in a good mood.

Dave nodded. Much better. Neeta had nearly clipped his car pulling into the parking lot and had driven on by, oblivious to his horn blast. When he saw her schlepping to the canteen, he'd called Sharon to do something about it. The last thing he'd needed was his star host in a funk on today of all days, when he was about to unveil his grand finale. Most stars would have a snit fit—Neeta would more likely express her objections with a chainsaw.

Sharon had sent Ted after her.

He again congratulated himself on his choice of personal assistant. Brilliant. Sharon was simply brilliant. Such a masterful judge of character—almost on par with him! A little flighty at times, what with her new rabbit craze, he thought as glanced behind him to see her swaying and lightly stroking the scene on her DoDroid, but otherwise...

I should do something nice for her, he thought as he went through his pre-meeting routine. Something relaxing before we go to New Orleans for *ZDE II*.

As he jogged slightly to get the blood flowing and shook out the tension in his arms, he ran over ideas. When was that Day of the Dead celebration in Mexico? Nice irony there. Could be fun.

Nah. Something different. Unrelated, but bigger. White water rafting? Scaling the half dome at Yosemite? Did she do mountain climbing? He could get her a guide. Nah, still too small.

Personal! He chided himself. *Got to make it personal. She likes bunnies....*

"Sharon, baby. There are rabbits in Australia, right?"

She looked up, caught by surprise for once. "Sir?"

He held out his hand. She slapped his drink into it. He guzzled it down, thinking, Safari in the Outback. Lots of wildlife. Camping. Camping's relaxing right? I'll have to get Lida to make the arrangements. Right now, though, got to focus. The producer is there. Even more, Neeta is there!

He swallowed the last, belched loudly and handed her the bottle. She took it and slapped his DoDroid into his hands, his talking notes already called up. He had to sell this and sell it big.

"Let's do this."

He pushed open the conference doors and strode in, his hands raised in victory.

"People, it's finale time!"

All conversation stopped, all eyes turned to him. Energy and anticipation crackled in the room. He held his pose a moment longer, not looking at them, merely taking in the energy like a god accepting homage. He lived for this.

"We will give our viewers a thrill that will leave them glued to their seats. Yes, even if their own homes are invaded by zombies, they will not want to miss a single minute! For we are going...back to the warehouse!"

"Okay," Neeta said mildly.

"There will be more suspense, more harrowing twists as our intrepid apprentices face the scene of their greatest tragedy—the death of one of their own. This isn't just for our viewers, however. It's for our own people! A chance for vengeance, a chance to confront their fears..."

"Sounds good," she added.

"Now hear me out! This is just what the…" He cut off his spiel as his brain caught up with his ears. He turned to Neeta.

"Did you say, 'Okay'?"

Neeta shrugged. "I've been thinking about it for a while. Vengeance is dangerous; play it on the commercials, but not on my plebes; but they do need to come face to face with the situation again. I don't want them to have a similar environment in the future and choke where there's no safety net." Her voice hardened. "But we will have a safety net."

Dave blinked. He could not believe his luck. He scrolled down his notes, moving past argument and counter argument, nodding distractedly as she pulled out her own pad and read off the safety protocols she wanted in place this time.

Alberts, the producer, cleared his throat. "And what's all that going to cost?"

Neeta raised an eyebrow at Sharon, who rattled off some figures.

He scowled. "What if we use animatronics again?"

"No," both Neeta and Dave chorused. When they met each other's eyes, they saw they mirrored each other's bemused grins.

The producer shrugged. "Can we get this done in a week?"

Neeta said, "I've talked to ZERD. They have plenty of experimental AH foam ready. I went back through the warehouse last week and have marked the best areas for traps and safe zones."

"The Sam Richards' *Destroy-Rebuild* crew is available this week," Sharon added. "Sam's apparently out with an infected hand from a splinter he got at some party. Grabbing a souvenir, his assistant Allison said?"

Ted choked on his latte.

"Anyway, they said they'd do it and film it as a special if we let them tear some stuff down in the process."

Dave beamed at his assistant. Genius. Definitely an Outback safari. He wondered if he could schedule some rock climbing and white-water rafting, too?

Again, he spread his hands, offering them his blessings. "Well, then, people, what are we waiting for? Let's make some magic!"

After six hours of pouring over three-dimensional schematics of the warehouse, psychological and character assessments of the plebes, and reports from ZERD on their latest "crop" of zombies, they had designed a great episode of "capture the flag," zombie-style. They decided to split the plebes into teams of two, Dave nearly having a paroxysm of joy when Wang suggested they invite Lacey in to team with Spud.

Neeta, however, nearly jumped out of her chair. "Are you people out of your mind? What part of 'keeping everyone alive' wasn't clear? She's injured—and you want to set her against a horde of zombies."

Wang shrugged. "Thanks to nanite knitting, broken bones take about two weeks to heal. I know because I busted my hand last year and was back on the job by then."

Neeta leaned over and spoke with deceptive calm. "Wang, what do you do for a living?"

"Uh, screenwriter?"

"Screenwriter. And, as a screenwriter, how much heavy lifting do you do with that wrist?"

"Er…"

"And if I'd given you a 15-pound chain saw to swing about for half an hour, how would that newly-healed wrist of yours have held out? Enough that you'd be able to take on the zombie that waited thirty-two minutes before attacking?"

He looked at the table.

She turned to Wang's partner. "Gary, how fast have we seen zombies run?"

Gary almost jumped when she first called on him, but relaxed. He knew this one! "They've been recorded as fast as 15 miles an hour. And, they don't tire."

She nodded, then leaned back to take in the whole group. "And you want to send in a recently injured, still lame girl to battle them. Do you want Spud to lose? Because most likely, you'll lose your knight and your damsel—permanently."

Dave threw his hands in the air. "Fine, then! Who do we put in?"

"Ted."

"What?"

"Huh?" Ted looked up from where he'd been dabbing his spat-out latte with a napkin.

"Ted?" Alberts gasped. "The cameraman? You don't want to send an experienced exterminator in, but you'll send *Ted?*"

Neeta nodded. "He's been training with me privately for the past few weeks and with the crew the whole series. In the warehouse and the 9-1-1 call, he showed good instincts and courage."

Alberts opened his mouth to protest, but Dave shrieked.

"I'm seeing it, really! The unlikely candidate! The wild card! We have outtake footage—we'll make some flashbacks... Chills! I'm getting chills! Are you getting chills?"

The rest of the crew responded with silence until Ted purred, "Oh, yeah!"

"Beautiful!" Dave gushed. "Neeta, baby, we're making music, sweet music! I can't say enough wonderful words! Oh, crap!" His expression turned from ecstasy to panic. "We're going to be late! Sharon, get Neeta to wardrobe and find her something less casual. And call the car!"

"Why?" Neeta asked.

He grinned. "Small surprise. You'll love it. Sharon will take care of you. Hurry now; we're going to be late. Too much synergy in this room, totally threw off my time sense! Sharon, baby—Australian outback wildlife: summary in my pad tomorrow!"

"Where are we going?" Neeta demanded, but Dave was calling out orders in quick succession to the rest of the staff.

Sharon put a hand on her shoulder, and she followed her out.

"Sharon," Neeta protested as they headed down the busy hall to wardrobe. Sharon was calling up nature videos of Australia on her DoDroid, navigating the turns and opening doors automatically.

Neeta said. "I don't like surprises. Surprises usually mean I have to kill something."

Sharon shuddered, but it seemed to be at something on her screen.

"Sharon!"

She typed some commands into her pad and said without looking up. "*The Tonight Show* had a guest cancel. Miley Cyrus's hair nanites are still malfunctioning—can't decide if she's blonde or brunette. Completely confuses her performance. I hate snakes!" She moaned.

"So?"

"First zombies, now snakes. I don't sleep at night. Did you know I don't sleep at night?" She muttered more than spoke to Neeta. Her hands never stopped calling up video after video of extreme animals: snakes and crocodiles, a kangaroo lashing out with its legs at a tourist, a spider the size of her hand.

Neeta set her palm over the image of a bushwhacker about to strike the camera. "Sharon?" she asked.

Sharon blinked. "Um, sorry. Right. *The Tonight Show with Rus Mobi* needs a guest. You and Dave are on. You get ten minutes to talk finale and zombie extermination. You want something practical and tough but sexy—do you like leather pants? No? Well, Colleen will set you up. I'll give you some talking notes as you change, but don't tell Dave. He likes to surprise people."

They entered the wardrobe room and Colleen met Neeta with a hug and dragged her to a rack full of "tough, practical but sexy" clothes, which mostly ran to leather and microweave plastidenim. Sharon trailed behind.

"Bunnies. Something with bunnies," she muttered. "Spiders, poisonous lizards…I need a new job."

Backstage, Dave nudged Neeta as they waited for Rus to finish his monologue about the Chitter movement to get Conan to host the show again.

"Surprised?" he asked, grinning like a schoolboy.

"Very." Neeta grinned back, but she thought it probably looked more sickly than surprised.

Onstage, Rus said, "All I'm saying is that being able to tell a joke in two hundred and eighty characters or less might not be the best of qualifications. #Idoitbetter" The audience laughed.

She did not want to be there, especially wearing tight plastidenim pants. At least she'd talked Sharon into letting her get a company polo shirt from the car. The tight-sleeved lace blouse and leatherish vest Colleen had suggested might have been good, if she were Miley Technicolor Cyrus, but if she was going to talk zombie extermination, she wanted to look professional.

Rus wrapped up his monologue and reaped in the applause. "Listen, we have a great surprise for you tonight. I know you were expecting to see Senator Cyrus, but she had an unforeseen emergency."

He paused for the staged moans of disappointment.

"Yes, it was a hair-raising ordeal."

Rimshot and laughter.

"Anyway, we have a treat for you tonight. You've been watching *Zombie Death Extreme*, right? Right? All right! That's what I'm talking about! Well, you know the season is about to end, and the finale promises to be the best ever. And here to talk about it is Reality TV Czar David Lor, and the Queen of the Zombie Exterminators herself, Neeta Lyffe!"

The band struck up the theme song to *Zombie Death Extreme*, and as directed, Dave and Neeta started across the stage to the seats. Dave trotted across in a bouncy half-trot, waving, blowing kisses and generally playing the crowd, while the crowd chanted "Lor! Lor!" Neeta followed, hand up in a shy wave, wondering if her face was glowing red through what felt like a layer of paint the make-up crew had plastered on her face.

Suddenly, Dave rushed back to her, grabbed her arm and held it up, like a victorious prize fighter. The crowd roared its approval.

Neeta gritted her teeth into a smile.

After what seemed an eternity of standing center stage, feeling like Dave's prize show dog, he lowered her hand, and still holding it, led her to their host. Rus leaned over the desk to shake their hands. Dave gave her the seat closest to Rus, then took the one next to her.

"Dave, Neeta, thanks for being here. Dave, congratulations on another great show."

He paused for the applause.

"Neeta, I love what you do and the flair with which you do it. You can protect my house anytime. But the backyard…"

He paused while people laughed at the lighthearted reference to her lawsuit.

Neeta tried to keep the snarl out of her voice. "Well, Rus, are you planning on inviting any zombies to a barbe-que?"

"Uh, no. I'd rather serve the food than be the meal."

Remembering Sharon's briefing, Neeta waited for the swell of laughter to start dying then spoke over it. "Then you should be fine. But the fact of the matter is, nearly half the zombie attacks in America are what we call 'targeted attacks.' That means someone has done something to draw them out—like serving pickled beets outside near a graveyard."

"So, you're saying these can be prevented."

She grimaced but didn't pause in her answer. Sharon had warned her: *Talk about the show and you can get your points across. Dave likes to sit quietly like he's just there to support the stars. But get off the show or hesitate, and he'll take over.*

"Well, in the case of the zombie LaCenta took down, who was a murder victim come back for revenge, sure. However, in general, the answer is Yes and No. We still don't know what causes the dead to rise, so there's no preventing that except with spinal severing after death. However, yes, there are ways to prevent zombies from making a beeline to you pool party."

"Is it true one yelled, 'Cannonball!' as it jumped into Twiddle's pool?"

Neeta smiled, sweetly feral. "I wouldn't know. I was trying to extract my chainsaw from some vermin's prosthetic arm. Fortunately, it didn't swim well."

Dave shifted position—slightly, but enough to draw Rus's attention—and Neeta knew she'd spoiled her chance.

Rus said to Dave, "So, here we are—a week away from the final episode of *Zombie Death Extreme*. What can you tell us?"

"Three words: location, location, location," Dave teased.

Rus leaned forward. "You got to give us more than that!"

Dave tossed his hands in mock helplessness. "We just left a major strategy session. Details are still in the works."

"Give us the broad sweep. Anything. Come on. We're dying to know—aren't we?" Rus directed the last toward the studio audience, who obliged with applause and hoots.

"Well…" Dave hedged, tossing a brief glance at Neeta, is if seeking permission they both know he neither needed nor wanted. "I can say this: our dear, departed Bergie will at last be avenged."

This time, the audience needed no prompting to explode into thunderous applause. As Dave lapped it up, the whole time with a humble, self-depreciating expression, Neeta tried to keep her own face neutral.

Inside, she wondered yet again what had possessed her to join this circus.

Dave monopolized the rest of their ten minutes, so that Neeta only managed to get one more comment in. Even that came out as a lame reassurance that her plebes were smart enough now that they wouldn't get themselves killed for points. She thought she'd heard actual expressions of disappointment in the audience. Fortunately, Rus then introduced the next guest, an up-and-coming singer/actress Kirstie Stone. Thrilled to share her time with a couple of reality show people instead of her competition, she kept up a sparkling and vibrant dialogue, flirting with Dave and preening for Rus and the camera. Neeta sat back and tried to look interested until the theme song played, they made their last waves, and she was released.

She drove home with her eyes intent on the alleys and corners, wishing for something she could re-kill.

Brian called her just as she was walking to her porch.

"Honey! You didn't tell me you were going to be on *The Tonight Show!*"

"I didn't know until Sharon dragged me into wardrobe." She rested the phone against her shoulder as she reached into her pocket for the key.

"You could have called me from the green room. Cassie called me, screaming, 'Turn on *The Tonight Show*! Turn on *The Tonight Show*!' You looked great, by the way."

Neeta smiled as the lock turned and the door slid open. "Thanks."

"You didn't really look like you were having fun, though."

Neeta paused, her hand on the doorknob, and waited, letting silence be her answer.

"I just don't get it. You're a celebrity now, Neeta. People know you and admire you. You should be lapping it up. Why won't you let yourself have some fun?"

"It's not my idea of fun," she said.

"What is your idea of fun, Neeta?"

Her mind flashed to yesterday's lesson with Ted and how hard they laughed as he tried to roast a marshmallow from thirty paces.

"Neeta?"

Sitting in the Cuthbert's living room, sipping a Corona and swapping stories about 'Oscar,' the zombie fisherman who always seemed to slip their grasp, while Lacey and Spud held hands on the couch.

"Neeee-ta?"

Oh, Mom, am I really so warped that these are my ideas of fun?

"Neeta!"

"I have fun with you," she offered.

His voice softened. "All right, then. Cowboy's coming back day after tomorrow, so I'm off the hook for the evening shift. Want to catch a movie? *Double Indemnity* starring Cole and Dylan Sprouse is out."

"The Disney remake? Are we talking about a special showing or just an ordinary old theater?"

Brian laughed. "You pick the theater. No stars. Just you, me, and overpriced popcorn."

"Now we're talking fun!"

They made their plans and he hung up to get back to work. She hummed to herself as she closed and locked the door. She wandered into the bedroom, reaching into her pockets to empty the contents into the tray. She pulled out the door limiter.

I do have a door, she thought, and went into her utility room after screws and a drill.

Chapter 14

"Lyffe Undeath Exterminations, Neeta speaking."

"Neeta, this is Brian St. James with K-RTH 101."

"Yeah. I think I know who you are."

"Well, I'm calling on official business. Yesterday on *The Tonight Show*, you and director Dave Lor announced that you're going back to the warehouse where Bergie was killed, but we heard precious little from you about it. All due respect to Dave, we want to know your side of this story!"

"Yeah, Neeta! Helloness! You told everyone that 'Warehouse Eight' was going to be the toughest challenge they faced on the show. Are you taking that back, now?"

"..."

"Neeta, we're not looking for anything sensational. Just tell us your side—the side you didn't get to tell last night."

"(Sigh.) Look, five weeks ago, we made a mistake. They weren't ready, and the conditions were too much for their level of experience. They knew but they didn't *understand* how to use their supplies. And, to be quite frank, some, like Bergie, were still treating it like a show and not an extermination.

"Now, they know better. They understand better. They'll be better equipped. They'll perform better—as exterminators, not as reality show contestants. Frankly, it wouldn't grieve me one bit if this turned out to be the most routine, boring episode in the series."

"Wowsers! So, no one's going to die?"

"Can you guarantee a fireman won't die on the job? Or a policeman? I've said it before and I'll say it again, Cassie. Zombie extermination is dangerous. There are no guarantees. But they've come a long way. I'd have any of my plebes by my side on an extermination."

"Neeta, you are so hard core!"

"Uh, listen, are there any more questions? I have another call coming in, and I'm hoping it's a nice, quiet job I can do before going to the studio—ants or rats or something. Oh, and Brian St. James with K-RTH 101?"

"Here, Neeta."

"See you at the Metroplex. You owe me an extra-large Raisinets for this."

Neeta pulled up to the warehouse, humming along with the radio. The call had been from new owners of a home who had found a nest of ants along the garage. Not owning a television, they'd simply picked her because they liked her website. They saw the link to *Zombie Death Extreme* but hadn't followed it. They were interested in ants, not zombies. She'd been so happy, she'd done the job for free and signed them up for her regular inspection program. In all, a good morning's work.

Now, to use the afternoon to keep her plebes safe.

She found the assessment crew from Destroy-Rebuild hanging out at the warehouse. One crewman was walking around the building, pointing an instrument that looked like a cross between a radar gun and a tricorder at the walls and doors. The rest had crowded around a folding table, consulting blueprints and a holographic design of the interior of the building.

A broad, bearded man in a flannel shirt with the sleeves chopped off broke from the group and went to meet her. He started to hold out a bandage-wrapped hand, caught himself and laughed self-depreciatingly.

"Sam Richards, I presume?" Neeta asked.

"In the flesh! And the, er, gauze. It's supposed to come off Monday. Don't worry; we'll have the place knocked out and redone to your specifications in time for the show. Dave already gave us some general specs."

Had he? "Well, I hope you understand that what Dave wants and what I get may be two different things. Just because I have faith in my plebes to meet this challenge doesn't mean we're not going to put in some safeties just in case."

"Works for me. Just tell us what you want us to do— and what we can smash in the process."

Neeta heard a familiar roar and turned to see a Kawasaki weave between two cars as it entered the parking lot. The UV shielding hid the rider from view, but there was no mistaking the crossed swords and shield on the tank. "Perfect! Here's our technical advisor now."

The motorcycle pulled up easily beside the two, giving them a glimpse of the ZERD parking sticker before presenting its profile. The UV protection faded as the engine died, revealing a slim young woman in riding leathers and plain T-shirt. She pulled off her helmet, letting her blond hair fall in easy, springy curls around her face.

"Sorry I'm late," she said as she twisted to pack the helmet into a side saddle. "You wouldn't believe the traffic once I hit LA. I got stuck behind a couple of GM Entitlements for half an hour. Stupid things take up so much of the road, no way I was going to try to squeeze between them. Makes me wish for when Hummers were the road hogs."

She paused to pull off the leathers, revealing Capri's with a swimming fish pattern, and tossed them in with the helmet, then turned to offer her hand to Sam. "Elouise Shieldmaiden, ZERD civil engineering, at your service."

They walked over to the table, and Neeta again explained the basics of the challenge: eight zombies would be set loose in various parts of the warehouse. Fifteen minutes later, the plebes would go in, in teams of two. Their objective would be to reach and capture one of the flags placed in the warehouse and escape without needing to trip any of the safeties set up in the area. They earned points for time and for number of zombies encountered and re-killed.

"What I want," Neeta concluded, "is to minimize the hidey-holes and ambush points that a zombie might use to its advantage and set up safeties—they can be as simple as buckets of Porcelain Sparkle or as fancy as safety-glass barriers. You can decide what's appropriate—"

"—and showy enough to suit Dave," Sam added. "Can we have a little fun with them?"

Elouise giggled, "What, like some *Zombieland*-style stuff?"

Neeta shrugged. "As long as they work."

"Oh, let's do the falling piano! I love the falling piano!"

They spent the next couple of hours walking through the building, making plans. They even found the perfect spot for a falling piano, though Elouise suggested filling it with a thin-skinned balloon of anti-zombie repellent to be sure the job was done right. Soon, they had marked the interior with directions and cryptic signs that signaled the destruction and rebuilding of Warehouse Eight into a playing field for the world's most dangerous game of capture-the-flag. Finally, they agreed on a time to meet again early the next morning to re-enact the whole planning session for the cameras.

Heeding Elouise's warning about the traffic, Neeta left a little earlier than she'd planned and headed home to prepare for her date. Before she left, however, she had them burn her a copy of the plans they'd made. If Dave tried to make any changes for "dramatic effect," she was going to enlist Lawyer Eugene in giving him more drama than he could handle.

VoiceofReson:
Subject: Back to Warehouse Eight?
Clip from *The Tonight Show with Rus Mobi.* So, one guy gets killed there, and they want to go back for another episode? Maybe they've already slated there next victim. Got to bring the ratings up, after al.

I can't believe you people watch this stuff. It's like the roman Circuses all over again.

MANIC_MIND

Oh, look, moderator! The troll (or should I say, Tro-1-1-1) is back! Didn't getting kicked off once teach you anything?

Unlike you, I actually watch the show and read the blogs. I've seen how careful Neeta's been in training her plebes. They aren't trying to get anyone killed, but like she said this morning on the radio—can you guarantee that a fireman won't get killed fighting a fire? I liked Bergie, I really did, but he was careless and more interested in showing off. Look at his performance in episode three. And here, where Neeta took him aside and called him on it.

Neeta's a pro. She's trying to train these people, not get them killed. She's not in this for ratings.

VoiceofReson

I don't know what you're talking about—Trolll, who? I just happened across this forum and thought I could talk some sense into you people. Obviously, I was wrong.

If Neeta isn't interested in being a celebrity, why was she on The Tonight Show—and in tight flashy pants? Why's she doing this show at all?

Rigormortis:

I'm with Voice. I don't like the idea of them going back to the warehouse. I'm scared to death. Maybe they won't use real zombies—maybe they'll use animatronics like before?

BrainDeadHead

This is reality TV, not simulation, guys. After next week, they'll be going up against the real thing on a regular basis. I don't think Neeta's going to coddle them. Hey, StudleyWithSwords—got any scoop for us?

And Voice, funny how you don't know who we're talking about, but you spelled his name correctly.
MANIC_MIND
Roman circuses? You want sensationalism, what about the news? Remember the Phoenix riots? 48 hours of seeing the same fights, the same violence. Analysts talking about the violence. Interviews of the victims showing off their wounds. Remember the #1 YouTube video of that week, the grenade that went off in the guy's hand? Made all the major news shows. Bet you were glued to the set.

And you think this show is Roman Circus? Get off this forum until you have a clue.
VoiceofReson
That was news. There's a difference, even if you can't fit your puny mind around it.
MANIC_MIND
News. Yes, I feel so much better informed after watching the same footage of people tearing each other apart and destroying property for two days straight while the commentators recite the same lines. "It's just tragic...let's see that clip again."

Did you know Berkley did a study that found that people who watched television news were five times more likely to need counseling for disorders ranging from depression to post-traumatic stress disorder?
Rigormortis:
So, they're real? OMG, that's so horrible! I don't know how I'll stand it!
VoiceofReson
Yet you're going to watch, aren't you?
Rigormortis:
Of course, aren't you?

Kissing Brian on her doorstep was a lot of fun, too, Neeta decided.

He pulled away enough to rub noses with her. "So, are we going to go in and watch the movie?"

After 20 minutes of *Double Indemnity*, they'd left the theater. Neeta found herself annoyed at the environmental subtext—Dietrichson owned one of the few coal-burning plants still in existence. Brian couldn't get past the comedic moments of mistaken identity between Dietrichson (played by Cole Sprouse) and his wife's new lover, Walter Neff (played by Dylan). By mutual agreement, they decided to take their popcorn and Raisinets and head to her house and watch the 1940s original on her media center. But the heat of the day was finally breaking, and the breeze across the porch had felt so good.

"You know," Brian teased, "I don't think you like people in your house."

Neeta leaned her head on his shoulder and thought about the people who had crossed her threshold the past few months. Dave, Eugene, that lawyer from Bottum's Up diet drinks...

Ted, Brian...

"Depends on the person," she answered, then added before he could take offense, "but in this case, I just miss sitting on my porch swing. Why do you think I was waiting for you out here? I used to sit here all the time with a book."

"Let me guess: equipment manuals?"

She smacked his shoulder.

He laughed. "Don't tell me you're the trashy romance type?"

"Military sci-fi, if you must know. Honor Harrington is my favorite series. That and the Gem Flight series—

you know, dragons and mystic stones? Fun, escapist stuff. What about you? Celebrity biographies and tell-alls, right?"

He rolled his eyes. "Guess I deserved that, and I'd be offended if it weren't true. But it's not just celebrities. People interest me. That's why I'm in this biz. And I like noir, too, which brings us back to the movie."

"Let's go then." She pushed herself off the swing.

Brian followed. "So, when are they coming to take care of your door?"

She tilted her head. "What do you mean? They did. Hasn't looked this nice since I was a kid."

He frowned, his eyes brooding. "You could have gotten a new one. I told them to give you whatever you wanted."

"They did. I wanted a new paint job. They guy even planed it down, see?" She opened the door, but although it slid open for an inch, it then stopped abruptly.

She laughed. "Oops! I forgot I put the limiter on and went out the back. Come on."

She shut the door and took his hand, but he didn't budge, still staring at the door as if it offended him.

"So, I offer to replace your door, let you have the fanciest one you could ever want even, and all you asked for is some paint and a door stop?"

"It's called a door limiter, and actually Ted gave that to me. It's got kind of a funny story—"

"Ted? You asked Ted to fix your door?"

"What? No! See he got the door limiter at this wild party—Seventh Day Inventists, surely you know about them—and I own a door and he doesn't so—"

He pulled his hand away from her and gestured at the door. "I could have bought you a door limiter if you'd wanted one."

"I didn't! At least, it never occurred to me—"

"Yet there it is!"

Neeta looked at Brian's face, flushed from heat that had nothing to do with the day. Her jaw dropped. "Are you jealous?"

He opened his mouth, closed it, opened it again, then burst out, "Yes! Yes, I guess I am!"

"Of a door limiter?" she asked slowly.

Again, he opened and shut his mouth, looking something like a giant carp, but this time nothing came out.

Part of Neeta seethed, but mostly she just thought he looked silly and pitiful.

"Wow. Maybe next time, I'll ask Roscoe to get me a doorknob."

A pause, and then his anger turned from real to mocking. "Forget it, babe," he said. "If anyone provides the doorknobs in this relationship, it'll be me."

They burst out laughing then, and Brian held open his arms. Neeta stepped into his embrace.

"How about we go in the back way and watch that movie?" she suggested.

"Good idea."

They never got to the movie, however. While Neeta booted up her media center, Brian turned on the television, which was set to iNews.

"Neeta, you need to see this," he said.

She looked at the screen, and her face fell.

Afghanistan had been hit by an earthquake, the biggest in recorded history.

Dave smiled with satisfaction as he surveyed the lounge set for *Zombie Death Extreme*. It looked much like the lounge where they'd filmed the reading of Neeta's fan mail, but with the addition of a television set that was playing their sister network's news channel. Lisa LaStrade was telling viewers about how the world was rallying to aid Afghanistan in its time of need, but he knew that soon enough, they'd return to the carnage. In fact, he'd personally called to work out the timing. He'd had Sharon call the plebes and bring them in early. As they gathered, LaCenta, Spud, Gordon—even Roscoe!—converged on Nasir, touching him, supporting him, eyes always flicking back to the television screen. It was beautiful, really. Gave him chills.

They'd get to filming the finale later. Fate had brought him human drama to add to the show. How could he pass that up?

He directed Nasir to the seat directly in front of the screen.

"Just act natural," he directed. "Let the camera do the rest."

Nasir, baggy-eyed and frazzled from a long night of trying to contact his friends and relatives, let loose with a very natural stream of epithets, and the rest of the plebes gathered around him, adding their own barrage.

Dave smiled. "Yes! Exactly what I want to see. The raw emotion. The competitors becoming comrades in a real-life tragedy."

"I won't do this!" Nasir exclaimed. "I'm not going to sit here and let my grief entertain your audience!"

He turned to storm out, but Dave grabbed his shoulder. When Nasir spun to punch him, he grabbed his fist in a stunning show of agility and slapped a check into it.

"Think carefully," he advised.

LaCenta gasped. "You ass! You really think you can, can pay him off?"

Dave ignored her outburst. "Wouldn't you just be sitting around watching the television anyway? Think about all the damage those American dollars can repair."

Nasir looked from the check to Dave, and his eyes welled with tears.

"I hate what you have made me," he growled.

He stormed to the seat.

As he sat, the anchorwoman was using the last 45 seconds to sum up the two-minute speech made by the UN representative from Iran. "Once again, Iran says it's ready right now to offer medical and emergency aid to what Permanent Representative Riza Mohammad Danaii called 'their brothers to the East.' This is in response to the earthquake that devastated that country. We have reports that there are still smaller earthquakes—like aftershocks, but far worst—that continue to damage the country."

As she finished, the camera panned back to take in her anchorman partner. They gave each other sad, sympathetic looks.

"It's good to see someone taking decisive action," the anchorman said.

She nodded. "It's tragic, just tragic. Can we see that clip again?"

On the screen behind them played the jerky yet now-famous cell phone footage of a hospital collapsing.

Next she smacked her palm against the off button of the television, cutting off Lisa LaStrade's sympathetic noises as she commented again on the cell phone video.

As if she'd broken the spell, the others looked at her, then at the cameras, then back to her before ducking their heads in embarrassment.

She squatted in front of Nasir and took his hands.

"Do you want to go home? I can make that happen."

His body trembled in a shiver she felt more than saw. "Do I have a chance of winning?" he asked.

She wanted to tell him yes. She wanted to give him the money right then, but that was hardly fair to the others. "As much as any of you," she replied.

He straightened his back, threw back his chin. "Then I will see this to the end. I…cannot help there right now, and here, I stand a chance of doing more good in the long run."

LaCenta, sniffling like she used to tease Katie about, threw her arms around Nasir, while the others patted his shoulder.

"Beautiful!" Dave cried, breaking the moment. "Poetry! I could not have scripted it better! Pity about the cameras. Can we go for a second take?"

"No!" Everyone yelled in unison.

Chapter 15

Anchorwoman Lisa LaStrade shuffled the papers that she never read and smiled at the camera.

"In other news, thousands of people have crowded around the BUDDy theater, where the premier of *Unwashed Unholies 10: This Time, We Get It Right!* is expected to start at six o'clock. Preceding—and more important than the movie—is Woody Forrest's press conference, where he is expected to announce his intentions to run for President of the United States. We'll be reporting that live at five.

"But first, this just in: While US veto has prevented a UN resolution applauding Iran's rescue efforts, Iranian Permanent Representative to the UN Danaii has announced that his country's relief teams have crossed the border and are on their way to Kabul. Here now is Pete Hicklin with more."

On the screen behind her, Pete Hicklin, dressed in clean if rumpled kakis and a light jacket, stood on the shoulder of a four-lane highway known as

"Independence Road." Behind him, trucks, personnel carriers, tanks and soldiers swarmed past. All bore a red cross symbol, but the soldiers also carried rifles.

"Lisa, behind me is the first wave of relief efforts on its way to help the people of Afghanistan. This is first of what Iran asserts will be several such movements. We've been assured by the commander of the relief efforts that the tanks and armed guards you see are only there to ensure the supplies get through in a safe and timely manner."

Lisa asked, "Pete, how is the situation in Afghanistan?"

"Lisa, it's just heartbreaking. The earthquakes have decimated this country. Entire towns just flattened. Families digging in the rubble for their loved ones. Horrible—painful to watch. Here's some footage we took earlier…"

Dave decided that to announce the final challenge, they should "go back to the classics," so Neeta stood on a raised platform on a black stage with her plebes lined up before her. She wore her actual zombie fighting gear: Hazmat suit and high rubber boots, chainsaw held at rest in her right hand, while her left cradled the motorcycle helmet against her hip, turned so her company logo showed. She thought that was the only part of her that didn't look ridiculous, but Dave insisted she looked intimidating.

"And hot," he added with a wink.

She was hot. Studio C had become unbearable in the heat, so they'd made arrangements with Disney to rent one of their smaller studios for the filming. However, its

AC had given out twenty minutes into rehearsal. Until the studio tech crews could get it repaired, they were making do with fans and ice. Naturally, having her hair blow would ruin the effect, so everything was directed toward her feet, which were getting uncomfortably cold even as sweat trickled down her back.

They'd already filmed her announcing the challenge—four times, because since everyone already knew what the challenge was, they'd had a hard time getting the right amount of surprise and horror in their reaction to suit Dave.

Before her, LaCenta, Nasir, Spud, Roscoe and Gordon waited, each with two duffle bags in front of them. LaCenta and Spud both watched her with confidence born from their experiences in the last episodes. Nasir did his best not to appear preoccupied with the problems at home; she thought Dave must love how well he was failing. Gordon stood at strict parade rest, belying his nervousness. Roscoe shifted his weight as he tried to appear bored but nervous. Neeta suppressed a smile. His contract said he wouldn't win, but she wondered how far he would go.

He really is a good actor, she thought. Could be a good exterminator, too.

Their Wild Card, Ted, stood in the wings, dressed and carrying his flamethrower. She tried not to look in his direction.

"Action!" Dave called.

Neeta forced her face to an impassive expression.

"So, you five remain. You have trained. You have studied. You have faced challenges equal to and beyond what an average apprentice faces in their training. You have been briefed on the final challenge. Now you must decide.

"You see the bags in front of you? They mark your final decision. In the smaller one on the left is $30,000. Choose that bag, and you are out of the game. You may take the money and your experiences and walk out right now. The bag on the right contains a state-of-the-art extermination suit fitted for you. Choose that bag, and you are accepting the final challenge. Once you decide, there is no turning back.

"Before you decide, know this: In my judgment as Master Exterminator and your trainer, you are all worthy to be called Exterminator. You may have some local requirements to fill wherever you go, but you can do this job. I'm proud of each of you."

She paused to let that sink in—and for the cameras to record their reactions—then nodded. "Choose now."

LaCenta, Spud and Gordon each grabbed up their suits without hesitation. Nasir wavered, eyes darting to each of his companions as if assessing the competition, then he, too, picked up the suit duffle. Roscoe bent toward the money, almost grabbed it. He clenched his left fist, grabbed the suit with his right and stood.

He was sweating. Neeta wondered if it was the heat, the acting, or actual fear.

Didn't matter. He'd perform—like an exterminator.

She grinned, satisfied. "All right, then. As each of you chooses to remain, we have one more order of business.

"This challenge calls for you to work in pairs. As you know, exterminators usually work in teams of two. Having someone watch your back could save your life. The final challenge is geared toward that reality. However, there are an odd number of you. Therefore, we are bringing in an additional participant."

None of them spoke, but she could see their reactions. In her mind, she heard Dave's scripted narrative and imagined whose expression would accompany it. Was it Crying Katie? Nervous Alexis? Had Heisman's foot grown back?

"Plebes, welcome your new teammate."

The spotlight snapped on, and Ted strode into the light and stood, legs spread, shoulders squared, flamethrower cradled in his arms. The rakish grin on his face made her heart skip, and she forced herself to keep a neutral expression lest Dave's cameras pick up her reaction.

She needn't have worried; her plebes gave enough reaction for Dave's cameras.

"The cameraman?" LaCenta howled.

"You can*not* be serious!" Roscoe joined in.

"You're not saddling me with that fobbit!" Gordon snarled.

Neeta held up one hand, and they quieted.

"Ted Hacker has been undergoing a private apprenticeship and has been involved in some of your challenges. Gordon, you may not recall, but in Warehouse Eight, he used his camera to knock back a zombie that was headed to you. While he's not had the academic training, when it comes to the practical aspects of fighting, I would be glad to have him at my side—and I am confident enough to place him at yours."

LaCenta asked, "Does this mean he gets a shot at the million?"

Ted laughed and hefted his BelchingDragon M2-7. "Hell, no! I just want to take 'my girl' out for a spin."

LaCenta rolled her eyes. "Well, all right then."

Ted whooped and strode forward. He smiled at Gordon.

"Semper fi!" he told him.

Gordon glared. "Don't say that. You have not earned the right to say that."

Ted shrugged. Roscoe jerked his head to the spot between himself and Spud and both scooted over to make him a space. As he passed, Roscoe held out his fist, and Ted smacked it above and below with his own.

Neeta turned her head and nodded to someone off stage. A leggy blonde wearing a parody of a hazmat suit consisting of a halter top, hot pants and high-heeled rubber boots, strode up with a velvet bag in her hands.

"LaCenta, Spud, Roscoe. Step forward," Neeta commanded. "In the bag are the names of our three other plebes. You will draw to select your partner."

The blonde held the bag to LaCenta, and she dug her hand into it.

"Ted," she read.

Behind her, Gordon clenched his fist and pulled it in, in victory.

Spud gave the busty assistant a quick smile before pulling out the strip of paper.

"Gordon, it's you and me," he said.

"Yes!" Gordon cheered.

Roscoe turned and gave Nasir a flirty look. "Well, Afghan man, looks like it's up to us to show these losers how it's done."

"Oh, in your dreams!" LaCenta snapped.

"Honey, you are not in my dreams," Roscoe retorted. "Of course, I totally understand if it's true the other way around."

Dave called, "Cut!" as LaCenta sputtered, and sent them off to individual corners so he could film their reactions separately.

Neeta called to the warehouse and spoke to Elouise. They were checking the last of the safeties and would be able to loose the zombies on schedule. Left to her own devices for the next half hour, Neeta peeled off the shirt of her hazmat suit and squatted in front of the fan, letting the ice-chilled air cool her skin and dry her muscle shirt. One of the stage crew whistled. She ignored him.

"Neeta! 9-1-1!" her phone suddenly called out.

"What the—?" She reached into the suit pocket and pulled out the phone. The ID said "Hoffman Exterminations" rather than the 9-1-1 switchboard. That meant real trouble. She sat back from the fan and pressed the button.

"Neeta. What is it?"

"Big pile up on West Burbank and Front Street. Blue cheese dressing truck—broken bottles everywhere."

"Oh, no. Which way's the wind?"

Hoffman laughed in an ugly, resigned way. "What little there is? Right to Bedder Rest."

Neeta swallowed back the rising panic. ZERD last estimated nearly two hundred undead in that factory. "Where's the LA Z-Mat?"

"Political rally. Woody Forrest is running for president—you know there's going to be undead trouble there. I'm stuck in Anaheim on a 409. Once we finish, we'll get there, but we'll need to resupply first. Neeta, you and those plebes of yours are the best defense we've got. It's a huge pile up—thirty-two cars last count."

"Are they on the move?" Neeta didn't say zombies. She didn't need to.

"CHP has a uniform with binoculars watching the factory. Last call, he said he'd seen some stirrings, but none had exited yet. That was about five minutes ago. Neeta, they're doing their best to evacuate everyone, but traffic is backed up thanks to the rally. 9-1-1 has put out an all-call, but you're closest. I know LaCenta is good; what about the rest of your plebes? Can they handle this?"

"I trust them." Even Ted. But seven against two hundred undead—plus panicky civilians to protect? "I can't force them."

Hoffman swore, but not at her. "Take who you can and get there fast. Gotta go. Call Missy at dispatch when you're on the road; she'll get you details and clearest route.

"Right." She hung up and stood, striding fast towards the center stage.

"Plebes to me! NOW!"

The command in her voice caused them all to jump from their seats and hurry over. Dave, who was encouraging Gordon to express his rage at the addition of Ted, scrambled after them, overtaking the group and getting to Neeta first. He grabbed her arm.

"What do you think you're doing? We're not done!"

Neeta pulled her arm out of his grip. "Shut up. This is real! Listen to me—we have a Class One migration in the making. An HLV!"

"A what?" Dave demanded. "People, get back to your—"

"It means 'Helluva Lotta Zombies'! Now, shut up!" LaCenta yelled, and Gordon yanked him behind the group.

"Where?" Spud asked. "Is it a cemetery?"

Quickly, Neeta filled them in on the details she'd learned from Hoffman.

Behind the group, she saw Dave's eyes get big. She knew exactly what he was thinking. To the other side, one ambitious cameraman was still filming. Let him. He wasn't getting anywhere near the mess.

"I can't ask any of you to come. But I have to. I swore an oath. And if you take that same oath, you may some-day face this same situation. Even more, there are at least thirty-two cars involved in this accident. That's at least thirty-two drivers, plus passengers, plus the fire department and ambulance technicians who are there to help the injured. Fresh meat for the horde."

She stopped before her heart pounded its way out of her chest. "Other exterminators are on their way, but we're closest. We will be the first line. Who's with me?"

"Get me a chainsaw!" Gordon demanded. "And a su-persoaker of TidyToidy. OOH-Rah!"

Spud stepped forward, as did Nasir.

"Me, too!" Ted exclaimed, then looked at his flamethrower. "Hear that, baby? We're doing this in style!"

"Well, this is what we've trained for. Let's get a move on!" LaCenta said.

They turned to Roscoe. He stared back with large, frightened eyes.

"Oh, what the hell?" he said. "'Bout time I did something real. Let's go kick butt and re-kill things!"

Quickly, Neeta split them into groups. She, Ted, and LaCenta would go ahead in her van. Meanwhile, Gordon, Spud, Roscoe and Nasir would find Eloise at the warehouse and grab all the supplies they could, pack them into the ZERD van and follow. She took her group and headed out, pulling out her cell phone and dialing Missy to get an update.

"Thank God!" Missy said. "Get there fast, honey. Rooney said he's not seeing any movement in the upper floors. They're probably in shuffle mode, but as soon as one finds the door—"

"Has anybody called the National Guard about an air strike?"

Missy moaned. "Governor won't authorize it until an actual exterminator is there on the scene to evaluate. You know how he is."

Neeta swore. "Stalling. Give me the number?"

In the parking lot, Ted ran beside her. "I'll drive! You make calls!"

When they got near enough to her van, she pointed the fob at it and opened the doors. Ted surged ahead and threw himself into the driver's seat. He backed the van out and was tearing through the parking lot almost before LaCenta had closed the door. He made a left turn across traffic, cutting off a driver and knocking LaCenta against a storage box.

"Watch it!" she yelled. "I want to be able to fight when I get there!"

"No prob!" With a rebel yell of delight, he switched on the sirens and sped through a red light.

Neeta, meanwhile, dialed the governor's office and was promptly put on hold.

She glared sternly at Ted. "If you get Exterminator's Berserk…"

He laughed. "Me? No way! I just love having an excuse to drive like this!" with one hand, he cranked the wheel into a tight right turn. He slapped on the blinker midway through.

"Oh, Lord, have mercy on us and grant us safe journey," LaCenta began.

Ted glanced at her, and when Neeta yelped a warning, jerked his head back and swerved to barely avoid a slower car with Pasadena license plates. "Hey, I didn't know you were religious," he said.

"I am now!"

Ted hit the brakes and shouted something very unreligious. "Can you believe this traffic? We'll never get there!" Suddenly, he jerked ahead, only to get cut off. A lady in a business suit opened her window and flipped him off.

"Can't you hear the siren?" Ted shouted at her. Neeta snarled at the phone. "The governor's aide put me on hold. He's listening to Forrest's speech. He's about to have a major infestation of undead and he's listening to some tired actor with political aspirations!"

Ted surged ahead, then careened left, taking the van the wrong way down an alley. "Time to call in the big guns, Neeta!"

"What do you think I'm trying to do?"

"Not those! We need to get the word to the people—clear the way and stay the hell off the highway. Call that boyfriend of yours and get him on the air!"

Chapter 16

"And that was Ricky Martin 'Living La Vida Loca' on K-RTH 101. And speaking of the crazy life, things are getting really crazy on Burbank near Front Street, where a GM Entitlement cut off a Lizzie's Organic Dressing truck, causing it to veer into the median and roll. Blue cheese dressing is spilled everywhere. There's a pile-up of over 30 cars. Apparently, that's not the worst of it. I've got Brian St. James, from our morning show, with more. What's up, Brian?"

"Cowboy, I just got a call from Neeta Lyffe, Zombie Exterminator. That pileup on Burbank couldn't have happened at worse place. There is a known zombie infestation not far, and while they're normally dormant, that blue cheese smell could draw them out."

"No way! Are they on the shamble?"

"Not last Neeta heard, but the real problem now is that there's no defense on that street. Police are trying to evacuate people, but traffic is backed up. That's why I'm calling.

"If you are listening and you anywhere near that area, get off the road. Also, clear Victory between Alameda and Burbank. Make room for any exterminator vehicles heading your way. Please! You'll save lives. If you are stuck in your car or live near there, lock your doors and roll up your windows. In a house, turn on the television low, then stay away from it. Grab any pesticides and household cleaners you can, ammonia or bleach-based are best. Believe it or not, they are your best defense."

"How many zombies are we talking about?"

"Hundreds. And right now, six exterminators—the cast from *Zombie Death Extreme*—and about ten police officers are the only ones on their way."

"What? What about the LAPD? They have a zombie-fighting team."

"Assigned to the governor and Forrest at the rally across town. Neeta's trying to get through to him, but not having much luck. Don't suppose anyone out there can help with that?"

Ted took the turn on two wheels and just missed the motorcycle of a California State Patrolman that was setting up roadblocks.

"Sorry!" he called to nobody, then slammed on the brakes, throwing them all forward as the van skidded to a stop near the patrolman who was watching the warehouse with binoculars and calling in the numbers and positions of zombies shambling their way.

Neeta stuck her phone into her pocket as she turned to the others. "I want to see the situation myself. In the meantime, start with the defensive perimeter along the exit lanes like I told you. There are CHiPs with shotguns to handle the other areas until we get help."

"Rooney's counted fifty so far," LaCenta said, her voice high. "All heading this way."

Neeta spoke resolutely. "And we're going to contain them. Brian came through; the governor's calling in the air strike, but it's going to take time. We have over a hundred people to protect. Right?"

LaCenta nodded and muttered. "Draw them out. Grenades first, then flamethrowers and squirt guns. Get the leaders."

"And activate your helmet cam!" Ted added. "Dave is going to love this."

Neeta regarded him with narrow eyes. "You could be enjoying this too much."

"Never!" He gave her that grin that sizzled through her, then jumped out, shouting, "Who's with me?"

A half dozen police officers joined him in making a left flank.

"Oh, he is *not* showing me up!" LaCenta declared and grabbed her equipment. She jumped out the back.

"Let's go, people! Saving lives and killing zombies!" She ran down the exit ramp, her corps of policeman following.

Neeta rolled her eyes and pulled open the car door. She looked around her, taking in the situation.

West Burbank and the top part of the I-5 exit were littered with dented cars. The GM Deficit that couldn't slow itself down in time was still wedged into the trailer of the truck, where organic blue cheese oozed and ran in the hot afternoon sun. EMTs and firefighters were hard at work evacuating the wounded and getting the survivors to a central area away from the truck. Glass bottles, the hallmark of Lizzie's "Down with Plastic—Organic Deserves Glass" philosophy, were broken everywhere, making people move slowly and carefully. She heard a choppy roar and saw a medivac chopper coming in for a landing in a roughly cleared spot.

It wasn't as bad as she'd imagined, she tried to tell herself. Oh, there was a lot of twisted metal and broken glass. She'd rather have seen the chopper farther back, but at least the blue cheese dressing was between the landing area and the warehouse. That might slow the zombies—maybe long enough. Plus, West Burbank was raised slightly at this point. If they could keep the zombies contained in the bowl of the Bedder Rest parking lot, they might have a chance.

She remembered playing a game once as a child. Her mother had bought a bunch of ladybugs for their garden, and she'd tried to see how many she could keep cupped in her hands. She'd laughed as they'd scrambled through her fingers. It had tickled.

She shook herself. Zombies don't tickle. Failure was not an option here.

Officer Rooney hurried to meet her and handed her the binoculars. "About a hundred out so far. Most are staying together, but we've got some heading toward the highway and South Front."

Neeta thought hard. "Got any marksmen? We need to pick off the stragglers. Even if they just lame them, those zombies that don't get discouraged will become hamburger for the others."

Rooney paled. "Like sharks?"

"Exactly."

He gave her an odd look. "Do you always smile like that on the job?"

She hadn't realized she was grinning. "Only when I have to work for my victory," she said. Hey, it sounded good.

He chewed on his mustache, deciding if he really wanted to say what was on his mind. She raised a brow.

"I watch your show. I always thought you'd have to be half-crazy to want your job. Now I know I'm right."

"Good crazy?" she asked hopefully. The last thing she needed was for these people to lose confidence in her.

Fortunately, he grinned. "Oh, sure. What do we do next?"

Right then, a familiar voice cleared her throat, and Katie Haskell joined them. "I was just about to ask that myself."

"Katie! What are you doing here?"

"Didn't I say I didn't want to see people die? We were on our way to a SAMs Club for a promo when we heard about the accident. I have a whole truck of B to Z products and two brave defensucators. Where do you want us?"

Neeta hugged her and told her to split the supplies among Ted's group, LaCenta's, and the civilians. "Then you all stay with the civilians. Show them how to use the stuff."

Katie gave her a winning smile. "That's our job!" She ran back to the truck.

Neeta watched her trot back to the truck enviously. She looked so cool in her sandals and Bermuda shorts, even her T-shirt was cool greens. Despite the heat, the waves of her perky ponytail bounced.

Neeta sighed. "Someday, they'll make rubber that breathes." She checked her helmet and breathing mask, then rejoined Rooney at the fence. At six-six, he could see easily over the scrub brush, but not so, her. She stood on a junction box and looked down. She felt vertigo that had nothing to do with her position.

A swarm of zombies flowed out of the factory.

She clicked on her radio. "Everyone copy? Ted, La-Centa, give me a copy."

"Copy!"

"I'm here. Damn, but it stinks down here."

"That's good. The smell will draw them but watch for stragglers. They're going to vector toward the crash, but you have about fifty feet of eight-foot-high wall. That'll discourage them until it slopes down to jumping height. The fence will stall them, too, but we know for a fact they can scale it when motivated. Move your teams farther down the ramp, nearer the gate. That's the weak link, and they'll realize it, eventually.

"If they breech the fence, fall back. Do not engage them in the trees and brush. Like Roscoe said, it's a stupid idea with one zombie, much less a horde."

"Quit rehashing what you told us in the car and tell us something new!" Ted said.

"We have strays coming out other exits. Rooney's getting some sharpshooters to pick them off. Might distract some others."

"Well, let's do that, too!" LaCenta told her team to each pick a spot in the horde and fire.

From her vantage spot, Neeta saw five cops (then ten as Ted got his team on board) pull out their service revolvers and fire into the swarm. The sharp cracks of the gunshots were followed by a rising moan from the zombies. The foglike stream of zombies wavered and dense pockets of undead eddied as they turned to devour their own kind.

"Oh, that is sick!" Ted crowed. "Neeta, when you coming to join us?"

Neeta pulled out her phone and glanced at the time. Had they only been there five minutes? "Soon as the rest of our team arrives. In the meantime, Katie's brought us presents. Arm as many of your team as you can and pour the rest in a thick line in front of you."

"What about reloading our squirt guns?"

"You really think you'll have a chance?" Neeta heard the chopper roar overhead, taking another handful of living to safety.

"Listen to me. If they get past the blue cheese truck, they will go for the victims. At that point, the job is to draw them away. Bring them back up Burbank to me. Got it?"

"Got it!"

"You're the boss!"

"Ted, can you set fire to the trees?"

"They look awfully green, but I'll try."

Neeta sighed in exasperation. The city kept the plant life around the factory green and well-kept to hide the horrors it contained. "Only if you think you have time. Otherwise, save your fuel. We can napalm it when the others…"

She heard the screech of tires and the roar of a Harley and turned to see Elouise Shieldmaiden and Gordon driving up, a *ZDE* truck close behind.

"About time! Hang on, the others are here."

"Hang on, the others are here."

LaCenta felt a wave of relief wash over her—a small wave, granted, but she felt very alone despite the officers and Ted. "Tell them to hurry up!" she snarled into the mike.

Heat and fear made sweat stream into her eyes, but no way was she removing the visor to wipe her head. Wasn't that part of what got the damfool Bergie into trouble? "Got to show off the hair." What last words.

Concentrate, woman. They ain't gonna be satisfied with mangling each other for long.

A horn sounded behind her, and she saw a B to Z truck drive up behind the line. The side doors rolled open and a man in a light green shirt with the B to Z logo shouted. "Got supplies."

The police started to run to the truck.

"Wait! Only three of you from each group!" LaCenta shouted. "The rest keep your eyes on the horde!"

Quickly, the officers started loading up their buddies with a couple of bottles of B to Z All Surface Cleaner. They tucked them into their gun belts by the triggers and slung them over their shoulders with the straps that B to Z placed on each bottle "for easy carrying whether defending yourself on the run or just running from one spill to another!"

One of the B to Z reps came up to her, his dark skin making the bright cheery green of his T-shirt almost too bright to look at—if it weren't for those muscles. He had a nametag, but she barely noticed it for the broad shoulders and perfect eight-pack that his tight T-shirt didn't hide.

He held out two bottles of toilet cleaner to her. "For you, LaCenta. I... think you're amazing."

Wow, he had gorgeous eyes! She hoped he couldn't see her jaw dropping behind the helmet. "Oh! Uh, thank you."

She took them from his hands. They were shaking. She looked back to his face and realized he was terrified.

"Don't you worry. We'll keep them under control. But do me a favor and pull that truck behind the wreck, then leave the doors open so we can get to the stuff, and then you get out of here and get to somewhere safe." She slid the straps over her shoulder.

He nodded quickly. "Good luck," he whispered.

What a voice! Was he naturally that sexy or was near death heightening her senses?

If I survive this, I am so going to find out!

"Hey!" Ted called. "She doesn't need luck. She's got skills!"

The man smiled but didn't take time to say anything more as he ran back to the truck.

One of the officers said," Maybe we should douse ourselves?"

"No," LaCenta replied. "Remember what Neeta said—if they get past the wreck, we need to draw them away from the victims. I'm sorry, but they need to smell fresh meat."

Beside her an officer moaned.

"Steady, Adams," the female cop beside him said.

"They're at the fence!" someone else cried.

The zombies had indeed made it to the fence line, but rather than reaching up to climb the chain link, they just bumped against it. In the meantime, the press of bodies still following the alluring scent of spoiling salad dressing was pressing them against the fence, making it harder for them to move.

Maybe they'd stay that stupid, LaCenta thought. Oh, please stay too stupid to climb.

"Be ready," she called.

Adams pulled out his pistol.

"No!" LaCenta cried. "Spray bottles. Bullets now will just tick them off!"

He fired.

Several others followed suit.

The force of their bullets pushed the struck zombies against those behind them. Those zombies in turn grabbed the injured and started tearing them apart. As zombies collapsed into pieces and others bent to grab the remains, the ones behind them began to climb on their backs and reach for the fence.

"Neeta!" LaCenta wailed.

Gordon jumped off the bike even before Elouise had stopped, and ran up to Neeta. He handed her a sheet of paper. "List of assets, Gunny. What's the plan?"

Gunny? Neeta scanned the paper. Only six napalm grenades? She growled under her breath. Meanwhile, the others gathered around. She saw several people jump out besides Spud and Nasir. Good. They needed help.

"Right. Ellie, there's a sharpshooter on South Front. Take the paintball gun and the antihistamine balls. Those'll work better than bullets.

"Gordon, grab everything you can and head to the accident. If they have to fall back, direct them away from the evacuation area. Spud, lay down a defensive line that repels them away."

Gordon glanced at the exit and pointed. "Spud, if you can cut it between that blue Toyota and the red Challenger, we might be able to funnel them in. Then we can take stations on the cars there—" He pointed. "—and there and pick them off like ducks in a pond."

"Good," Neeta agreed. "Make it happen. Nasir, take all the napalm grenades. Once they breech the fence and as soon as you think the others are clear, blanket the trees."

"Right," Nasir said grimly.

Spud looked over the area Gordon pointed out. "N-neeta, what do I use? We d-d-don't have enough for that area."

"See the B to Z truck? Empty it if you need to."

"Ca-can we put people in it and drive them out after that?"

Neeta blinked. "Spud, you genius! Yes, do that. Roscoe, join Katie."

"Katie?" Roscoe squealed. "She's here?"

"She brought the truck. Join her. Let her know the plan and protect those people. And take her a suit and sword from my van. You're the last line of defense."

Roscoe gave a smart salute with his own sword. "You can depend on me."

"Those people have to depend on you both. Tell her that. In the meantime…" She looked toward the truck and saw two of the cameramen unloading some equipment.

"What are they doing?"

Gordon snarled. "Drone cams. Dave insisted. Stood in front of the truck until we agreed. I wanted to run him down, but..." He shrugged.

"They're remotely run," Spud said. "They p-promised to launch them and get out of the way."

"Those things had better get out of the way!" Neeta declared, "or I'm going to—"

Gunshots cut off her vow of cameraman mayhem.

"Neeta!" LaCenta's panicked cry came over the intercom.

Neeta jumped onto her perch just in time to see the fence toppling under the weight of the zombies.

"Pull back! Just run!" she yelled. "Nasir!"

"I'm going!"

Before she could say anything more, her team was running toward their assigned stations. She made one last glance at their fleeing defense before jumping off the box and dashing to her van.

Time to get to work.

Spud sprinted to the B to Z truck. He waved his arms as he approached the still-moving vehicle.

It stopped and burly black man in a lime green B to Z shirt and a name tag that said "Denzel, Level One Defensucator" on the front leaned out. "LaCenta said for us to park it."

"New plan!" Spud panted. "We have t-to evacuate the living!" He jumped onto the running board, grabbing the rear-view mirror for support, and told the driver to head back to the spot Gordon had indicated.

"Can you get in the back?" he asked Denzel.

"Sure?' but he looked confused.

"Start dumping things out when I tell you. W-we're going to make a d-diagonal line across the road to where they are." He pointed to where Neeta was running for her van. "Just dump the bottles. I'll b-b-break them. When you get to the end, shovel out whatever you can. Empty the truck, then go to fill it up with as many p-people as you can and get out. G-got it?"

The two men traded looks, gulped and nodded in unison.

"You've got to save those people. Go!"

Denzel slid through the window to the back as his partner, "Guy, Level One Defensucator," reached the starting point and spun the truck around. Spud hopped off. As Denzel started tossing out bottles, he hacked them open with his sword and kicked them to spread the contents.

"Faster!" he yelled when he noticed they were keeping pace with him. "Don't worry about me!"

But Denzel opened a bottle of Force One kitchen cleaner and, leaning over the tailgate, doused him with it. "Use the Force, Spud. The Force will protect you!" he said. He dashed to the back and told Guy to accelerate.

Soon they had left Spud behind with a row of unopened bottles for him to smash. He swung his sword like a pendulum, its razor-sharp edge slicing neatly through the environmentally-friendly thin plastic.

Boy, he hoped he was doing the smart thing.

He really hoped his mom wasn't watching.

But it might be nice if Lacey was.

Gordon roared the battle cry of his old division as he dashed toward the zombie horde. Adrenalin coursed through his veins, making a kind of angelic hum in his ears that almost drowned out the panicked cries of the officers and instructions of LaCenta and that pyromaniac cameraman. He could just make out zombies between the low trees, clambering over the fence and each other. The chemical defense line they'd laid hadn't worked—when the first ones stalled, the others pushed them down and walked over them.

Gordon could have told Neeta something like that would happen here. Now her brave exterminators and the LAPD were on the run.

Let them. He'd cover their retreat until Nasir had the place blazing. Oh, yeah! He was meant for this!

As the first cop sped past him, calling, "They're coming, you idiot! Run!" Gordon planted his feet on the asphalt, relishing the crackle of the glass breaking under his boots, and fired up the chainsaw.

"I want a piece of you!" He shouted at the zombies, then started singing the Marine Corps Hymn in a strong bass.

He heard a squeal and turned to see LaCenta tumble and fall on her hands. Her flamethrower went flying. She twisted, cussing but somehow missing the broken glass as she struggled to rise. One zombie, faster than the rest, was heading her way.

Without thinking, Gordon switched off the chainsaw and ran toward her, grabbing his squirt gun. He sprayed her first, then turned the spray on the undead reaching for her. It squalled and clawed at its face.

"Get up!" he shouted.

"Don't need to tell me twice!" she snapped as she rose and pulled out her sword. She swung, neatly decapitating the zombie and scoring the first re-kill.

Damn, but at least she was alive—and that was due to him.

Later, over a beer, he would think, "And about a half-gallon of TidyToidy. Figures."

Nasir looked over the scrubby barrier between the road and the mattress factory. There was not enough napalm in their little grenades to blanket the area. He needed to make a bottleneck, along the lines of Gordon's plan.

The zombies were already storming through the trees where they'd torn down the fence. He set the napalm grenades for maximum dispersal and lobbed two. They struck about where he wanted, and he was rewarded with a FWOOM! and blast of heat as the trees near him caught and flamed. This side was easy, but that was the limit of his throwing capability. If he didn't get some fire on the other side of that bottleneck fast, he'd just drive them toward Interstate Five.

He had to get to the other side, but that meant going past the swarm of zombies that were already starting to reach the road.

Nasir took a breath to calm his nerves and turned away from the scene at the factory to find the motorcycle cop.

He jerked back, almost striking the metal road barrier as he came nose to nose with the camera drone.

At first, he was going to yell, but then a wonderful idea hit him. He grabbed the drone in both hands.

"Hey!" the technician's surprised voice sounded over his headset. "Leggo!"

"Listen to me, cameraman! I need this drone and at least one more. We must deliver the napalm to the trees by the lower side of the exit ramp."

"Hey, how come you speak English so good?"

He howled in frustration. "Never mind that! I'm going to strap napalm grenades to the wings and you are going to crash these drones into the trees. Do you understand, or should I explain in smaller words?"

"Uh, that would destroy the drones, wouldn't it?"

"So?"

"I'll get in trouble with Dave."

Neeta cut in. "Dave's wrath or mine. Pick now." The roar of her chainsaw firing up emphasized her point.

"Um… yeah… uh, second drone coming your way."

"Thank you!" Nasir huffed and looked for the policeman. "I need tape—"

Rooney was already running up from where he'd been digging in the saddlebags of his bike, a roll of duct tape in his hands.

Neeta dashed to her van and drove it toward the zombies, zigzagging through the maze of cars until she came to the dressing truck and broken glass blew out all four of her tires. Cussing in all the languages she knew, she scrambled into the back, grabbed as many items as she could carry and flung the back doors open. She jumped out, squirt gun in hand, chainsaw at the ready by her side.

She heard a roar over the groaning and sirens and looked up, hoping to see the air drop. Her heart leaped for a moment when she saw two choppers heading their way—until she noted the iNews and CNN logos on the side. Figured.

A policeman ran full tilt into her and clung to her.

"It got me!" he blubbered. "Oh, God, please! I don't want to die and come back."

Neeta couldn't even swear. "Where?"

"Legs," he sobbed. "We were running and as we went through some debris, I felt someone tear at my legs. I'm cut! I'm infected."

Checking quickly to see that they were safe for the moment, she knelt and pushed away the torn fabric of his uniform to examine his wounds. Over the headset, Nasir was arguing with the cameraman about using the drones.

She sighed in relief. "You scraped on something. Debris, some kind of metal."

"Please, kill me first."

She didn't have time for this! She stood, grabbed him by the shoulders and shook him. "You're not infected. It wasn't a zombie!"

"No? You're, you're sure?"

"Yes, I'm sure! Now get out of here so I can do my job! No, wait!" She shoved him toward the van. "Grab any supplies you think you officers can use and hand them out. You'll run out of bullets soon enough."

"I am out."

"Then load up! I've got to get to work." And, because she thought he needed the image, she grabbed the chainsaw and fired it up.

On the mike, the cameraman was still arguing with Nasir.

Neeta swore, then said over the mike, "Dave's wrath or mine. Pick now."

Then she stormed toward the nearest group of undead.

Roscoe held the legs of the jumpsuit while Katie stepped into them.

Katie hissed, "Roscoe, this is crazy! I took the money and left. I'm not cut out for this!" She was shaking, all the confidence she'd been showing the frightened people around her eroded by the sight of a rubber hazmat suit and a zombie hacker.

"Girlfriend, you're more qualified than anybody else in this group, present company excepted, of course. If the others fail, we're all these people got."

Behind them, Katie had organized the living, with children and wounded as far to the back as possible, parents next, then the rest, with the volunteers closest to the front. She'd armed as many as she could with B to Z bottles, and everyone was damp from getting sprayed with B to Z All Color Laundry Bleach—with Oxy! They watched the road with fearful eyes, sometimes turning their gaze to Katie and Roscoe as if hoping they could make a miracle.

"You're right, you're right." She fumbled with the sleeves, and he zipped the suit closed for her and helped her with the helmet. She did a quick comms check.

"Good to have you on the team," Neeta said. They heard her chainsaw and splattering in the background.

"Thanks," Katie squeaked. Her face was scrunched up and she held the sword in a death grip.

Roscoe grabbed her shoulders. "Deep breaths, girl. We just got to stand guard. Come on. Open your eyes."

She obeyed, looking first at his roguish smile he'd plastered on just for her, then past him to the accident scene. "What are they doing with the B to Z?"

"Making a barrier to corral the zombies away from us. Then the truck is coming here. You load it with as many living as you can, get in and get out of here, 'k?"

Katie's eyes widened as if realizing something. She grabbed his elbows. "Roscoe, you, too! You never meant to seriously become an exterminator. You're really just a contestant."

He laughed. "Oh, honey—this is the Final Challenge. You think I'm going to turn tail when that witch LaCenta is out there swinging her sword like she thinks she's got a chance at the million? Oh, no. I can't let her show me up! I'm seeing this through."

Behind them, they heard the wailing siren of an ambulance heading their way.

"Now, go meet the ambulance and tell them our plan. Then make sure the kids and wounded are ready to jump in that truck. Pack in tight—they only need to go a couple of miles, so weight is no problem. I'll stay here and send the truck back."

She nodded and turned to the crowd. "Don't worry! Help is on the way!" she cheered, then ran to the back.

Roscoe smiled, bemused. What a lady. And she even made the suit look good. 'Course it didn't hurt that her waist was smaller than Neeta's while her bust was somewhat bigger.

He banished such thoughts and turned back toward the front, striking a hero's "at rest" pose, feet slightly spread, sword pointed down and away, body loose but ready to spring into action. Posing he could do.

And if it comes to a zombie fight, I can do that, too.

Realization struck him, and he swallowed hard.

I've gone crazy, he thought. I've gone insane. I've gone *native!*

But for the first time in a long time, he felt he'd gone *real.*

"I love when reality TV gets real!" Ted shouted as he let loose with another barrage of flame from his girl. Behind him three officers kept a steady rain of gunfire.

They'd retreated to just behind the first line of cars, some of which had sped past the twisted wreck of a truck and were now being swarmed by zombies. Most continued on toward the living, but several undead had stopped at an antique '57 Chevy and were leaned under its open hood and grunting. To the left, one knelt by a Toyota with a leaking fuel tank and was sniffing so hard, its head slumped back with each breath.

"Heads and neck!" the female officer, Angelina, called out. "Body shots just tick them off."

As if to demonstrate, she fired straight into an approaching zombie's neck. Her high-caliber bullet punched a hole in its neck on entry and tore through its spine on exit. The zombie twitched once and crumpled.

"Woooo!" Ted cheered. "I want to have your babies!"

Angelina laughed. "Have to buy me a drink first."

"Deal!"

"Enough chatter!" Neeta's annoyed voice sounded over the headset.

"Got it, Sensei!"

"Fall back to the next line of cars! I've got a looky-loo I need to drive off."

"Yes, boss! You heard the lady!" Ted roared a rebel yell and let loose a wide spray of flame to cover their retreat. He twisted toward the sniffer.

"No!" Angelina yelled. "Run!"

As the officers turned and sprinted away, the spilled gasoline caught fire. Even the sniffing zombie had the sense to back away.

"Oh," Ted started. He backpedaled quickly.

The fire crept up the side of the car and ignited the tank.

A huge spout of flame billowed out of the tank.

"Oh!" Ted shouted. He smacked his helmet with one hand.

Pushed by the small breeze, the flames set fire to a group of zombies shambling in their direction.

"Oh! Oh!" Ted cheered. He pumped his flamethrower in the air victoriously.

"Ted! Fire discipline!" Neeta scolded.

"Oh," he moaned and got back to work.

Neeta growled over the mike, but inside, she was laughing. Ted was a loon, but he had good instincts, even when he didn't realize it. That car fire has taken out five zombies that she could see and was driving them further into their second bottleneck.

She should be there, at the next bottleneck, but she'd spotted a red Lexus driving the wrong way up the exit ramp. Idiot must have made a heckuva U-turn.

At first, she'd entertained the unlikely thought that the person was some kind of visiting exterminator coming to help, but all the *gwah!* had done was pull out his cell phone and start taking pictures.

And now, his shiny fancy car had attracted the attention of a group of zombies.

She couldn't run fast enough to get to him in time. No one was closer. The damfool was talking on the phone now, head down while he wrote notes, oblivious to the danger approaching. Even Ted's fireball didn't attract his attention.

Think, Neeta! She started toward the car, looking around her for something to get his attention. She saw a glint of metal coming from the BMW that was half-under an H5 on her right and realized someone had left the keys in their car. Maybe…

She jumped up and yanked open the door of the H5. The tricked-out model had more dashboard controls than a fighter jet, but they were lighted and the engine was running. Bingo!

Oh, this would be fun!

From her vantage point atop a '29 Mustang, LaCenta could see the spray of fire emit from the burning car and strike the zombies. "The man's a menace!" she complained between pants. She saw movement to her right, fired a shot of 409 from her squirt gun and was rewarded by a zombie shriek.

On her left, Gordon fired at another. "Getting the job done. This is war, Dane."

"Don't 'Dane' me! If that maniac don't save us, he's gonna kill us all, that's all I'm saying!"

Gordon didn't contradict her. "We've got to get down from this car before they totally surround us. Ready to switch to swords?"

Despite the lightness of the nanoblade that Hollerman had loaned her for the original final challenge, her arms were achy from all the swinging. When Gordon had seen her tiring, he'd told her to climb to the top of the car and switch to guns. The squirt gun was heavier, but at least she wasn't swinging, and it did get lighter with each use. She didn't want to think about what she'd do when it emptied, other than to toss it away and lighten her load when she ran. She had no doubt that at some point, she'd have to run, that they all would.

She was so tired.

And Neeta carried a chainsaw. Now she understood her Amazon biceps.

"This is crazy! They're everywhere!" Something grabbed her ankle and reflexively, she cut off the zombie's hand.

Gordon laughed. "We got them right where want them; now we can't miss."

"Stupid Jarhead!"

"Once a Marine, always a Marine! So, ready to bolt?" Gordon asked.

"You leading or me?" she demanded.

"Go, go, go!" Gordon cried and ran down the trunk and leapt off, swinging his chainsaw and decapitating the zombie trying to get them from behind.

"Semper fi!" he yelled, and a zombie with a "Death Before Dishonor" tattoo on his arm turned away from them.

"Yaaaa!" LaCenta yelled and ran after him, taking out a zombie at the right and maiming the one behind it. No way was she losing to that pumped up jarhead. She needed the money to buy a home gym!

She heard the roar of an engine and saw an H5 tearing across the road, its combat grade, totally reinforced and puncture-proof safety wheels kicking up glass and its front bumper mowing down zombies as it raced toward a Lexus parked at the side of the road. She saw a helmet with Neeta's logo.

She felt really sorry for whoever was in the Lexus.

Katie lifted up her visor to smile at the children. "Don't be afraid. It's just me!" Several of the smaller children, already terrified beyond reacting, simply hid their faces in the legs of a parent, while others glared at her scornfully.

"Everyone, listen to me, please! In a few minutes, the B to Z truck is coming here to get us out!" She let them cheer a moment and held up her hands. "Plus, another ambulance is coming, and we'll have them take as many wounded as they can carry. Uninjured people will crowd into the truck. We want to cram as many people as possible, so please skooch in!"

"Lady!" a child cried. She stood near an unconscious woman, holding her hand so tightly her knuckles were white.

Katie knelt down. "Oh, is this your mom? You can go with her. It's okay."

The child shook her head. "Don't want to go. The ambulance is sick!"

Confusion made Katie laugh. "Sorry. What?"

"The ambulance is sick!" The child pointed.

Katie turned just in time to see the ambulance, swerving along the road like a drunken thing, hit the median and go into a spin.

Behind her, Roscoe led a cheer at something happening on the front. Their voices drowned out the screams of surprise of those in the back as the ambulance flipped and slid toward them.

It stopped mere yards away.

Immediately, a couple of EMTs left the group and ran for the ambulance. Together, they pulled at the doors, opening the bottom one, and one peered inside.

"Run!" he screamed and backed away.

"What?" Katie yelled. "What is it?"

A hand too pale and stiff for the living clawed spasmodically at the door as a zombie in torn clothing crawled out of the ambulance, tugging IV tubes and EKG wires with it. It rose and forced its mangled body toward them, groaning.

The child beside her whimpered.

"No," Katie whispered, then with growing force: "No. No, no, no, no—NO!"

She whipped out her sword and ran toward them screaming, "You will not take the children! NO!"

Roscoe was leading his "civilian troops" in a cheer as LaCenta jumped down from a blue Mustang when he heard children screaming.

"Stay here! Guard the front!" he shouted to the nervous group, then ran to the back.

It took only moments to round the group, but when he got there, Katie was already making mincemeat of the zombie, having sliced off its arm and a leg and its head in three places. She was still hacking at it with the sword, screaming incoherently.

Everyone was staring at her, now more afraid of her than the zombie.

He approached cautiously. "Katie!"

"No, no, no! You will not do to them what you did to Bergie!"

"Katie! It's over!"

"You horrible, unnatural—" She stopped swinging to kick the corpse.

"Katie!" Roscoe ran behind her and grabbed her, pinning her arms. She continued to kick and scream and try to slash at the air with her sword.

Because of that, they didn't hear people shouting that a second—and third—zombie were approaching.

Roscoe tried to drag her back and finally arched his back, picking her off the ground entirely. "Oh, honey! You weigh more than you look!" he grunted.

Katie, thrashing, kicking and now screaming epithets she'd blush about later, twisted, and Roscoe saw the zombiefied ambulance attendants reaching for them.

Roscoe turned and put Katie between them. Her wildly swinging sword sliced through the face of the first one.

Roscoe dumped her to fight that one and pulled out his bottle of Porcelain Sparkle to take on the other, a lovely 30-something woman but for the dazed, angry expression.

"Bring it, baby!" he found himself yelling. "Let's get real!"

Neeta was swearing in Dari, enjoying how the syllables tripped off her tongue. It was oddly relaxing and made a nice counterpoint to the corpses bumping off her fender. She'd have preferred the radio, but when she started the engine, *LA's Philharmonic Plays ABBAs Greatest Hits* was in the CD player, and she couldn't find the off button. In fact, all she'd managed to do was activate the loudspeaker so that it broadcast the music.

Of course, it did get some of the zombies stopping to sway together in groups.

A zombie leapt onto the hood. She turned on the windshield wiper fluid and it screeched and fell off. She bounced in the seat as the rear tires bumped over it.

She kept accelerating toward the still-idling Lexus until she wasn't sure she could brake in time, then stomped on the brakes with both feet and jerked the wheel to the right. She could hear the squeal of the tires over her swearing, the zombie groans, even the enthusiastic all-violin rendition of "Dancing Queen."

She panted as if she'd ran the entire distance, took a deep breath to slow her heart, and took in her surroundings.

She came to a stop beside the Lexus, its side mirror mere inches from her door.

And in the process, she'd somehow bumped the off button for the CD. All right!

In front of her, lining the shoulder of I-5 just past the police barrier, a half dozen looky-loos were standing outside their cars, holding up cell phones to record the massacre.

Not all right!

She grabbed the mike and cranked the volume to full.

"Listen up over there!" she called in her most commanding voice. "There are about a hundred undead heading your way, so unless you want to join them, get in your cars and go! I repeat—"

Something knocked on her window. Her jaw dropped.

Bruce Twiddle, Attorney at Law?

I could go, she thought. Drive back to the fray, save those worth saving…

She lowered the window. Everyone was worth saving, even Twiddle.

All part of the job.

Even as she was drawing a breath, he started, "Do you mind? Some of us are working here."

"Get in your car and get out of here!" she shouted. "The zombies are headed…"

Her ears caught up with her brain and she shrieked, "Working?"

He continued self-importantly. "When all this is done, there are going to be a lot of people who will need representation, and Wanker, Wanker and Twiddle prides itself on…" He paused, his own brain doing catch up.

"Neeta Lyffe! If that's your car, I'd say you're not doing so badly."

"Look, Twiddle, you have to get out of here. Zombies are coming!"

He sneered. "You mean other than the ones crawling up your bumper?"

She swore as she saw a head pop up from the grail. Ignoring Twiddle, she threw the car into reverse, cranked the wheel hard to the left, just missing Twiddle's Lexus again. She hoped he appreciated that, unintentional as it was.

Then she shoved it into drive and rammed the fender into the cement wall.

"Whoa!" Twiddle yelled, holding up his cell phone to get a shot.

Neeta kept her foot on the gas until she was sure the midsections of the zombies were nothing but goo. Then, she hit reverse, spun around and smashed the backside of the H5 into a wall. She was rewarded with a crunch and a groan.

She leaned out her window. "Twiddle, can't you see—"

But he did see. He leaned out of his window, frozen and staring at the crowd of undead shambling his way.

"Get in your car and drive!" Neeta yelled.

For once, he listened. He ducked into the car. She heard it give a couple of mechanical clunks and die.

With a scream of frustration, she pulled up next to him again.

"It's dead!" he shouted.

How long had he been idling in this heat? part of her wondered. The rest said, "Try again!"

"I have been!"

"Then take this one! Just take it and drive! Worry who it belongs to after you're sure you'll live!" She jumped out of the van, pulling her chainsaw with her.

He dashed out, gathering his iDoAll and phones. When he saw the seats, he stopped.

"I can't sit in that. It's covered in…gross."

"I'm covered in gross! Excuse me for working!"

"I'm not sitting in that. I might get contaminated. Do you want that on your conscience, too?"

"What I want—" she started, then caught herself. Didn't matter. The zombies were coming while she argued with this *baka tare*. She grabbed the passenger door and tugged it open. Under the seat, as she expected, she found an unopened winter emergency gear kit.

"Unless you want me touching the tarps, pull them out yourself and drape the seat."

"I hardly—" he started, when a moan cut him off.

"Duck!" Neeta yelled, and raised her squirt gun. She shot the zombie full in the face and it fell onto its rump, shaking its head.

"Get in, use the tarp, get out—and take those idiots with you!" She swung the butt of her gun toward the couple of cars still hanging around.

Again, he obeyed, and while she made real music with her chainsaw, he clambered in and locked the doors. A few minutes later, he drove off, ABBA again playing on the loudspeakers.

The zombies paused, watching him go. Then, deciding Neeta made a better target, they advanced, slowly, as if each one had loved *Night of the Living Dead* in life.

"I could use some help by the red Lexus!" she called over the radio.

"Neeta, get out of there!" were the replies she received.

She looked around her. The only way out was I-5 and she was not luring the horde that way. She yanked the top off a bottle of B to Z and poured it over herself then threw it toward the horde.

"I can't! Backup, please!"

Static answered her.

She bared her teeth behind her helmet and sprayed the area in front of her. They stopped, torn between the repellent scent of the toilet cleaner and the lure of her own sweat.

For the first time in a long time, she prayed. *I don't want to die, God, but if I go, let me die fighting.*

And please make them bury me with my severed head in my hands.

Spud heard Nasir swear as he struggled with the duct tape. "I'm sending the last bomb Neeta's way. What else have we got?"

Gordon replied, "Try to vector it between LaCenta and me and Neeta. Maybe we can cut through."

"That's stupid!" LaCenta countered. "We'll all be killed. There are too many. We need a vehicle."

"Neeta's van?" Roscoe chimed in.

"Tires blown out. Zombies swarming it."

"The news choppers!" Katie called. "Maybe they can land?"

"No place safe," Gordon replied.

"I'll call anyway," the new cameraman offered. "Maybe they have a ladder."

"Spud here. There's an ambulance c-coming this way. I'm going to flag it down and take it." He trotted down West Burbank.

"Oh, Spud, be careful!"

"Will do. I got too much to live for." Despite himself, his hand went for his pocket, making sure the ring box was still in his jeans under the exterminator suit.

Regardless of their jobs, he didn't think a gore-splattered engagement ring was all that romantic.

"Spud, you stud, we've almost got the victims packed in. Pick me up and we'll get her together!"

"Roger, Roscoe!"

Nasir said, "Until then, what can we do to stall?"

"Neeta, you can't die!" Katie shrieked over the radio. "Just run! For the love of everything, just run!"

"Anytime, guys!" Neeta grunted, and they heard the chainsaw grinding through zombie flesh.

"Neeta!"

Gordon cut off Katie's frantic calling. "Neeta, do you copy?"

All were silent, but all they heard were her grunts and the sound of zombies and titanium chain.

"Her comms are out," LaCenta gasped.

"You'd better fear me! I'm Neeta Lyffe, Zombie Exterminator! I am your doom!"

"Go, girl! Oh, gawd, she's hardcore even now. I'm so in love! Well, lust."

Spud rolled his eyes at Roscoe's comment as he waved his arms to stop the ambulance. That was Roscoe, right to the end.

"Roscoe, shut your hole!" LaCenta snarled.

"Nasir, just bomb her an escape route. She'll know what to do." Gordon said. He pointed to another car closer to Neeta's position. They jumped to it.

"I'll blast cars!" Ted said. "Angelina can shoot the gas tanks and I'll ignite them! She'd rather brave fire than zombies, right?"

"Right! Hey! Gordon, sing the Marine song, quick!"

"From the halls of Montezuma, to the shores of Tripoli…"

LaCenta hollered in a drill sergeant voice. "Norks at eleven o'clock. Get them men! OOH-Rah!"

Even from where he was climbing into the ambulance, Spud could hear an undead chorus shout "OOH-Rah!" in reply.

"Napalm away!" Nasir called.

The cameraman broke in. "I sent the other drones to harass the zombies. So, uh, don't do anything too spectacular, 'k?"

"Air Force," Gordon snorted, then continued with the second verse.

"Guys! I hope you're planning something! I don't want to die a virgin here!"

"Look!" LaCenta paused in her swinging to point in Neeta's direction.

One brave zombie crossed Neeta's line, and the rest followed. As she backed around the car, spraying and slicing, they advanced, cautiously, almost as if they knew who she was.

"You'd better fear me! I'm Neeta Lyffe, Zombie Exterminator! I am your doom!" she shrieked.

She didn't make any feints, couldn't waste the energy. She had to keep alive until help came—because she knew, even though she couldn't hear them, that her plebes would find a way to save her.

She hoped they'd be in time.

The zombies lunged toward her one at a time, like in a bad karate flick. Like in those flicks, she howled and kicked and swung, knocking one back, spinning and chopping the arm off another, months of training in the simulator allowing her to now move on reflex. No trick shots now, though. Decapitate or incapacitate. Her body knew. Adrenalin and effort made her feel feral and dizzy.

But there were just too many, and after they'd backed her into the wall, not far from the smeared remains, fear began to get a fingerhold.

"Guys!" she called. "I hope you're planning something! I don't want to die a virgin here!"

Suddenly, a camera drone dropped between her and the zombies.

"This is what you're going to film?" she shouted, but instead the drone plunged into the thickest part of the zombies. They fell back, partly from surprise.

Then a horn blared, and a van with a zombiefied cockroach on the top drove into the fray. The roach tilted as the hatch in the top opened and two Hollerman and Co. Exterminators popped out the top and started spraying the horde with 409.

Neeta cheered and cut a path toward them.

A moment later another drone dove into the horde on her right and exploded. Bits of zombie, aflame from the napalm, rained over the rest. Some tried to stop, drop and roll, bumping into their neighbors. Further back, she heard gunshots paired with explosions. Ted, no doubt. And did she hear the Marine Corps hymn? What were her plebes doing?

She climbed onto Twiddle's car and made a running leap for Hollerman's. Jason caught her.

"Am I glad to see you!"

"I'm glad to know you've kept your virtue intact, Little Girl," he said, and for a moment, she was torn between laughter and tears.

A thunderous droning sound distracted her, and she looked up.

"Yes!" she screamed as the CL415 Superscooper soared past, circled fast and dumped 1600 gallons of ZERD-created antihistamine foam on the area.

"My truck!" Hollerman wailed as some of the foam leaked in through the open hatch.

Now sitting on the top, her legs dangling over the hood, Neeta wiped foam off her helmet and laughed as two hundred and thirteen zombies sank to the ground twitching and groaning and finally falling still.

Chapter 17

"The LA Zombie Massacre. That's what local historians are already starting to call the incident at West Burbank and South Front Street where nine exterminators and a handful of police officers took on—and defeated—over two hundred undead..."

Steppenwolf's "Born to Be Wild" sang over the news anchor's report. Not taking her eyes off the screen and trying not to disturb the ice pack on her knee, Lacey reached toward the table by the couch for the phone.

"Mom! Yeah, yeah. I'm watching iNews, too. Yes, the boys are there. Well, obviously, they left me here. No, they missed all the fun—sorry, Mom. Okay, okay. I know, I'm sorry. I just meant that they got stuck in traffic and didn't get there until after the plane blanketed the area."

On the screen, footage from a news helicopter showed the accident scene swathed in white foam save for a few smoking cars and the brightly colored hazmat suits of the people working to clean up the twice-dead and make sure there were no undead missed.

"Victims of the accident say the exterminators, primarily the cast of the well-known reality TV show, *Zombie Death Extreme*, performed a minor miracle, with only four deaths and three cases of zombie-ism. Those were due to a spontaneous regeneration of Gloria VanBuren, 35, an accident victim who died and came back *en route* to the hospital."

Lacey leaned back, waiting for the interviews. "They're doing the cleanup," she told her mother, then laughed. "See why I said they missed the fun? I dunno. City's paying, I guess. Yeah, I know. I suppose it's a good thing, but we were making such good money."

The announcer continued, "But what do these intrepid exterminators have to say?"

Lacey leaned forward. "Mom! Mom! Hush and listen a minute. It's him!"

Gordon was standing on the fender of Neeta's battered van, which had been towed away and hosed down. He held a zombie's head in a plastic bag for all to see. The rest of the team was gathered around him, including some of the officers and the B to Z team. All were dripping wet from the decontamination procedures, and those who did not have suits were in hospital gear provided by a supplier only three blocks away.

"We came. We saw. We kicked zombie ass and took heads!" He held the head high.

Around him the others cheered and laughed.

Sitting beside him, one foot propped on the fender and an arm resting on the knee, Neeta chuckled and shook her head, like a bemused schoolteacher of an unruly but high-achieving class.

"We're not taking the heads," she said for the reporter's benefit, "except to ZERD for research or the incinerator."

Gordon pulled the head close and caressed it. "Spoils of war! I love this head!"

"It's leaking," Roscoe said casually.

"Yah!" Gordon tossed it away, toward the reporter in fact, who jerked back with a screech of his own. The others started laughing, and Roscoe and LaCenta did a high five—down low because their arms were so sore from waving the swords around. Neeta reassured the reporter that the bags were ten times the rated industrial strength and airtight enough to keep viruses out—or in.

The reporter, trying to regain his composure, asked the group what the biggest surprise of the day was.

"No, Mom. Not that moron! To the right. Blue muscle shirt, short blond hair. Shy smile. 'Smitten?' Jeez, Mom! Who says 'smitten,' anymore?"

Roscoe was waxing poetic about Neeta's lunatic drive to save the looky-loo. "It was breathtaking! Edge. Of. The. Seat! I'm sooo sorry for whoever owns that H5, but, oh, gawd, such heroism! And when she jumped out and just gave it to that guy to make his escape while she faced the horde alone!" Roscoe pretended to swoon into Gordon. Instead of snarling, Gordon laughed and pushed him upright.

Neeta shrugged. "His car died. Vapor lock, probably." She glanced back at the soiled Lexus. Every officer, out of spite, had stuck a ticket for a different traffic violation under its wiper. She shouldn't get joy from that. Really.

The cameraman caught her smirk.

Lacy said, "All right, maybe I am smitten. Here! Here! Listen!"

"I'm just glad to be alive," Spud told the reporter. "Really, tha-that's the largest surprise of all. Uh, can I say something to someone? Lacey, I hope you have t-time to see me tonight. There's something we need to t-ta-ta." He ducked his head, grimacing, then took a breath and looked straight at the camera.

"I have to ask you something," he finished.

"What?" demanded the reporter. The others joined in.

"What?" Lacey yelled at the television. "What? What do you want to ask me?"

On screen, Spud just shook his head, blushing slightly.

The camera moved back to the reporter. "There you have it—the heroes of the day. Crowing their victory, keeping a level head, patting each other on the back…and hiding secrets." He smiled at his last comment.

LaCenta grabbed the mike and stuck her head next to his.

"And now, we are going to ride into the sunset, like heroes do. See ya in a bit, Mom, Jamal, Moe!"

The anchorman laughed his well-practiced laugh. "This is…"

Lacey smacked her uninjured leg in frustration. "Mom, what could he possibly..? No! Are you sure?"

She grabbed the remote and backed up the feed.

"There's something we need to t-ta -"

She froze it, dragged the cursor to his front right pocket, and enlarged.

Just as her mother suspected, there was a small, square bulge in his pocket.

"Yes!" she screamed at the television, dropping the phone, whamming her fists against the couch cushions joyously and bouncing so that the ice pack slid off. "Yes, yes, yes!"

Hollerman pulled his truck up to Neeta's curb and unlocked the doors. She looked at the door handle. It almost seemed too much effort to open it.

"Need help, Little Girl?" he asked.

She shook her head tiredly, but with affection. "I'll be fine." She leaned her head against the seat and tilted it toward him and his partners in the back.

"Thanks for saving me."

Jose shrugged. His cousin, Elina, kissed her own hand and caressed Neeta's cheek. Hollerman gave her a fatherly smile but merely said, "All part of the job, right?"

"All part of the job," she repeated. They all held up their helmets and clicked them together in a toast.

"Now get on out so I can get home. That AH spray really is making me drowsy."

She got out and shut the door on the second try. As she dragged her duffle and herself toward her welcoming green door, her eyes were on the sidewalk and her mind on what would happen next: a shift on cleanup, no doubt, then figuring out the damage to her van, and seeing if Eugene could recommend a good lawyer. No doubt, Twiddle was lining up the owner of the H5 to sue her…

She mounted the steps still on automatic. Of course, tonight, she had to toss her gear into the sterilizer and scrub everywhere. A steamy shower sounded good for her sinuses, too.

"Hey, hero."

Her key halfway in the door, she stopped and blinked at the man smiling invitingly from the porch swing. He wore dark jeans that were just a bit too tight in the right way and a white silky shirt that was unbuttoned, showing off a smooth, tanned chest.

"Brian?" She paused to shake her head. Had they planned a date? "Um, what are you doing here? You do know what I've been doing?"

"Of course. Why do you think I'm here?"

Her eyes widened. How much of their recorded conversations had been aired already? "Brian, if this is about the virgin comment…"

"Virgin what?"

She raised her hand dismissively. It hurt. "Never mind. Why are you here?"

He laughed, a warm, mellow, patronizing sound. "Neeta, honey. You don't have to pretend with me."

"What?" She was going to need all her energy to figure out what he was talking about. She let her duffle drop.

Taking that as an invitation, he rose and moved toward her, slowly. "Come on. You put up such a brave front for the others. You don't need to for me."

"Front?" She seemed to understand one word in three and found herself repeating even fewer.

"I understand. You have to be tough. But it's okay around me. I know how traumatized you must be."

"Traumatized?" she repeated, then mentally slapped herself. "Why would I be traumatized?"

"All those people you killed today."

"What?" Anger gave her energy to yell. "Is that what the news is saying? We only took out the undead."

"Right."

Her next statement started as an incoherent "buh." She tried again. "What people, then?"

Now he stopped, his whole demeanor twisting in confusion. "The zombies, of course."

She gaped at him. Didn't they already have this conversation? "Brian, they're not alive. They're not people. They're like cockroaches."

"Come on…" he coaxed.

"I feel worse about exterminating ground squirrels."

"You are not so cold."

"Cold?" she squawked, then her voice did turn cold. "Listen, Brian. I am exterminator. That's my job. I remove pests, whether roaches or fluffy-tailed ground squirrels or shambling rotting remains of what once was a human being. And I don't feel remorse. I don't feel pity. Well, maybe for the squirrels, but not the roaches and certainly not the zombies."

His face clouded and he lowered his arms. "How can you…?"

"What I do feel," she pressed on, "is filthy and tired and worried about how I'm going to deal with people out there who think I can destroy a shambling horde without collateral damage."

His crossed his arms, his whole body tense in anger under the soft folds of his shirt. "You just don't get it, do you? I've tried. I really have. Neeta, I just want to be here for you!"

"Be here for what?" she demanded.

"To comfort you. To hold you. To hear your troubles and help." He stepped toward her, then suddenly turned away, waving his arms and pacing. "All right! I get it! You are Neeta Larger-than-Lyffe, Bane of Zombies. The Great Hero of our era."

"Hey!"

He spun back.

"Don't you think, just once, you could let someone rescue you?"

For a moment, she gaped at him, stunned. Did he really say what she just heard him say? Had he bothered to watch the news all the way through, or had he decided to doll himself up to be ready to "comfort" her?

His voice gentled. "Neeta, love…"

She cut him off, her voice low, low in a way that the *ZDE* writing team knew meant "scoot your chairs back and duck!"

"What do you think Hollerman did?"

Brian just stepped closer. "Let's not fight."

"*What do you think Hollerman did?* Were you watching when he pulled my *posladko* out of the fire?"

"Okay, um, I meant—"

"And Jesse and Elina. Or what about my plebes? Didn't you see how they tried to blast me an escape route?"

He jerked back as if struck. "Oh, are we on Ted again?"

What? "Yes, Ted! And that officer—Angelina. And Nasir and the cameraman—" Shoot! She didn't even know his name. "And what about Roscoe and Spud? They were going to hijack an ambulance and barrel down zombies to get to me! So, you want to tell me again that I need to *let* people rescue me?"

"You don't understand what I'm saying," he yelled.

She shouted back, "And you don't understand me!"

The neighbor's dog barked, startling them both. Neeta again realized she was standing on her front porch, arguing with her boyfriend, in full view of Mrs. Westerman and anyone nosey enough to have followed her home. So much for low profile.

She pinched the bridge of her nose, trying to regain her composure. She was so *goram* tired.

"Brian. I'm not trying to be a hero. And I don't need to be comforted for doing my job. I don't put on brave fronts. This is who I am."

Suddenly, she felt shaky and completely uninterested in continuing this conversation, now or ever. She pressed her *posladko* against the door in an effort to keep standing.

"Brian, you're a great guy. We've had a lot of fun, really, but…"

"Right." He spoke through gritted teeth. He turned on his heel and marched past her and down the steps. Then he turned, his eyes soft and melting her heart—or trying to.

"Have a good life, Neeta."

She watched him until he got into his car, in part because she had to gather her strength. When he drove off, she wearily opened the door and forced herself to do her post-job errands. She took a long, hot shower, scrubbing her skin and under her nails and behind her ears and washing her hair three times.

And if she chose to cry there, it was her choice, not some man's.

Her last act was to turn off her phone and set her alarm. She didn't remember hitting the pillow until she woke up drooling into it the next morning.

LaCenta left the small party her brothers had arranged, claiming weariness, and made her way to the spare room her mother still kept up for her. She shut the door, sat on the edge of the bed, and looked at her cell phone.

"Oh, just eat the crow, LaCenta!" she snarled to herself after a good two minutes of debating and dialed the number Sharon had given her earlier.

"Hi, this is Katie Haskell."

"Katie! It's LaCenta, girl. I didn't wake you? Oh, now don't be like that. It's a reality TV show. Someone's got to be the snarky one."

"What you were, *Placenta*, was a—"

LaCenta pulled the phone away from her ear a moment, then made herself laugh into it. "Girl, I do not believe you just called me that! You got hidden fire, that's all I'm saying. No, no, I'm not mad. I guess I deserved it. Bygones, right?

"Anyway, we just saw you on the TV, battling that zombie—no, the other one, the one that was still moving. Girl, you had some sweet moves."

"Really?"

"Yes, really."

"So, I can come back? You're asking me to come back?" Katie squeaked.

She did not just say that! LaCenta again forced a light laugh from her lips. "Oh, no, I'm not! You walked off the show. You gave up your chance at the mil'. Let's not take bygones too far. Besides, you've got yourself a sweet gig, doing something important and hanging out with those hotties!"

Katie laughed. "I know! Talk about fringe benefits!"

"Well, I just wanted to let you know, you know, that you did good, and I'm glad you were there—and those guys you brought with you. What were their names?"

"Guy and Denzel? Weren't they the best? I mean, they are brand-new defensucators just moved here from Sacramento to help me promote B to Z, and lickety-splickety, they're helping fight zombies!"

"Their wives must be worried!" It was an obvious hint, but she knew Katie. The girl would natter on and never get to the point.

"Oh, no wives. Corporate likes single reps. All the better to flirt with the customers. I don't really agree with it, but sometimes, you have to deal with the boss. Dave taught me that!"

She laughed and LaCenta joined in with a real laugh of her own.

Katie sighed. "Guy is so dreamy, with those big blue eyes. I wish I could find a way to connect—outside of work, I mean. But I just couldn't come out and ask him!"

LaCenta lay back against the bed. How much easier could the girl make this? "Well, girlfriend, maybe we can help each other there."

Her business phone woke her half an hour before her alarm. Groaning and cursing herself for not having turned that one off, too, she answered and mumbled something she hoped sounded professional.

"Just as we thought," Dr. Spice said over the line. "Neeta, I'm calling you because we all know you, and too well. You are not to return to the massacre site today."

"Massacre?"

"Oh, yes. That's what the press is calling it—crediting some unknown local historian. Pfaw! At any rate, we have the cleanup under control. Your services are not only unneeded but if you should come by, anyway, you will be returned to your home—under sedation, if necessary."

"Cory, I'm fine." In fact, she felt more than fine; she felt a growing warmth in her chest at her friend's concern. And Brian thought she needed rescuing.

"Nevertheless, sleep in today. You deserve it."

"Doctor's orders?"

"Doctor's orders."

He hung up then, and she put the phone in the charger and leaned back against the pillows, thinking that she could take advantage of the extra time and…

That was the last thing she remembered until the sun woke her an hour after her alarm should have gone off.

Chapter 18

Notes from: *The Zombie Syndrome*

A Documentary

By Gary Opkast

Episode: Zombie Exterminators

Clip from several past segments showing different ways of fighting off undead, ending with *Zombie Death Extreme* footage of Neeta whacking away at the zombies. NOT THE BERGIE SCENE!!! DO NOT LET ANYONE TALK YOU INTO USING THE BERGIE SCENE!!!

NARRATOR

Despite efforts made to stem the tide of undead, the zombie syndrome remains—and probably will for a long time. While the average person has some means of defense, when it comes to tackling the problem—and decapitating it—you need a professional. The Zombie Exterminator.

CAROL LYFFE

(Be sure to credit the iNews Personality Profiles for the testimony)

I never intended to become a zombie exterminator. I didn't want to do the single mom thing as a Marine. I used my GI money to get exterminator training and set up a business with a classmate, Jerry Lee. Those first years were tough. I did a lot of overtime then to make ends meet.

It was February, and it'd been raining steadily for a week. The Sunnyside cemetery was having a problem with rats—they were just pouring out of there in droves, it seemed. We know now that that's a sign that an area's infected with zombie-ism, but at that time, everyone blamed the rains. They had some big-wig getting buried there in a couple of days, so they needed the place cleared fast—and, of course, after hours.

We were in rain gear setting traps and other "non-standard" ways of getting rid of the pests—stuff I'd picked up in the Corps and adapted—when Jerry noticed one of the graves just, well, writhing. There hadn't been a lot of zombie sighting yet, but it's not hard to figure out what that meant. I grabbed Jerry and ran to the groundkeeper's shed.

NARRATOR

In the shed, they found what would become some of the tools-of-the-trade for zombie exterminators: chainsaws, machete, even motorcycle helmets.

CAROL

There was a riding lawn mower. Jerry called the police. I found some duct tape and strapped anything I thought would be useful to the mower or to myself. I was a weapons master and defense instructor, and I taught my Marines to think of everything in terms of its use as a weapon.

NARRATOR

By the time they got the mower started, something was scraping at the door. With Carol wielding the chainsaw and Jerry at the wheel, they busted through the shed door, mowing down the two undead that had been seeking entrance.

Split screen here of Carol and Jerry running down zombies and footage of Carol discussing the incident. Maybe the trial footage?

CAROL

Look, at first, we were just intent on getting out with our lives. Call the police, let them handle it. But then the lightning flashed, and we saw how many were clawing their way out of the ground. I only live a few blocks from there, your honor. I had a five-year-old girl at home. What if one of those things wandered that way while I was worried about my own skin? I wasn't leaving until I knew none of them was making their way to my house or any other house.

NARRATOR

With Jerry mowing down those on the ground and Carol hacking through those standing, they cut down the horde until the police arrived to join the fight. By morning's light, the area had been cleared. Once the limbs were collected and the holes in the graves counted, police determined thirty-three zombies had risen that night—and nearly half of those had been re-killed by Jerry Lee and Carol Lyffe. Although the cemetery tried to press charges for damages, they received the Medal of Valor from Governor Cyrus of California.

NEETA LYFFE

(In her home, pan to some childhood pictures of her and her mom.) Mom was a hero, no doubt. But like a real hero, she didn't care about that. She just wanted to keep people safe. It's all part of the job. Most of our money went into training and researching new ways to fight off the undead. She helped found ZERD. She pushed for re-kill licensing, and the Dead and Decapitated Act. She wasn't always just whaling away at reanimated corpses—though I have to admit, sometimes, I think that was her favorite part.

My favorite part? I...I'm not sure. I suppose, just succeeding. Every time a zombie is re-killed, the world's a little safer. That's what I like best—knowing I've helped make the world a little safer.

Neeta had just finished some stretches to loosen up her muscles and was again scrubbing down her suit. Not like she needed to worry about her van, after all. Cory had called earlier to let her know that despite the fact that it had made a good perch for the TV interview, the interior was too badly damaged by a flaming zombie, and she'd have to total it. How ironic could you get?

The phone in her cleaning room rang. She wiped her hands on a bleach towelette, but let the machine pick it up. Reporters, clients, neighbors—everyone had been calling her. And she thought being on a TV show was bad!

After the tone, a rich voice with a slight Hispanic accent said, "Ms. Lyffe. I'm Miguel Hernandez of Hernandez HumVees. We own the H5 you—"

She snatched up the phone. If she was going to get sued again, she'd take it like a pro. "Yes, Mr. Hernandez. This is Neeta Lyffe."

"Ms. Lyffe, I hope you do not mind if I have you on speaker phone. My staff is with me. Let me start by saying that this morning, they released footage of what you did with our car yesterday evening."

She took a breath and sat down on the stool in her cement washroom. *Here it comes...*

"It was nothing short of incredible."

"Listen, I'm really sorry, but there wasn't any other vehicle I thought could do the job."

There was a pause, then a cheer!

"*Bien!* We had hoped you'd say that!"

"*Escusame?*"

"*Ai, mia!* You are a hero, Neeta! You and your team saved my sales associate, Shirpa." He paused for her to call out, "Thank you! Bless you!"

"You saved the couple who were test driving the car with her. Then you saved that man in the useless Lexus, giving him your means of escape and facing the zombies alone. What were you thinking?"

"I," she started and paused. This conversation was not going as she'd expected. "I had to keep the zombies away from the Interstate. Without live bait, they'd have followed the car and we'd have had a real massacre. I... You know, it's all just part of my job."

There was silence on their end as they processed her statement.

"Neeta, we want to thank you."

She found herself slumping with relief. "You're welcome!"

Miguel laughed. "No, you don't understand. We want to thank you, tangibly. We heard your van was damaged."

"Oh, um, wow, but it's too badly—they said it can't be repaired." She stopped as anxiety clutched her chest. How was she going to run her business? Her car could hold some things, but not enough for a full raid. Besides, it needed a new transmission.

"Perhaps we can help each other?"

She tried to laugh. "I'm afraid even with a discount, I couldn't afford a Hummer."

"Not what we were thinking. Neeta, how would you like to own the HumVee of your choice, outright?"

"What? What's the catch?"

He laughed again. She liked his laugh. It was boyish. "You've dealt with car salesmen before, then?" he teased, then turned serious.

"Neeta, the footage of you in our car went worldwide. Our phones have been ringing off the hook. We shut down to have this call with you. Corporate e-mailed to tell us the same thing is happening everywhere and to make you this offer."

"Any car you want—off the lot or made to order. Yours, if you agree to drive it, and promote it for the next five years."

Despite herself, she snorted. "Brian's gonna love this," she muttered.

"Who is Brian?"

She hadn't realized she'd spoken aloud. "What? No one, never mind. Miguel, this is tempting, really. But, well. Look, it was a lot of fun to drive and it did get the job done and I adored the bumpers, but well, I need something lower to the ground and with a big back where I can put my equipment and get at it easily. That's why the van—"

"Did you know Hummer makes vans?"

"—is so much better for… They what? When?"

"The first model came out last year. Slightly lower chassis, longer in the back. A little narrower, but not much. This is a Hummer, after all. We can't have jokes of shrinking the designs in the wash," he said, referring to a joke Rus made on *The Tonight Show* about the failed HumMini.

"Listen, do you have time today? Let me have one of my associates pick you up and bring you to the dealership. We have a floor model. Take it and the proposed contract for a week. If you don't like it, bring them back—consider it our thanks to you."

"Serious?"

"You need something for your job, no?"

"Oh, si! All right. Okay. I'll look. No promises, but I'll look."

"When is good?"

"Now?"

She imagined him waving one hand in a "why not?" gesture. She heard a female voice in the background.

"Shirpa will get you. She wishes to thank you personally."

Nasir paced in his small hotel room like a caged lion, one fist clenched so tight, his short nails were digging into his skin. The other hand had the phone pressed so hard against his ear, the edge of the casing was making an impression in his cheek.

"Answer!" he said and swore again. "Please, Badria, answer!"

On the TV behind him, footage showed the Iranian "rescue" forces opening fire upon a zombie horde that made yesterday's look like a Hollywood publicity stunt.

And the announcer was saying the undead were rising throughout his country.

When the doorbell sounded, he roared in frustration and threw the phone against the bed. If it was another reporter asking what he felt!

He flung the door open to find Gordon standing at parade rest. He jerked his chin at the TV.

"You're going to need help. Count me in."

Two hours and an embarrassing number of thanks later, Neeta drove off the lot in a 2042 HumVan Sport, a contract on the seat beside her. She'd forced herself to keep composed while at the dealership, but once she'd turned the corner, she let loose with a stream of cheers. She called up traffic on the GPS, decided she could ask Eugene about the contract tomorrow, and used the Bluetooth to call Hollerman. His wife said he was at the cleanup, so she decided to take a chance and head over there.

The policewoman at the roadblock looked at her ID, and tears filled her eyes.

"My husband's an EMT," she said, her voice cracking. "He was here last night. Your plebes saved his life. I thought *ZDE* was just a show, but..." She mashed her lips together, then stepped aside and saluted as Neeta drove past.

Neeta did her best to commit the woman's face to memory. All too soon, she knew, people would forget what they'd done, spectacular as it was. Life would go on, and exterminators would become forgotten heroes. It was just a job.

She found Hollerman consulting with Spice at a tent set up where they'd gathered the living just fifteen hours ago. They glanced at her irritably as she pulled up, but their looks turned to full glares as she rolled down the window and leaned out.

"You were warned!" Cory said.

She held up her hands through the window in surrender, then slapped the door. "Hey! I just came for some advice. What do you think of it? I can get a sweet deal, but will it work for extermination?"

Soon, everyone who could get a few minutes off was swarming around her van, careful not to contaminate it, but examining it thoroughly, suggesting modifications, discussing pros and cons, most clearly envious. Neeta rocked back and forth on her toes, feeling more giddy than she had in ages.

Finally, Hollerman stood over her and demanded sternly. "And how are you affording this?"

The others gathered in to hear her answer.

She bit her lip and hoped she didn't sound like a complete sell out. "Advertising. I have to promote the brand for five years, and I can get my own van, custom made."

"Noooo!" Gregory howled and sank to his knees, hands up in supplication. "Why do I never have such fortune?"

Boris and Karl wrapped their arms around their brother and pretended to weep.

Neeta leaned against the side of her loaner. Guess she had a keeper after all.

Spud stood on the small stoop to Lacey's townhouse and took a breath. He'd lost his nerve last night, and after calling his mom to assure her he was safe, he'd called Lacey to ask if they could talk the next day. She'd suggested a picnic on the beach. Even though he was relieved that she wasn't angry, he'd spent the night tossing and turning.

What was he going to do? He'd seen a jewelry store on the way to the studio and had bought the ring on an impulse. He'd planned to put it in a safety deposit box the next day, save it for when they knew each other better.

He raised his hand to knock, drew his fist back to press against his mouth instead.

Why did he make that stupid statement on television? They'd only known each other a few weeks. He'd planned on waiting, invite her to Idaho to meet Mom.

It was the zombies. All those monsters shambling toward me. I thought I was going to die. All I could think of was that I hadn't told her how I felt, but this!

What do I do now? I'm committed.

What if it's too soon? What if she says n-n-

He was so nervous, he was stuttering in his thoughts.

Mom was right. Never make a hasty decision.

Too late now. Just do it and hope for the best. Unless maybe he could ask her something else?

He was still trying out questions that were close to the one in his heart when Lacey opened the door and threw herself into his arms.

"Yes!" she squealed. "Yesyesyesyesyes!"

Roscoe was standing in front of the mirror, examining his outfit. A pile of discarded shirts, slacks and robes sat by his closet door. This was going to be his first vidblog after his "Thank you, God, that I lived!" post he'd made before collapsing into bed. Now he was having trouble deciding which outfit projected the best "day after" image.

"Should have done this in the morning," he scolded himself. "*Ask Loreli* always said, 'White fluffy robe, such a symbol of goodness and casual sexuality for mornings or hotel getaways—and getting "surprised" at the door. Any other time is just tacky.' Well, the moment is lost now."

He undid two buttons, examined the effect, then threw up his hands and tore it off. It was just too refined.

It was too hot for the college sweatshirt trick, but what about a tie-dye T? And his "Give me Woody!" button, just to show that there were no hard feelings about his having the Z-Mat team when they really needed them at the massacre.

He'd just finished checking the text of the button with a small level to be sure it was straight when the doorbell rang. He found a man with a suit and a posture that said "hired security" holding out a small square envelope.

"Like the button," he said as Roscoe suspiciously took the envelope and pulled out the heavy ivory parchment card within.

Woody Forrest would like to personally invite you to a reception in your honor
Luxe Sunset Boulevard Hotel
6 pm -10 pm
RSVP to Mr. Michaels
A limo is scheduled to pick you up at 5:30 unless other arrangements are made

Roscoe screamed like a crazed fangirl and fainted.

Chapter 19

Gary cracked his knuckles and stretched his shoulders before letting his fingers hover over the keyboard. This was it! He was going to sell *The Zombie Syndrome!*

Sharon had e-mailed him that morning with a phone number to the Discovery Channel's main offices and a time. "With the LA Massacre and the Zombie Defense of Afghanistan, there's no better opportunity. Pitch it, hard, Gary."

Halfway into his fifteen minutes, Mr. Olesker had told him to come to the offices next week with a script and treatment.

He could kiss that woman. Maybe, when he had the contract, he would.

But first, he had to finish the script.

"Shitty first draft," he told himself. "Just get the ideas out, fix it later."

Notes For *The Zombie Syndrome*

A Documentary

By Gary Opkast

Episode: Bring Out Your Dead!

Footage of a hand stretching out of a grave from a 2028 surveillance camera at the Leavitt's Memorial Gardens in Lucky Acres, North Carolina. Rather than dramatically clawing its way out to stagger off in revenge, the zombie dragged herself out of her grave, then rose onto hands and knees, coughing and spitting like someone who had half-drowned. Next, she sat hard, clawed dirt off her face, then her hair. Finally, she sat for several minutes looking around stupidly (speed time here) before rising and shambling off camera.

NARRATOR

> We don't know what causes the dead to take on liv-
> ing abilities, and we don't know what gives them the
> strength and agility to claw their way out of the most
> seemingly inescapable of graves. However, we do
> have some idea what motivates their actions. Dot-
> tore Virgilio Dante, foremost expert on undead
> psychology, explains his seven levels of living dead
> motivations.

VIRGILIO DANTE standing in one of the open plazas in the University of Turin. In the background, students rush back and forth between the arched walkways, some getting close to Dante and ducking expertly as his hands swing in their direction.

DANTE

> Now, naturally, we cannot interview zombies, so all
> assumptions of motivation are made based on

observed behaviors. I admit that I have made a nod toward my ancestor's work, *The Inferno*, of course, but I have categorized the basic motivations into seven levels.

Need a graphic, maybe V. Dante standing at the gates of Hell and looking into a vortex, divided into seven levels. Each level full of undead, and signs highlighting the level as the narrator lists them.

NARRATOR

V. Dante's seven levels…

- Improper burial, which may not be a cause but simply make it easier to arise
- Denial of death
- Habit
- Vengeance
- Unfinished business
- Fear of crossing over, mostly found in certain religious groups
- Type A Personality

DANTE

Sometimes it's a combination—for example, the case of Giovanni Feliciano, who worked in a rather anonymous job at a Fiat factory near Brindisi. With no family and no friends, no one took much notice when he died in a car crash. Or when he returned, undead, three days later, to resume work as a quality control specialist for dashboard auxiliary power systems. Only when they found his finger caught in a cigarette lighter did they suspect something was wrong.

NOTE: Wonder if we can get Sprint to sponsor? That'd be great if they ran the commercial of a zombie with an unfinished wireless plan commitment. *Minuuutes…*

Of course, once Neeta was at the site, she couldn't help but demand that she help "clean up her own mess." After some finagling and not a little whining that staying home made her victim to reporters and lawyers, Spice agreed to an hour. One hour turned to four; after which, he found her, a syringe in his rubber-gloved hand and a threat on his lips. Laughing and feeling tired but content, she went to the decontamination station, then headed home to repeat the same routine of last night. This time, however, her mind was full of happy thoughts except for one.

A winner. I have to pick a winner.

Gordon's learned so much, she thought, remembering what LaCenta had said about his dousing her with TidyToidy.

LaCenta—brave and smart, and has been since the beginning.

Spud kept his head as always. He's not flashy or innovative, but you seldom need that on the job—sometimes, it makes things worse. Like giving your only means of escape to a lawyer who tried to talk the dealership into suing you, with him as the rep.

(When Miguel related what he'd told Twiddle to do with his lawsuit, she'd almost signed the contract unseen.)

And Nasir—not a real stand-out, but more than capable, and he came from so far for this.

She was sitting on the toilet lid in her white bathrobe, combing back her hair and mulling over her decision when the doorbell rang. She got up and lugged herself to the door and peeked through the peephole. If it was a reporter, she was going to disable the bell and go settle down with a book.

Instead she saw Ted and Roscoe jostling to peek back at her.

She undid the door limiter and pulled it open.

"I have got to knock on this door more often!" Ted said before she could ask what was up.

"Oh, gawd, do you read *Ask Loreli*, too?" Roscoe asked.

Behind them Gordon stood with arms behind his back and eyes looking at the porch ceiling.

They were all dressed up, even Ted, who wore a silky white shirt and dark jeans. She was so glad he'd topped it with a vest patterned in flames.

"Nice vest," she said.

"Like it? I got it today. I love it!"

There was also a new guy, wearing a suit and an admiring smirk on his face. In his hand was an envelope.

"If you've got a subpoena for Neeta Lyffe, she's not here."

"Oh, girlfriend, you are so all there!" Roscoe purred.

Some days, she didn't understand that man. "What's going on?"

"What's going on?" Ted repeated. "Honestly, did you check your phone messages at all today?"

"Well, I—" Her hand dropped to her jeans pocket. She touched terry cloth instead.

Her hands went to her rapidly heating face. "I don't believe this," she muttered. She peeked through her fingers just enough to catch Mrs. Westerman's face in the window across the street. She had a cell phone to her ear. Great.

Gordon smacked his lips. "Situational awareness not so good off the job?"

"Not that we're complaining!" Ted added.

The suit cleared his throat. "Ma'am, perhaps this will explain our presence." He handed her the invitation.

"Oh," she said as she read, bathrobe again forgotten. Then "Wow. So, what about the others?"

"Spud and Lacey are being embarrassing in the car," Roscoe said with a roll of his eyes but a grin. "LaCenta and Katie are coming in another limo. They have dates. Oh, uh, we talked to Brian. He… said to uh, have fun. Oh, girl, I'm so sorry."

"It was wrong for both of us," she said. "Nasir?"

They glanced at each other. "You didn't see the news? Zombies are crawling all over his country. He and Sharon are making arrangements for us to wrap up filming tomorrow and to get him and Gordon to Afghanistan."

"Gordon?" She looked up at the big veteran Marine.

He shrugged. "Teams of two. Safer to have someone at your back. You taught us that, right?"

She felt herself choke up. "Absolutely."

He glanced at the others then added. "And we know you get to pick who wins, but we'd like to discuss that with you."

"But on the ride!" Roscoe threw his hands up like an Italian grandmother and waved her back in the house. "We need to get you dressed and dolled. Woody is waiting!"

He hustled her into the house, then stopped the others as they tried to follow them.

"Oh, no, boys. This is our time. Go wait in the limo— or out of it if Spud and Lacey are too much for you."

He slammed the door in their faces and put on the limiter.

"Hey!" he called to Neeta, "That thing on the door...?"

"Don't you start!" Neeta said. "Just pick me a nice outfit while I do something with my hair."

"A little gel and a little fluffing," he advised. "We don't have much time and trust me, you will look so vogue."

He opened her closet, frowning over her clothes until he looked down.

"Neeta! Love the footwear!"

"They're in order!" The bathroom door muffled her voice. "By comfort. The farther right, the less time I can wear them and actually stand and walk."

"And when do you plan to have shoes like this and not stand and walk long?" he asked, eyeing a pair of peg-heeled black suede boots.

"Dinners, award ceremonies, that sort of thing!" Even the door couldn't muffle her ire. "Don't get ideas."

"Of course not, Miss Neeta Virgin Lyffe!" With so few really good outfits, he was able to choose quickly. After all, you could never go wrong with the little black dress, and hers was darling! Now if only...

He squealed when he found a wide leopard print belt with matching shoes near the center of the row. True the heel was a little low, but they were platforms and there was a peep hole.

"You have red nail polish?" he called.

"Somewhere. Do we have time?" She popped out, hair and make-up done, holding a small bottle.

He gasped. "You're a vision! Maybe we should send the others ahead."

"Stop that, or you'll lose any chance of winning the million!" she growled, her face turning red.

He handed her the dress and shoes. "Honey, I'm an actor. I live for camera, not the prize. Besides, the winner is already picked. That's what we want to discuss. Now get dressed and we'll do the nails in the car. We have important people to grace with our presence."

Date: August 3, 2042
FROM: Sharon Peterson
TO: ZDE Forum members
SUBJ: Important announcement

Hi, Everyone, Sharon, the ZDE Admin here!

I'm e-mailing to let everyone know that the events in LA and Afghanistan have led to a serious change in schedule for the cast and crew. Not only will Nasir Haq Qalzai be returning tonight to his homeland to help battle the infestation that's ravaging his already torn country, but Gordon Makepeace will join him.

As a result, the winner of ZDE will be announced LIVE at 9:45 a.m. tomorrow in a publicized ceremony where Los Angeles Mayor Gruberman will be awarding medals for heroism to each exterminator, along with the emergency personnel who participated in the event. If you are in Los Angeles, please come and support the ZDE crew and all who helped save 124 lives yesterday and prevented a zombie contagion from invading the city. Those unable to come, it will be shown on all the major news networks and via live streaming on the ZDE website.

We will be having a final episode! "The People's Choice" will feature favorite clips and funny outtakes of the season. Missed Hu's toilet snafu? Want to see Spud fall in love. (They're engaged, BTW!) We're collecting votes until Wednesday, so get on the ZDE website and rate your favorites! In addition, Neeta talks candidly about the ups and downs of each episode. If you've been watching, you don't want to miss it. If you've not—it's a great way to meet the Heroes of LA.

You are receiving this e-mail because you are registered on the Zombie Death Extreme Fan Forum. If you do not wish to receive further announcements, please click here to unsubscribe.

Chapter 20

ZDEAdministrator
SUBJ: Apology from Tro111
I got this in the e-mail late last night and wanted to share with you:

Dear Sharon,

Thanks for the e-mail. Yes, I'm also VoiceofReson. Sorry for the deception. This, however, is genuine.

I, with my nine-year-old son, were part of the accident on West Burbank. We were there until the B to Z truck helped us all escape. It was the most harrowing hours of my life, made even more so because of the presence of my son, whom I was not sure I could protect. Any fathers in your group will understand.

The ZDE team was...surprising. Professional, brave, positive. Even that Roscoe showed a mettle I didn't think he had, no offense. They kept us together, they kept us alive, and when we were off the scene, they did their best to keep the zombies at bay until real help arrived.

I still stand by my words about reality TV. But the plebes of ZDE? They're more than contestants. They're real.

And that's why I'm even alive to write this apology. I'll be at the ceremony. Part of the adoring fandom, but here are real people who deserve real fandom.

Troy Llamé

The heat wave finally broke at 9 p.m. the night before, and the morning stayed cool—if 85 degrees Fahrenheit could be considered "cool." Still, it was enough that Neeta's skirt wasn't sticking to the plastic seat nor her company polo to her skin as she watched the mayor give the last of the medals to the ambulance technicians.

From the corner of her eye, she caught Roscoe making pucker lips to the audience. She smacked him on the leg with her fingers, hoping no one would see, then did a double-take as she saw LaCenta doing something similar but more subtly to a man standing in the front row. Past her, Spud fingered the medal around his neck reverently, while Gordon sat ramrod straight. Nasir squirmed, obviously eager for the day to end so he could board the first of several C-130s bringing troops and supplies to help his nation not only repel the now-acknowledged invasion, but also the zombie threat. Katie sniffled, and Ted reached down and grabbed her another tissue.

The mayor and EMT shook hands, and everyone applauded lightly until he invited all the heroes to stand and receive one last round. Even in the open air, it thundered against Neeta's ears.

She remembered what her mother had told her when she was eleven and her mom had received some kind of national award for her work. The crowd had thundered then, too, and she'd leaned over to speak in Neeta's ear.

Lap it up now, Neeta, because the accolades come few and far between in this biz. Better that way. Can't work with a big head.

"Gawd, I live for this! What are you laughing about?" Roscoe leaned over to ask her.

She just shook her head in reply.

The mayor held up his hands and the applause died down. "Now you've all been standing here for quite some time. You've seen our heroes awarded. You've listened to the stuffy politicians pontificate."

He paused for the laughter.

"But now, I think you won't leave until you hear one more thing! So, without any further ado, here is Ms. Neeta Lyffe, Master Exterminator, to announce the winner of *Zombie Death Extreme!*"

The screams and cheers struck the stage like a gust of wind, then fell into muddled chants of contestant's names. Neeta stood and brushed her hands on her skirt. She looked back at her plebes and saw them drinking in the adulation. Maybe she should change her opening.

She walked up to the mike, and the cheers didn't so much die down as stop, like someone had pushed a mute button on the whole audience.

She pulled the mike to her level. She twisted her head just enough to look at the *ZDE* team while speaking. "Before I start, I have a message for my plebes—for my exterminators—that my mother gave me as a child. Big heads don't fit in motorcycle helmets."

Everyone laughed. Roscoe stuck his tongue out at Neeta.

"Having said that, I want to remind you of something else Mom said. Take the accolades when you can. They will be too few, but they are inevitably deserved."

She straightened and addressed the audience. "I've also been instructed by my producer to remind everyone that, even though I'm announcing the winner today, we will be having a season finale on schedule Friday. It's being dedicated to the memory of Bergie Eidelberg, so I hope you'll watch.

"Thank you, all of you, for being here and for watching the show. We never expected this to happen. We never expected a lot of things to happen! But like real professionals, these people rolled with the punches, bounced back, and when it came to a real emergency, put aside fear, ambition, and rivalries to work together for the real reward: saving lives.

"That's what was making it so hard for me to decide on a winner. And never have I been more grateful to have a decision taken out of my hands."

As Dave had instructed her, she paused there to let the audience squirm. Then, one by one, she called them to stand beside her:

"Roscoe Glaser, you came to this show seeking glory. Instead, you discovered self-sacrifice.

"LaCenta Dane, you wanted to make your family proud. You've done that, and so much more.

"Pippin 'Spud' Frost, quiet and dependable. You had some people fooled, hiding in the background. You have what it takes to stand in the forefront.

"Gordon Makepeace, you may have been taken out of the Marines, but the Marine will never be taken out of you.

"Nasir Haq Qalzai."

He stood and started forward, but she held up a hand.

"Nasir, you have come so far and sacrificed so much to be here. And now your country needs you. And, in the opinion of your competitors—"

She heard the gasp of realization from the audience.

"—of your *teammates*, you not only need but *deserve* the prize of one million dollars."

Nasir staggered back, stunned. Katie sprung from her seat and hugged him, sobbing loudly enough to be heard over the cheers.

The rest of the team ran to hug and offer slaps on the back. Neeta stood at the mike, watching and trying to ignore the tears running down her own cheeks, until someone reached out and pulled her into the group.

Not just someone.

Ted.

Chapter 21

"It's a cool 81 along LA's miracle mile in what experts are calling clear proof that the government is not taking enough measures to stem global cooling."

"Global cooling? Snort. Helloness! I like being able to wear sleeves."

"Don't we all? Hey, we've called up someone who's always going to be hot in my book, Ms. Neeta Larger-than-Lyffe, Zombie Exterminator, who's also the new spokeswoman for HumVees."

Sounds of chainsaws and zombies moaning "Braiiiins" before a honk and a thunk.

"I told you to stop calling me that!"

"Where are you?"

"My new HumVan! I just picked it up today. I can't believe how well my equipment fits. I even have a little fridge for AH grenades!"

"That's the stuff they used to stop the LA Zombie Massacre, right?"

"The very! Saved a lot of lives, but not easy to keep in a foam form, which is why I'm loving the fridge!"

"The fridge? You're driving Motor Trends New Design of the Year, and all you can say is it holds a fridge?"

"And the bumpers! I love the bumpers. If I get in with a swarm of zombies, I can mow them down. And the smart airbag means I won't have it going off in my face. Everything about this van is smart. The only thing it won't do is come when I whistle."

Brian laughed. "How's it handle?"

"Nice! I took it on the track fully loaded to try it out."

"How fast did you go?"

"I'm not saying. I don't want anyone getting ideas. Let's just say faster than any regular driver needs to go. Scared myself a couple of times on the turns—scared the instructor, too. Glad they strapped on safety bars for the training, or we might have rolled and wrecked my paint job! But you know, the point is, it doesn't handle like my mom's van. I know I said I was never going to promote products, and frankly, I wish they'd cut the price in half so average people could afford one, but seriously, it's a sweet machine."

"I don't know, I've seen plenty of average people driving the new Hums."

"Not in my neighborhood. Good thing this has my logo all over it or I'd probably lose it half an hour after leaving it on the street! Not really—the tamper proof alarms are fuze core. That's what my friend's brother said after he tried to pick them for an hour."

"You had someone try to break in your car?"

"Wowsers, Neeta!"

"Yeah, well, if I'm going to endorse something, I'm going to make *goram* sure it's worth endorsing. Anyway, I've got to go. We're doing a photo shoot with it before I get it all gored up from work."

"Neeta, thanks for your time."

"Thanks Neeta. And since we're on the subject of cars, let's find out the latest in traffic…"

The background sounds of the station muted, and Brian said to Neeta. "See? That wasn't so hard."

Neeta breathed out through pursed lips and turned on her blinker to take the exit. "I hate advertising! Did I do okay?"

"Well, they might want to talk to you about that 'average person' comment. But don't worry. First time and all. Hey, did you get the flowers I sent?"

She smiled at the dashboard camera, even though Brian didn't have his on. "Yes, thank you. The doorknob was a nice touch. I'm going to see if I can get it put on tomorrow."

"Good. I meant what I said on the card. If we can't be a couple, let's be a couple of friends. So, who'd you hire as your apprentice?"

She sighed as she came to a red light. "Still looking. Hollerman hired LaCenta, and Spud's working with Lacey until they earn enough to start a business in his hometown. Roscoe said he'd freelance now and then, but you know him. He lives for reality TV."

"Well, someone will turn up. Listen, I know what you said, but if you ever need a shoulder."

"Thanks, Brian, but I have two of my own."

After the shoot, Neeta pulled into the parking lot of a mom-and-pop grocery store. She had just enough time to grab a couple of things before meeting Eugene to go over Twiddle's new payment schedule, and the fridge was good for more than ammo, after all.

She walked past the register, with its wall of cigarettes behind a cage and the sign "Smoking—the Addiction that Kills." The guy at the register smiled at her in a dreamy, unfocused way that made her hurry to the dairy section. Before she got to the milk, she had to stop and admire the big standup sign advertising Longevity.

Spud and Lacey stood with their arms around each other's waists and chainsaws hanging from straps on their shoulders. In their other hands, they held cans of BUDD drinks—Longevity for Spud, Supercharge for Lacey. In front of them, roughly a dozen undead lay in pieces.

"BUDDies for life—and the living," the caption read.

She looked more closely at the zombies and snickered. She'd have to tease Spud that if he was going to pose with the mangled dead, he'd better make sure they were all properly decapitated. For her rep as a trainer if nothing else.

She snagged some bread and milk, then headed down the pharmaceuticals aisle to the other checkout. When she saw a familiar face—and flaming vest—in the "Medicinal Marijuana" section, she hastened her steps.

"Long time no see!" she said.

Ted spun and spread his arms. "Whoa, hey! Blast from the past. Doing good? Any lawsuits?"

"Actually, not bad. Wanker called threatening another lawsuit, but I just have to pay for repairs to Twiddle's car. Sharon helped me find someone reputable and cheap."

"Cool. She's on Forrest's campaign committee, did you know that? Dave got her a safari in the Australian Outback to help her relax, and next day, she'd cashed it in and given him her resignation. Got the Forrest job right after. And a bunny. He's promised to make her Secretary of Zombie Affairs if he wins."

"That's great!"

"Yeah. Gary's with Discovery working on his documentary. Then he's been asked to write *Zombie Death Extreme: The Musical*. Did you know he's dating Sharon now?"

"Seriously?"

"Yeah. Looks like a lot of folks found romance on *ZDE*. Go figure."

They fell silent. Neeta looked at the signboard. Happy people of many walks of life—doctors, businesspeople, surfers—smiled and held their fingers in the classic reefer hold. "Safe. Easy. Medicinal," it read. "We love to use Mary Jane. Shouldn't you?"

Ted said, "I love this section."

Her face fell. "You do?"

"I've got a friend, writes the labels for the shelf. See?"

She looked at the bright yellow labels: Headache Hits, Bammy for Bloating...

"Here's his latest: Menstruate with Mary Jane." Ted chortled.

Neeta snorted, too. "Quite a sense of humor."

"Yeah. I never use this stuff. See the kid at the register? He's on Ace, the Antidepressant. Been giggling at the cash register for half an hour. Weird. So, I don't go in for homeopathy. When I have a headache, I want a regular old aspirin, not something that grew on a tree."

She looked at him, and when she saw he was sincere, started laughing. "Aspirin is made from a chemical that comes from the willow tree."

"Whoa! Serious? See, that's what I liked training with you. I learned so much. Oh, speaking of my 'girl'…"

"Looking for things to set on fire?"

He shuffled nervously. "Well, it's like this. Dave wants to go to Louisiana for *ZDE-New Orleans*. I'm really not interested in the Deep South. I'm a Pacific guy, right? So, I'm kind of out of a job, and camerawork is cool and all, but I think at that Massacre, I found my calling."

"Demolition?"

"Well, yeah. Zombie demolition, so…"

Her head pushed past her teasing. "Wait. Are you asking me for a job?"

"Depends. Do I have a chance?"

"You have to get your license."

"Testing in October."

He smiled again, that rakish smile full of mischief and fire, and she found herself smiling back. "Come to my office tomorrow. Let's talk."

Suddenly, her phone rang.

"This is the lifeguard at the Ketchum downtown YMCA. Please, help us! There're three of them in the Donald Eidelberg Memorial surfing pool. We thought they just needed a shower, until one took off his shirt and these maggots started spilling out. We're evacuating, but hurry!"

"On the way!" She flipped off the phone. "Did you bring your girl?"

"Trunk of the car! Got my suit, too!"

"You're hired! Meet me at my van!"

She dropped her basket where she stood, and together they dashed out the door.

As she fired the engine and threw the car into reverse, Ted whooped and turned on the siren, only remembering to put on his seat belt after she took a turn on two wheels.

She'd have a boatload of paperwork to justify bringing an unapprenticed, unpermitted trainee on the re-kill, but damned if she wanted to go alone against a couple of decaying surfer wannabes who were too stupid to know death meant the end of hanging ten.

If she could handle them, she could handle paperwork.

All part of the job.

Acknowledgements

The question shouldn't be "Where do you come up with ideas?" but rather "How do you decide what to write next?"

I'm blessed with an overflowing cup of ideas and also with good people to give me a push to bring them to life. Neeta Lyffe is one example.

Kim Richards, publisher of Damnation Books got the ball rolling with her anthology, The Zombie Cookbook. She asked us authors on The Writers Chat Room (www.writerschatroom.com) to send her zombie stories. Personally, I've never cared much for zombies, so while I wanted to write for Kim, I didn't have a solid idea and kept procrastinating.

Then while house hunting in Utah with my husband, Rob, my friend Rebecca Butcher from the chat room IM'd me. "We need to write something for the Cook-book. Kim's getting worried!" I didn't have any zombie ideas, so much as a few wise-cracks, particularly about election fraud with the dead voting. I was also feeling sarcastic about environmentalists, as my daughter was in a debate with her science teacher in California about this sacred cow. Chatting with Becca brought out the idea of a zombie exterminator having a hard time doing her job because of a new law that replaced her useful zombie repellent with less effective environmentally friendly stuff. It turned out to be such fun, I wrote it completely in an hour, giggling the whole time and sharing the jokes with Becca as I went.

Neeta Lyffe made her appearance in "Wokking Dead" in The Zombie Cookbook. I figured that was the last I'd see of Neeta and the shambling undead, but it turned out people liked Neeta, and someone asked Kim when I was going to write a novel about her.

Once again, I put it off. I had two other novels I was working on. But Kim mentioned it during the Wednesday chat in The Writers Chat Room, and others agreed it was a great idea. In that chat, we also talked about reality TV and someone mentioned the best opening lines he'd recently read: "They ate Jorgenson first. They were gnawing on his leg, his fine, white leg…" I think that story was about people resorting to cannibalism to survive, but like so many serious things, it got stuck in my head and demanded to be twisted. So, the project went into the back of my brain, to be started sometime after my current work in progress.

On the way to Long Beach to go whale watching New Year's Day, I decided to give it a start and wrote the scene on my little netbook. Soon, I was giggling as Neeta Lyffe, Zombie Exterminator led her plebes on a zombie run for a reality TV show. I enjoyed it so much that when my computer died, taking the back-up (including my serious sci-fi work-in-progress) with it, I decided I'd rather have fun writing something that I knew a publisher wanted.

So, thank you, Kim, Becca, and all the folks at The Writers Chat Room, for bringing Neeta to life.

And thank you, Audrey Shaffer, for creating The Writers Chat Room and for working so hard to make it a place where authors of all levels can meet to learn, to gripe, and to build friendships and support. You're awesome, my friend!

A lot of folks helped in the development of the story:

Rob Fabian, my idea man, my pun partner, my support and my true love. He came up with the zombie cell phone commercial in the book, BTW.

Tony Valdez, our neighbor who is in the LAPD. He and his wife, Christine, took the time to educate me on some of the finer zombie-fighting areas in the city.

Jason Carrier and Walt Staples, who by example as well as by answering questions, helped me flesh out veteran Marine Gordon Makepeace. OOH-Rah!

My children, Steven, Amber, Alex and Liam, who always listen to me read my manuscripts aloud. (Amber, 15 at the time, caught all the jokes and was both proud and a little appalled at Mom's humor.)

Ann Lewis, my writing buddy and best friend, who took time to read some snippets, share her ideas and just be there for me.

To my critiquers: Becca Butcher, Walt Staples, Devon Ellington, for catching typos, noting what didn't flow, and polishing it until it was brighter than a zombie on Porcelain Sparkle. Special thanks to Devon, who teaches the best workshops on dialogue. She taught me just how fun dialogue among a large group can be.

Please take a few minutes to leave a review. Just take 20 words to say what you liked or even disliked about Vern's battle with Shogzallie. It helps readers and helps with Amazon ratings which makes author and dragon happy.

If you want to keep up with my adventures in person and in print, sign up for my newsletter. You'll get a free ebook for joining.

https://fabianspace.substack.com/subscribe

There's More Fun in FabianSpace!

ABOUT THE AUTHOR

Karina Fabian is easily freaked out by horror films and Stephen King novels but does enjoy comedy horror. She enjoys comedy in just about anything, and it shows in her writing. She married a rocket scientist who is now COO of Vaya Space. They live in their dream home which has been pimped out in Geek Chic. She has four adult children, two dogs, and more stories in her head than she can get out in one lifetime. But she's trying!

www.ingramcontent.com/pod-product-compliance
Lightning Source LLC
Chambersburg PA
CBHW070622260626
47161CB00007B/2551